PRAISE FOR VIKKI WAKEFIELD

BALLAD FOR A MAD GIRL

'Everything you already love about Vikki Wakefield—
plus a spine-tingling supernatural mystery. *Ballad for a
Mad Girl* is brilliantly creepy and thrilling.' Fiona Wood

'There's a dark side to being the funny one in the group.
This is a piercing, creepy tale about a wild girl who could
lose herself to a ghost. Vikki Wakefield's writing never
fails to give me chills.' Emily Gale

'A ghost thriller with a literary feel from an
Australian author we love.' *Readings*

'*Ballad for a Mad Girl* is brilliant, edgy and unsettling. Grace
is a tough and sympathetic anti-heroine. I felt her grief and,
even when I cursed her curiosity, was compelled to follow
her to the story's satisfying, cinematic end.' Simmone Howell

'I'm obsessed with Vikki Wakefield's words. Seriously—I'd be
happy reading her grocery list.' Danielle Binks, *Alpha Reader*

'Fans of intelligent, unflinching, spine-crawling thrillers
will love this book.' *Books+Publishing*

'Vikki Wakefield is one of Australia's best YA writers.
I couldn't put down *Ballad for a Mad Girl*.' Cath Crowley

FRIDAY BROWN

'When I finish a Vikki Wakefield novel I get a tiny ache in
my heart because I'm already missing her gutsy characters.'
Melina Marchetta

'*Friday Brown* will haunt you long after you've turned the
last page…It will break your heart then put the pieces back
together in a new way. I absolutely loved this book.' Libba Bray

'*Friday Brown* is every superlative you can throw at it. It's a masterpiece…There are no words to describe this novel adequately. There is only humbled, awestruck, heartbroken silence.' *Mostly Reading YA*

'Vikki Wakefield writes the tough stuff…Her characters are so vivid and endearing, or vicious and infuriating, that she makes you feel everything down to your bones.' *Alpha Reader*

'The gripping story and rich characters took me to places where I didn't expect to venture…I devoured each page.' *Australian Book Review*

'This is a pull-no-punches story about learning the truth and growing up, full of the preciousness of friendship and love.' *Herald Sun*

'This novel is Australian young adult fiction at its best. *Friday Brown* will blow your mind.' *Viewpoint*

'A tense, multilayered tale about loyalty, memory and survival… Lyrical, suspenseful and haunting.' *Kirkus*

INBETWEEN DAYS

'An utterly gripping read with authentic, complicated and relatable characters.' *Sydney Morning Herald*

'Memorable, intriguing, perceptive and often very funny, this is an unforgettable YA novel and a most unusual love story.' *Magpies*

'Vikki Wakefield writes stories that will break your heart… A gritty, heartfelt read for teens and adult readers alike.' *Readings*

'I just adored *Inbetween Days*—really complex, raw, beautiful characters.' Melissa Keil

'Wakefield gives her fictional landscape the same haunting quality that she achieved with her novel, *Friday Brown*, and her writing is full of insight and feeling.' *Age*

Vikki Wakefield writes realist fiction for young adults. Her work explores coming-of-age, family, class, relationships and the lives of contemporary teens. Her novels *All I Ever Wanted*, *Friday Brown*, *Inbetween Days* and *Ballad for a Mad Girl* have won and been short-listed for numerous awards. Vikki lives in Adelaide, Australia.

vikkiwakefield.com

THIS IS HOW WE CHANGE THE ENDING

VIKKI WAKEFIELD

TEXT PUBLISHING MELBOURNE AUSTRALIA

textpublishing.com.au
textpublishing.co.uk

The Text Publishing Company
Swann House, 22 William Street, Melbourne Victoria 3000, Australia

The Text Publishing Company (UK) Ltd
130 Wood Street, London EC2V 6DL, United Kingdom

First published in 2019 by The Text Publishing Company

Book design by Imogen Stubbs
Cover photograph by MEM Studio / Stocksy
Typeset by J&M Typesetting

Printed and bound in Australia by Griffin Press, part of Ovato, an accredited ISO/NZS 14001:2004 Environmental Management System printer.
ISBN: 9781922268136 (paperback)
ISBN: 9781925774900 (ebook)

A catalogue record for this book is available from the National Library of Australia

This book is printed on paper certified against the Forest Stewardship Council® Standards. Griffin Press holds FSC chain-of-custody certification SGS-COC-005088. FSC promotes environmentally responsible, socially beneficial and economically viable management of the world's forests.

For Roan

You cannot buy the revolution. You cannot make the revolution.
You can only be the revolution. It is in your spirit, or it is nowhere.

URSULA K. LE GUIN

PROLOGUE

Dec said we wouldn't start hunting until dark. Pitch black was better for shooting. Hard to aim fast and shoot straight when you had to sort heads from tails—when it was just two beady eyes you could aim for the middle. You don't want to nick them, he said, especially the young ones. They never forget. Can't chance having a wounded animal come back for you when it's grown with a full set of teeth.

I was eleven. It was about eight degrees but it felt like zero. We were somewhere north of a town called Fiston—me, Dec, his mates Jarrod and Brett, one ute, two tents, three eskies, and a gun—and all I knew was it took five boring hours to get there and we could have stopped way sooner and still landed in a spot that looked the same: no fences, red dirt, sick-looking trees and lumps of moonrock. It was the furthest I'd ever been from home.

Dec told me to pitch the tents and get a fire started while they sat on the back of the ute, drinking beer. I'd only ever pitched a tent in our backyard; here the ground was rock-hard beneath six inches of dust, nothing to make the pegs stick. When they weren't looking, I weighed the pegs down with rocks and covered them with dirt. I made a circle of stones and tried to light a few dry sticks, but I burned my fingers. The fire went out.

'Like this.' Brett reached into a toolbox on the tray.

'Let him do it,' Dec said. 'Only way they learn.'

Brett ignored him. 'Watch.'

When I wasn't around, they made Brett fetch the beers. Dec and Jarrod talked about him behind his back and laughed to his face. It made them feel big to make him feel small—part of me hated them for it, but I knew if I had to pick I would rather be like them.

I expected Brett to rub a couple of sticks together and *whoof*, fire, but instead he squirted Zippo lighter fluid onto a greasy rag and poked it underneath the pile I'd made. He flicked his lighter and the sticks went up like they'd been burning for hours.

'Add the big stuff when the small stuff's caught. Right, kid?'

I glanced at Dec.

Dec let it go. 'Get on with it.'

I ran off to gather more wood. I didn't have to go far. I dragged a dead branch to the pit and dropped the leafy end into the flames; sparks shot skyward like a swarm of fireflies. I stacked medium-sized pieces in one pile, big ones in another. The stack of wood grew, and so did the pile of empty beer cans.

The way to please my old man was to keep doing whatever he asked until he told me to stop.

Dec looked on with flat eyes, the gun across his lap. He wore shorts and a singlet and his feet were bare. He never seemed to feel the cold. I counted eight empty cans on the ground, but that was between three of them; I'd taken my eye off Dec so I wasn't sure where he was at.

Three was okay. Five was borderline. Eight was dangerous.

Dec had shown me how to use the rifle at home, twice, unloaded. I remembered everything he showed me: *back straight, chin up, steady, aim, breathe out, squeeze. Never aim if you don't mean to shoot. Both ends can hurt you, loaded or not, and plant your feet or the kick will put you on your arse.* But the way his fingers fumbled and his tongue poked from the corner of his mouth made me worried the gun knew him better than he knew it.

'That's enough,' Dec said finally. 'We don't need a bonfire to tell everyone we're out here.'

He handed me the last of his beer. He'd been giving me the dregs for the past year or so—said I needed to start getting match-fit. I was sure it was ninety per cent spit, but I swallowed it anyway. Jarrod laughed when I screwed up my face and gave me his, too.

One minute it was bright, cold daylight; the next, the sun blazed and fell. It was almost dark when we set off. Brett drove, with me in the passenger seat. Dec and Jarrod stood in the tray, aiming the spotty. There were a few rabbits here and there, but one sniff and they darted underground. The ute bounced over jagged rocks and sandy mounds that Brett said were wombat burrows; we made new tracks where there were none and I hung onto the dash, trying not to bite my tongue, wondering how we'd find our way back to the campsite when every tree-rock-fencepost looked the same.

I'd only eaten a packet of chips since lunchtime; if this was hunting, I worried we'd starve.

'Fucken useless,' Dec said after an hour.

3

He ordered Jarrod to drive, like it was Brett's fault the rabbits were too quick. Brett got in the back. I wanted to get in there too, but there wasn't room.

'Be quiet,' Dec warned, though I hadn't spoken a word since we'd left the campsite.

Jarrod drove fast. We came across a clearing with more burrows. The ground moved: a wombat—fat, sluggish, unafraid, until Jarrod drove straight at it. I heard Dec whoop in the back, which meant Jarrod should stop. He braked hard and I braced myself on the dash.

Dec let off a shot. Dirt sprayed, just left of the wombat's head.

The wombat looked over its shoulder and waddled off, slow as a turtle but still too quick for Dec's second shot. He fired again, missing its backside by a mile. I prayed it would get away and it did, but Jarrod edged the ute forward and nudged the mound with the bull bar. The entrance crumbled and caved in.

'Bury the sucker,' he said.

I didn't know my heart could bang that hard without busting my ribs. I imagined the wombat suffocating down there—it wasn't like we could eat it, so why was Dec shooting?

I got out of the ute and stood in the dust-swirled glare of the headlights, gulping down the lump in my throat.

Brett put his hand on my shoulder. Under his breath, he said, 'Dug its way in—it can dig its way out. Got claws like a bear.'

I nodded and climbed back in the cab. I'd had enough hunting, but Dec wasn't done. I turned around, saw the glint of the barrel, his body swaying. He slapped the roof twice and whooped again.

We drove over the slack wire of a broken fence and entered a new landscape: flat, dry paddock with tufts of weed, a muddy waterhole in the middle. A few rabbits scampered from cover and took off, dodging left and right, searching for somewhere to hide.

But Dec didn't shoot—he'd spotted something bigger.

'Goats,' Jarrod said.

They were bigger than any goats I'd ever seen, with full beards, yellow eyes and curling hooves. I counted eight, clustered around the waterhole. At first I thought they were blinded by our headlights, but then I realised they were curious, and not at all scared. They'd probably never come across people like us before.

Dec couldn't miss, not at such close range. Not with the goats just standing there, waiting to be executed.

'Sitting ducks,' Jarrod said. He crawled the ute towards them and stopped about forty metres away. 'Roast goat.'

The ute heaved. Dec had jumped off.

The smallest goat in the middle took a step forward. It pawed the dirt.

I took a breath and held it. Stuffed the urge to cry down deep. It was as if I'd landed on a different planet—there were no children here, only grown-ups. I closed my eyes and when my nose stopped burning, I breathed again.

I wouldn't look. If I didn't look, I wasn't part of it.

The passenger door clicked. A rush of cold air and my eyes flew open.

'Man up,' Dec hissed, tugging my shorts.

'I can't.'

'Come on. Quick.'

I shook my head.

The ute heaved again. Brett came around to the side. 'Might be better to let him take a rabbit his first time.'

'Did I ask you?' Dec said.

Brett drawled, 'Come on, man—he's a kid,' and gave me a crooked smile.

I climbed out before Dec could wipe the smile off Brett's face. I let him arrange parts of me to take the weight of the gun. He cupped my left hand under the barrel and hooked my right forefinger around the trigger, and neither hand shook because I had already decided I would aim to miss—just a fraction too high over that distance should be enough to send the bullet way overhead.

'That's yours—the dumb one in the middle. Right between the eyes. Don't nick him.'

Dec stepped away and my body went cold.

'Aim.'

I lined up the sight.

'Shoot,' Dec said.

I made the adjustments—a twist in my shoulders, a dip in one knee, a slight tilt to the barrel—and I squeezed. The shot sounded like a jet had flown over. I staggered backwards and dropped the gun in the dust.

Dec swore and hauled me back by the elbow.

The other goats were restless now, but the little one lowered its head and stared back.

Dec picked up the gun and aimed.

I willed it to run. The goat *knew*, but it didn't do anything.

—

They killed four. We left three of them lying by the dam. I threw up twice. Dec made me ride in the tray with the one he picked. Its eyes were still wet.

When we arrived back at our camp and they hauled its body from the tray, I said I was tired and felt sick. I crawled inside the sagging tent and stayed there, heard them laughing, heard everything through the nylon walls and here's what I know:

goat skin comes off like a banana peel
the kid's got no idea
no stomach for it
no balls
no heart
no teeth.

ONE

Dec and Nance are fighting again. I lie awake, listening. It doesn't upset me as much as it used to—not like when it was Mum and Dec, when I was younger and on my own. Nance can look after herself. With the pillow over my head, their fighting sounds like beatboxing: all hiss and spit.

I toss the pillow aside and lean over the edge of the top bunk. The clock on the table reads nine thirty-six.

Otis and Jake are hard asleep on the bottom bunk, head to toe, curled around each other. My half-brothers, three years and two months old. With the door and window closed, our bedroom reeks of piss and stale breath. Fresh piss or old, I can't tell. O always stinks like urine or vomit or milk gone sour.

Jake rolls over, talking in his sleep, and Otis moves to fill the space as if they're two strange sea creatures inside the same shell. Twins. Jake has a bump on his chest and Otis has a dent on his; Nance says they were joined once, but Jake broke away and took a piece of Otis with him.

For fifteen minutes I ignore my aching bladder. They'll stop fighting if I show my face, but I don't really want them to stop. Maybe tonight Nance will win.

I throw back my sheet and slide off the bunk. The twins

only hear each other—not the fighting, the sirens, the crickets, or the Elvis music coming from Clancy's next door. Not my feet when they hit the floor.

I push the window up halfway and start peeing through the gap.

'Hey, Nate.'

There's a cloud of smoke rising above Nance's dying hydrangea bush.

'*Jesus*, Merrick. Let me finish.'

Obligingly, he looks the other way and takes another drag on his cigarette.

If I had to give a reason for Connor Merrick and me being friends for the last six years, I'd have to say it's more about proximity than personality. McKee and Merrick, straight after each other on the roll call, except for the times there was another McSomebody. The last picks for team—united by shame—me because I'm lethargic to the point of being coma-tose, and Merrick because he's smoked since he was twelve and it's probably stunted his growth. He lives in the upstairs unit across from ours, but he spends every second week with his mum a couple of suburbs over. He's a FIFO kid—he flits in and out. FIFO kids have two sets of stuff. I have a FIFO mum. Kids of FIFO mums have less of everything according to the law of diminishing returns.

Merrick always enters and leaves through our window. In the entire six years I've known him he has never come to our front door.

'Can I hang here for a bit?' he says when I'm finished. 'Senior's tossing my room again.'

His old man's a mean drunk. He throws things around,

9

including Merrick. He usually passes out before midnight, but he'd be hitting his peak about now.

I shrug. 'Dec and Nance are at it.'

'You mean...' He smacks his palms together.

'Nah. Like, brawling.'

'Oh.'

I check the twins: still twitching and dreaming. And I'm not getting to sleep anytime soon.

'We could kill some time at Youth? Might be some fresh meat.'

YouthWorks is the local youth centre, open every night until twelve. Merrick likes going there since he discovered that having a supreme mathematical mind pays massive dividends at the pool table. He looks hopeless with his tiny head and big ears, and sometimes you get meatheads who'll bet they can take him by slapping a whole pack of smokes on the table. Nobody can beat Merrick. I swear I can see glowing equations swirling above his head when he's plotting how to pot three colours off the white. Shame he can't apply the same genius when he's studying Trig.

Merrick nods. 'Good call.'

I grab my notebook, slip on my shoes and climb out, leaving the window open just enough for re-entry.

'Imagine how big your brain might get if you stopped depriving it of oxygen.'

I tuck the notebook inside the waistband of my jeans, at the back. Make sure my T-shirt covers it.

He brushes me off. 'I gotta slow it down until my head catches up. Or else my skull will crack.'

Plenty of people have tried to crack his skull. Merrick's

brain-smart but street-stupid—he'll get us both killed someday.

We squeeze between our row of sixteen letterboxes and thirty-two bins, push through the side gate, and head down Whittlesea Road. Three of five street lights are out; the two that work are swarming with bugs. Summer ended a while back, but Bairstal must get the memo late. A few weeks ago, we had six days straight over thirty-five degrees and we all looked like a new species with purple faces and bulging eyes; all we could do was talk less, pant like dogs and sleep under wet sheets.

'I got sixty-four per cent on my Chem test,' Merrick says. 'I'm officially an over-achiever.'

I shake my head. 'What'd I tell you? What's the first rule of high school?'

'Don't try too hard.'

'And what's the second?'

'Make fun of people who do.'

'Spoken like a true prodigy,' I say.

He screws up his nose. 'Who said that anyway?'

'The Wolf!'

'Not that. High school rules.'

'Channing Tatum. *21 Jump Street*.'

'Oh. Right.'

We've been working our way through the second-hand DVD collection at Youth for over four years; we can carry on whole conversations just using movie dialogue. Merrick and I know each other so well, we hardly have anything original left to say.

We stop at the main road between Bairstal and Rowley

Park. Two Subarus are nudging each other at the lights. We've got time to cross, but if one of them jumps the green we'll be skids. I throw out my arm to hold Merrick back.

He makes an L sign on his forehead. 'Give me an Evo any day.'

'Like you could ever afford an Evo.'

We cross.

'I'd tune up a Ralliart. Same motor, only detuned,' he says.

'Nah, it's a whole lot different. Chassis, I reckon. Brakes, too.'

'Point is it'll look like a shitbox until they're eating dust. Now that would be ironic.'

'No. It really wouldn't.' I've tried to demonstrate irony about a hundred times and he still doesn't get it. 'Anyway, face it. I'll never get my licence.'

'Why not? I can't wait.'

'Think about it—I have to log seventy-five hours, we don't have a car, and a driving instructor costs sixty-five bucks an hour. That's more money than I could scrape together in six months. Which leaves one option—steal a car and fake a logbook, but then I'd still have to come up with the money for the test. In that time, I reckon the person whose car I stole might have noticed their car is missing and I'll get busted for boosting and the licence I never got will be suspended for twelve months. It's a vicious circle.'

'Oh. Yeah, I guess.'

'For the record, that's not ironic either.'

'I know, but—come on. Tell me you don't fantasise about your dream car.'

'Whatever blows your hair back,' I say.

12

'My Evo will blow your hair *off*.'

'It's a dream car—it won't blow anything any more than your dream girl will.'

He thinks for a moment. 'We should definitely fake the logbook.'

'Sure, but then you'd be even more of a danger to society than you already are.'

Merrick mutters to himself, then changes the subject. 'Hey—when you marry Nance, you could adopt me,' he says, as if the thought just occurred to him. Only it hasn't, because that thought occurs to him frequently. 'Do you think she'll still be breastfeeding then?'

I give him a dead arm. 'Shut up. Anyway, she stopped.'

'Bummer.'

I add, 'O has an unpredictable bite reflex.'

'I'd still do her.'

'Mate, you wouldn't know what to do with it if it shouted instructions.'

'Yeah, I would…'

I grab one of his elephant ears and twist it until the cartilage pops. 'Get your hand off it.'

'Hey!' He rubs his ear with one hand and fumbles for a cigarette with the other. 'No wonder they stick out.'

I don't like him talking about Nance that way. Yeah, it's weird having a stepmother only eight years older than me, but no weirder than him having a dad ancient enough to be his grandfather. Merrick senior is seventy and my old man's half that age. Merrick's almost seventeen, six months older than me (though he doesn't act like it), and he thinks about sex *all* the time—about doing it, about watching others do it, about not having someone to do it with. Somehow he does this without mentioning that he's never actually done it. Even if I wanted to, which I don't, I couldn't. I have no privacy. I can't even take a piss without someone knowing.

'Did you know that organisms reproduced asexually for billions of years before sex came along?' I say. 'No mess, no fuss, no broken hearts—*boom*, clone yourself and get on with the important stuff.'

'What's more important than sex?' He makes a suction-ing noise with his tongue.

'Survival.'

Merrick points to my groin. 'You should get that looked at. You're not normal.'

I shake my head and walk on ahead.

Merrick got no challengers at the pool table. I shot hoops in the Rage Cage for a while, but my court buddies Cooper and Deng were no-shows and the bugs were swarming so bad I had to pick flying ants out of my pants. I sat scribbling in my notebook until Macy, the director, kicked us out.

I got a few words down. Not great ones, but that's not really the point. Mostly they're just random scenes, fragments of sentences or long letters to nobody. Ideas that probably wouldn't make sense to anyone but me. They're out of control, so they're not poems; they have no music, so they're not lyrics. I suppose they're a kind of alternative reality, a *possible* reality more than a parallel universe. Like it could happen to me, instead of a different version of me. My notebooks are like my own private well and my words are like stones: I drop them in the well so I don't have to carry them around. I need the well.

It keeps me from self-destructing.

Sometimes I wonder what might happen if I just threw stones instead.

When we get back to the flats, Merrick waves and disappears.

Nance is sitting on the verandah, sifting dirt through her toes. It's just past midnight. She's wearing a stained oversized T-shirt and her long brown hair is twisted on top of her head. She looks up. Her wide grey smiley eyes aren't smiling. Her expression is so blank it's scary.

'I thought you were in bed, bub.'

I don't know why she calls me that. I love it. I hate it.

'I was. I snuck out with Merrick. Went to Youth.'

'I would too, if I could.' She stands, dusting off her arse.

I know what she means. Nobody should be as old as she is at twenty-four. Dad—Dec—has locked her out again because that's what he does when she won't let up. He puts her out like a cat. When he's calmed down he'll serenade her with his guitar until she falls for him again. And she does. Every time.

A hacking cough from the balcony above makes us jump.

'Hey, Margie,' she calls, and waves. 'It's just Margie upstairs.'

Nance names everybody according to where they live: Clancy next door, Margie upstairs, Kath on the corner, the Merricks across the way. She says it's because she's from the country, where nobody has street numbers or letterboxes.

Margie flicks her ash over the railing and coughs in reply.

Dec tolerates Margie being upstairs because she minds her own business. She has a beagle cross called Kelly; Kelly has a chain smoker's cough too, and she's so fat her belly almost touches the ground. I haven't seen her downstairs in years, even though Nance said she could run around our yard because we hardly ever use it. The flats aren't pet-friendly, but everyone keeps Margie's secret because she loves that dog more than life. They sit at the top of the stairs every evening and Margie feeds Kelly people-food from a fork. (I worry about Kelly. I worry about the stains on our ceiling. I wonder where she shits and I've googled 'do dogs need sunshine'.)

'Dec in there?'

Nance shakes her head. 'He went out.'

This is a switch-up. 'With the twins locked in?'

'He probably thought you were there.' She smiles. 'They've got each other. They only need me for daytime.'

'I left the window up a crack. I'll open up for you.'

'He'll kill you if he finds out you leave it open.'

'I know.'

'Wait.' She grabs my hand. 'Read to me. Something happy.'

Nance is the only one I can read to, but I have to be careful what I pick. If I choose right, she gets this look like I've taken her far away and she likes it there. When she first came to live with us, I told her she could stay for a while but she'd have to leave when my real mum came home. She's had plenty of opportunity to score back the point, but that's not her style.

'I started something new. It's about Otis.'

She nods. 'What's it called?'

I breathe in and pull out my notebook. This one's falling apart and almost full. It weighs twice as much as a new one; it always surprises me that ink can be so heavy.

'For Otis.' Another breath. I riffle the pages.

'Read it,' she says, so low I'm not sure I heard her right.

'For Otis.' I clear my throat.

—*They say*

a piece of you is missing—

I stop. The last thing I want to do is make Nance cry.

'What comes next?'

'That's it. I've only got the beginning.'

Nance is quiet for a long time. She can't tell I lied. Her eyes are shining, or maybe they're just reflecting the sensor light.

'Let me know how it ends,' she says.

TWO

Our English teacher, Mr Reid, had this epic meltdown last year, when I was in Year Ten. It was Friday afternoon and nobody was paying attention—we were chucking paper and kicking chairs over as usual—when he stood up suddenly, white as, like he'd had a stroke. Smacked his palm on his desk so hard it sounded like a whipcrack. Everything stopped.

I memorised a few of his lines. Wish I could remember more. It reminded me of Matt Damon's monologue in *Good Will Hunting*, about the NSA and the bombing of the innocents and the clubbing of baby seals. Basically he said everything that's wrong with the world can be found in suburban-sized proportions right here in Bairstal: hate, racism, crime, dirty politics, segregation, terrorism, drugs, neglect, false religion, the wrong kinds of love, and more hate. A microcosm, he called us. *You're victims*, he said. *You think you're tough, but you're not. You're lost, and you're surrendering the only real weapon you have. Sure, you're pissed off that someone stole your iPhone or nicked your bike, but while you're fighting each other something else is being stolen and you don't even know it. You want to be angry, be fucking angry about that.*

I half-stood when he finished. I have trouble believing

anything that isn't scientific fact, but it sounded true.

Kobe Slater laughed first. Everyone else followed. One minute Mr Reid was upright, yelling at Slater to shut up, telling me to sit down; the next he collapsed like a sandcastle when the tide comes in—only the tide was us and our perfect disdain for anyone who drives an Audi but thinks he has the right to tell us our lives are shit.

Mr Reid never fully recovered.

'Angry about what?' I asked him when the class was empty.

'School's over, McKee,' he said. 'Go home.'

'I want to know. What was stolen?'

His eyes were dry and sore like he'd forgotten to blink. 'Your future, Nate.'

This year I have Mr Reid again. His walls are back up. After his meltdown, someone complained that he swore and he was made to apologise to the class. Some days I watch him watching us. I wonder if it would make any difference if I told him the reason I stood up last year was because I was about to start a slow clap, only I realised in time I was the only one who'd clap.

I'm a worrier. Nance says it's weird considering I grew up with Dec for a dad, his mantra being 'no worries'. Dec only wears Rusty or Billabong low-rise board shorts and singlets with droopy armpits, anything that shows off his pecs and that groin v-thing he's got going on. His head's shaved as close as you can get without a straight razor, and he's built like a cage fighter. Tatts, scars—he's got a story for all of them, and he rarely wears shoes except when he has to, like in the pub or the TAB. Our flat has an old longboard stuck in the dirt out front. Nobody would steal that board for two reasons: it's got a hole, as if something big took a bite out of it, and everyone's scared of Dec. Never mind that surfers surf and Dec doesn't. Never mind that we're forty kays from the nearest beach—no waves, just low tides and crabs and stinky black mud and old blokes in waders. No worries.

Yeah, I'm a worrier. I worry about pretty much everything, all the time. I worry about the big stuff: climate change, animal cruelty, the state of politics, boat people, whose finger is on the button, bigness, nothingness, all of it. Some nights I lie awake and think about the universe before it was a universe. Science says there are more than a hundred billion galaxies out there, and several hundred billion stars in our galaxy alone. But how do we *know*? Who counted? I get why people believe in God; how the *fuck* did we get here? What if just one of those chemical reactions never happened and we never existed, or what if cats evolved opposable thumbs instead of us? Some days I feel guilty for worrying about the small stuff: schoolwork, no phone credit, no cereal, the holes in my shoes, the stupid sensor light next door that's been left on for two years straight and beams right into our bedroom window, tricking me into thinking the sun is up when it's the middle of the night. My circadian rhythms are fucked.

I read a lot. Nothing but non-fiction, essays, scientific articles about evolution and adaptation, and hardcore news. Not poetry or fiction—there's so much bullshit in the world I only want to know what's true. Everything I learn I keep for later, because you can't know too much in Bairstal. Tough is the golden ticket. If you get tough breaks, tough going, tough luck, tough pills to swallow, well, tough shit. You have to accept tough love, talk tough, toughen up, tough it out, be a tough nut to crack, and when the going gets tough, sure, get going, but don't think you can leave.

I've decided sixteen is a nothing age. Too young to behave like an adult, too old to act like a kid. Doesn't help that my puberty took a timeout—my voice hasn't fully broken, my facial hair is fluff, and my bones grew too fast for my skin, so I look like I've spent a month on a medieval torture rack. Oh, and acne.

I'm treading water for now. If I can float long enough, maybe I'll wash up somewhere else. Nance says I have Dec's genes and one day they'll kick in. That's what I'm afraid of— that, and being numb. Sometimes I'll read long articles about child trafficking or the war in Syria to prove I still care.

I worry that it's too much hard work to be a good person. If I was truly good it should be easy.

It's Wednesday afternoon. We have about ten minutes left of English, and so far Mr Reid hasn't asked us to do much work apart from reading. He's kicking back on his chair, eyes closed, and every now and then he emits a deep *ahem*, which I'm beginning to suspect is a form of echolocation. Most of the class remember last year's rant, and we're not quite as feral as we used to be. It's not like he earned our respect or anything; perhaps it's just that unpredictability is a teacher's best defence.

'McKee, wait after class.'

My head snaps up so fast my neck cracks. I can't tell if I've done something right or wrong. It's better if I've done something wrong.

I pack my things away slowly.

I dread these after-class conversations. I'm not sure if it's all English teachers or just Mr Reid, but he inhabits another world, where every conversation has to be meaningful and anything we say must be tested to find hidden depth. If I told him there was a room in our house with a locked door and every day we walk past that door pretending it doesn't exist, he'd tug on his beard and say, *Hmm, tell me more about this door*, thinking it's a metaphor for something deep and unresolved in my family. He wouldn't believe me even if I said it's a literal room, with a literal door, and we're literally not allowed to go in there, and he'd spend fifteen minutes telling me off for saying 'literally' because he reckons it's a crutch word, like 'shit' and 'fuck'.

It's exhausting. Literally.

Mr Reid has forgotten I'm there. I clear my throat.

'You're not enjoying the war poets?' he says eventually.

It sounds like a trick question. 'They're all right.'

He has two handwritten signs stuck to the wall behind his desk, like giant Post-it reminders.

Revise.

Revise!

REVISE!

and

Dream—Goal—Plan—Action—Reality

They might as well tell me to fly.

'What can I do to engage you with the work, Mr McKee?'

I shove my hands in my pockets. 'Nothing.'

He thumbs through sheets of paper. 'Then how can I convince you that copying and pasting swathes of text does not constitute writing an original essay?' He finds the piece he's looking for and holds it up as if it's a soiled tissue.

Last week's essay. The one time I cheated, when I nearly missed the deadline and I'd been stuck with Otis all night, screaming, screaming because Jake had gastro and Nance had to keep them apart and Dec was off somewhere like he always is.

'It won't happen again.'

He hands me the paper. 'You have referred to Wilfred Owen as Wilbur, three times, and you call Robert Graves' muses "tarts".'

Since they're probably the parts I plagiarised, I have no idea what he's talking about. Beats me why we have to study dead poets and pointless wars anyway—it's not like the human race has learned anything from either.

'Sorry,' I say. 'I'll fix it.'

I just want to get out of here. If I miss home group I'll have to go to student services to sign out.

He stares at me. Watery blue eyes, full-face beard with leftovers from lunch, a comb-over like something dead on the side of a road. Apparently he's a Morris dancer in his spare time: dudes dancing around to folk music, ringing bells and waving handkerchiefs.

'We'll be working on something different over the next few weeks. I'd hate to see you so far behind that you fail to take advantage of this learning opportunity.'

'Different how?'

'Let's just say you'll need a clear head for a reckoning with your fatal flaw—s.'

'Plural?'

'Plural.'

Finally, he blinks. Pretty sure he has two sets of eyelids.

'A thousand words by next Tuesday. And a bonus

thousand-word piece on Bulwer-Lytton's line "the pen is mightier than the sword" as penance. Any form you like, but cite your references.'

I'm already wondering if he'll notice if I upcycle an essay I turned in last year.

'Oh, and McKee? Make it original.'

Shit. There's nothing original to be said about that line.

I sprint to home group, but take my time leaving the senior block. I prefer to wait for the corridor to clear out, that way I won't accidentally bump into somebody and start something. Eyes down, slow swagger. It's hard work pretending you don't care about anything when all you really want to do is scream in people's faces and push them down the stairs. Rowley Park High is a multicultural war zone and where the cultures cross turf, you get blood. There are metal detectors on the way in, but once you leave you're on your own. At this school, the pen *is* mightier than the sword. These days you can't get a knife past the school entrance, but that doesn't mean it's any safer. I'd run out of fingers if I had to count the number of students who've been stabbed with a Bic.

Merrick's waiting by the canteen window.

He won't walk home alone. It's not that he needs protection (like I could offer any) but he says he needs a witness. I get by if I keep my head down and my mouth shut, but Merrick's becoming a liability—too many wins at the pool table and he thinks freedom of speech is the prize, like a meat tray or something. He hardly does any schoolwork and I'm his only friend. I think he just follows me here out of habit.

He falls into step beside me, two for one of mine. You've

got to master the saunter, but Merrick always trots as if he's warming up for a sprint.

'Who'd you piss off today?'

'Won't know until I feel hot breath on my neck.' He laughs and starts thumbing through his deck.

Merrick collects the saddest Pokémon cards, the ones most people don't even bother trading. His reasoning is this: if they're so miserable they're being chucked, then nobody's collecting them, and one day they'll be rare and sought after. Problem is, he thumbs through them all the time, so they're not even mint.

'What'd you get?'

'Slowbro,' he says. 'Pacifist. Prefers not to fight. He's got a Shellder attached to his tail but if it's knocked off, Slowbro unevolves. The Shellder's poison stops him from feeling pain but if it bites down, Slowbro gets all psychic on yo' ass. Still, he's pretty pathetic. Worth keeping around.'

'Devolves,' I say.

'Whatever.'

I kick the oval gate open and hold it. 'Sounds like an unhealthy relationship. Shit, man, who makes this stuff up?'

He grabs the gate. 'Artists, Nathaniel. Visionaries. Humans with insanely creative minds, the likes of which the likes of you could never understand.' He lets the gate go and it hits a kid behind us. 'Sorry.'

I snigger. 'Bet none of them were born and bred in Bairstal.'

He licks the back of the card and sticks it to my forehead.

'Jesus, Merrick.' I flick it away and it flutters to the ground. 'Hepatitis B, coming right up.'

He bends to retrieve the card and slides it back in the deck.

We take the path through the long, narrow paddock that runs between the back of the school and the train line. In spring, you can hardly see the weeds for woolly bear caterpillars. In summer, it's snake heaven. A few late locusts click and scatter as we pick our way through the dry grass.

'Plague's coming,' I say. 'And all you can talk about is pool and Pokémon.'

Merrick gives me a serious stare. 'You should pay attention,' he says. 'Slowbro is basically you.'

Dec's in a good mood. He must have won on the dogs or ponies. When I get to the flat he's shirtless, Nance on his lap, Jake on the floor playing with his Lego.

I don't ever remember being allowed on his lap.

Otis is jammed in the space between the arm of the couch and Dec's rib tattoo, the one with our names being strangled by a snake and cut with a dagger. One day I'll ask him for that story.

'All right, Nate?'

I sling my bag in the corner near the door. 'Yeah.'

'They fill your brain with more useless shit? When I was your age I'd already been working with my old man for two years.'

'Doing what?' I ask, before I can censor myself.

Dec doesn't work, unless you count betting as a vocation or growing a hydro crop as primary production. It's his fault I can't use my own bedroom.

Dec's eyes turn slitty.

Nance crosses her legs and works on folding the hem of her dress into a concertina.

'Nah, I mean what did your old man do?' I smile to take the sting out. 'Wasn't he a boilermaker or something?'

I really wouldn't know. I have at least two grandparents somewhere, a grandfather on Dec's side and a grandmother on Mum's, but they're like mythical beasts. Mum is still alive, somewhere, but I've stopped counting the days until she comes back to visit. Now I count in years. That's why family is so important to Dec—he says anyone can hatch an egg but not all reptiles look after their young. He always says reptiles but it's not worth correcting him.

Dec doesn't answer. He's trying to figure out if I'm trying to be clever, or just continuing my long tradition of stupid. It's better for me if I'm not being clever. A week ago, when I forgot again and called him Dad, he said every time I did that it felt like he'd given me a gift I didn't bother to open.

'I'll make us something to eat,' Nance says. She swings her legs onto the floor, but he puts both hands around her waist to hang on. 'Dec!' She slaps his forearm and pulls away.

Otis slips sideways. He lands on his back, head in Dec's lap, and he starts bawling.

Jake springs to attention.

Nance leans down to pick him up, but Dec says, 'Leave him. Let him work it out,' and she freezes.

Jake does too, and it scares me that a three-year-old knows better.

Otis thrashes about like a flipped turtle, his muscles tense, but useless; it's like his brain sends messages but something gets in the way. *Wah, wa-ah-ah-ah-ah.* He sounds like a baby goat.

I'm still standing by the door, watching Jake's right

27

hand—he lets go of the Lego car he's holding and reaches for Otis, eyes on Dec, hand underneath the couch so Dec can't see. His palm flattens; his fingers flutter.

Otis's eyes glaze. He goes still, then slowly, slowly, kicks one leg over and rolls his body onto the floor.

'Good boy!' Nance says.

Jake gathers Otis under one arm and pulls him close.

The size difference is extreme now: Jake looks at least a year older. They both have Dec's chameleon eyes and Nance's shiny brown hair, but Jake has strong toddler muscles and Otis is flabby and weak; Jake hardly ever stops talking and Otis mumbles back-to-front words; Jake can kick a footy for miles and Otis has trouble holding a spoon. It's like the piece that Jake took away with him was a major connection between Otis's motherboard and his battery pack.

Dec has realised something has happened without his say-so. He holds us half-cocked with a grim smile until he decides we've had enough. He reaches for his guitar. 'No worries,' he says.

Jake claps.

Nance moves like someone pressed Play.

Otis smiles and drools.

My knees are knocking and I hate it.

THREE

On Thursday after school there's no one at Youth but me, Merrick, Tash and Mim, one of the volunteers.

Back in the nineties the building used to be a community hall. Outside, there's a long, curved brick wall facing the main road with the word YOUTH painted in graffiti. It's an ambigram: it reads the same right-side up and upside-down, but I've never stood on my head to confirm that. Macy always grumbles about how much it cost, saying she could have turned a blind eye and one of us delinquents could have done it better and for free, but instead the council commissioned a local artist.

That makes it art, I think, not graffiti. Art has permission.

The centre has double automatic doors with a glitchy sensor—from the inside, you have to pull off a dance routine to make them open. It has a kitchen and one gigantic rec room with a few old couches, beanbags, a big-screen TV, a pool table, two computers, a PlayStation, and a couple of bookcases with stacks of books, magazines and board games. At the back of the building there's a room where Macy sleeps sometimes, and two toilets, plus a shower, all locked. You have to ask for the key to the toilets, and if you don't come out within a reasonable time, you can bet one of the youth workers is coming in.

I figure something bad must have happened for that rule to appear on The Chart.

The Chart tells us what we can, can't and must do.
We can:
- use whatever we like as long as somebody else isn't using it
- watch whatever we like as long as it's rated G, M or MA15+
- eat or drink whatever we like from the group pantry or fridge
- say whatever we like unless someone asks us to stop
- borrow whatever we like as long as it doesn't leave the centre

We can't:
- bring drugs, alcohol or weapons onto the premises
- watch porn or anything rated R18+
- invade others' space or privacy
- be violent, sexist, racist, homophobic or offensive
- threaten or bully
- deface, destroy or steal property
- bring nuts, eat nuts or leave nuts lying around
- take too long in the bathroom (otherwise somebody's coming in)
- shout with raised voices (this is a new rule)

We must:
- share
- be respectful
- show kindness despite difference

- clean up after ourselves
- smoke outside in the courtyard
- and leave everything as we found it.

There's a three-strike policy. Strike one: a warning. Strike two: a suspension. Strike three: mandatory counselling and a possible permanent ban.

Mim's adding more *National Geographic* magazines to the pile on the bookshelf. I've never seen anybody read them but her. She has dark curly hair to her waist and she's tiny. Fierce, though. She's only here a few days a week. She stays in the background, talks fast and moves slowly, looks young but seems old, and she's watchful in a way that makes you feel safe, whatever happens. When she finishes her shift, a big guy picks her up from the door so she doesn't have to wait outside in the car park by herself.

'More magazines?' I say.

Mim smiles. 'I've read them all. They take up too much space at home.'

'Have you been to any of those places?'

'Europe. Egypt. Africa. France, for a year, when I wasn't much older than you. Twenty-three now and it seems like a lifetime ago. I'm saving while I'm studying at uni—next stop, Antarctica.'

'And you came here? Like, *voluntarily*?'

'That's what volunteers *do*.'

'I mean you came back here, to Bairstal.'

She shrugs. 'Someone once told me you can fly all you want, but you need a place to land. This is my place. Do you want to travel, Nate?'

31

I snort. 'No point deluding myself. Put that on The Chart, after no shouting with raised voices. "No deluding yourself." Anyway, isn't shouting and raising your voice the same thing?'

'I'd have to think about that.' She hands me a magazine. 'This is a good one. I see you writing all the time, but do you read?'

'Not really,' I say.

'*Cough*bullshit,' says Merrick. 'He reads everything. He stockpiles facts so he can shoot you down with them.'

'I mean, not books. News, mostly. Articles and stuff.'

'On the inside, he's an angry young man,' Merrick says.

'Ignore him. On the outside, he's a dickhead.'

'It's not my fault. I was born with foetal alcohol syndrome.' He looks at Mim and waits for sympathy.

'You can't catch that from pickled sperm. It has to pass through the placenta,' I say. 'And you'd probably have brain damage—oh, wait.'

Mim laughs and Merrick yells, 'What would you know? You don't *read*!'

'No shouting,' I remind him.

Mim glances at The Chart. 'I'm pretty sure there's a distinction between a shout and a raised voice. And maybe your delusions are dreams in disguise.'

I snort. 'Pretty sure they're just delusions.'

'Told you. Angry,' Merrick says, walking away.

Mim sighs. 'There's always a way out, even when you feel like you're walking around blindfolded. Just don't do what I did and think you have to close the door behind you.' The phone in the kitchen rings. 'I've got to get that.'

I tuck a magazine under my arm, find a comfy spot on

the couch and start reading an article. My eyes move over the words, but I can feel Tash's glare.

She comes here a lot. I don't even know if she goes to school—not ours, anyway. She has short black hair, cut like a boy's, and she wears op-shop clothing. No judgement, it's just that she goes out of her way to wear stuff that hurts your eyes: today, blue-and-yellow football socks with a long pink skirt. One time it was a men's suit jacket over a shiny dress that made her look like she went to a ball half-naked and her old man tried to cover her up. She's got dark eyes that show white all around her irises, so she always looks ready to jump out of her skin. Never says much—just burrows deep in a beanbag and watches TV, or plugs in her earphones and gives everyone her fuck-the-fuck-off face. She always makes sure her beanbag is backed up against the wall.

Merrick, for once, hasn't bothered trying to get Tash to talk. One too many burning stares from her, I guess, and manlier men than him have tried. Now he's got his cards spread out over the pool table in rows, like he's playing Solitaire. Every now and then he moves one to a different space and grunts.

'Merrick.'

'What.'

'Give me your phone. I need Spotify.'

I don't have Spotify. Too many choices, too much disposable shit. My music library is curated: only the top 100 songs by my top 100 artists of all time, at all times. There's something pure about having to weigh up whether a new track deserves to replace an old one—you have to test its staying power for at least three months. I've lost hours debating between a ten-minute anthem and a two-minute guitar solo.

But right now we need something upbeat, and my stuff is the opposite.

'Merrick.'

He gives me the finger.

Someone donated a jukebox a month ago. It's a Wurlitzer, really old, from the sixties or something, with faded lights and chipped buttons. It sits in a corner where the coffee machine used to be before someone didn't leave it where they found it. Macy has a coin stuck to a piece of Blu-Tack near the slot. The coin spits out after you choose a song and we're supposed to put it back after. Hardly anybody plays it, though—there's nothing on the playlist after about 1965, and the records jump and scratch.

I turn on the switch at the wall. The jukebox lights up. I push the coin into the slot, run my finger past the Elvises—at least a dozen of them—and press the button for Dion. 'Runaround Sue' starts.

Hey, hey, oh-oh-oh-oh-oh-oh—

Merrick says, 'Fuck's sake, Nate, turn it down.'

Mim looks up from drying dishes and smiles. She tosses her head, slings the tea towel around her neck, throws her hands out wide, and starts doing the twist from side to side.

Yeah, I should have known it from the very start
This girl will leave me with a broken heart—

Merrick nods his head.

I'm watching Tash.

She's got her headphones in, eyes down. She's focusing hard on the screen, squished down so deep in the beanbag half her body is swallowed up, but her index finger has curled,

34

hovering over the power-off button. She presses it. Her eyes flick to Mim. One corner of her mouth pinches, leaving a crease in her left cheek—it could be the beginning of a smile, or she might be preparing to deploy her fuck-off face. The toe of her left foot is tapping in perfect time.

At around six, a few more kids filter in, raiding the fridge and taking over the PlayStation and the computers—always the first choices.

Merrick brightens up and takes hold of a cue, waiting for a challenger.

Tash makes herself some toast and goes back to her corner.

Mim has her bag packed and waiting by the door, but Macy calls to say she'll be running late again. Mim puts her bag back inside her locker in the kitchen.

I go back to reading the *National Geographic* article. It's about the coy-wolf, a canine hybrid, the result of cross-breeding between dogs, coyotes and grey wolves. The coy-wolf *should* have been a genetic disaster, but instead resulted in a superior animal: bigger than a coyote, wilier than a wolf, and the dog-like part of its brain (roughly ten per cent) made it unafraid. So these wild creatures are roaming the suburban streets of North America in ever-increasing numbers. *Assimilating.* Probably wouldn't be long before people came home to find a coy-wolf reclining on the couch, hogging the PlayStation.

I laugh.

Tash looks up and stares at me.

I laughed because I had a thought: I'm a cross-breed, a genetic disaster. On the inside, I'm an outsider. I have to assimilate. But what if I'm like the coy-wolf? If only I could tap into the ten per cent part of my brain that wasn't afraid— shit, what if I have *potential*?

I open my notebook and write the thought down under the title: *Mongrels make good dogs.*

Mim looks across at me reading her magazine. She winks.

I turn the page.

Mim comes out of the kitchen.

Two younger boys leave.

Merrick chalks his favourite cue and places it back behind the bookcase so nobody else can jinx it.

Tash takes her plate to the sink.

I turn another page.

You hear sounds sometimes. They're common, so your brain thinks they're normal. Shouts, breaking glass—nothing to worry about, because whatever is happening is happening outside, or across the street, or over the back fence, so it can't touch you. And you can't change anything anyway. By the time you realise that, not only is it going to touch you, it's going to leave a crack in everything, it's too late.

It sounds as if the glass is breaking somewhere miles from here. When the doors burst open, nobody reacts. Not straightaway.

I don't recognise the guy. He's shirtless, bare feet and blue jeans, longish hair and red eyes, like he has a high fever. There's nothing in his hands—no weapon, no reason to think he will hurt anyone. He runs to the middle of the room and stops, as if he's trapped and he's looking for a way out.

Mim says, 'You need to leave, right now,' and steps towards him. 'Leave.' She points at the door.

The guy turns slowly in her direction.

She stands her ground. 'These are kids. This is not the place for you. We can find you some help somewhere else. Let me call somebody for—'

The man launches, chops at her neck with a flat hand, and she goes down. Her head hits the floor and she's limp.

But he doesn't stop. He straddles her and punches her, twice, so hard her cheek caves in and the bridge of her nose splits open. He spreads his fingers and stares at the blood on his knuckles, gets up, runs around the room grabbing things and smashing them onto the floor.

He leaves as suddenly as he arrived. The doors don't even glitch

'Call an ambulance!' Tash screams, and for some reason I can only think that her voice is husky and it doesn't match her skirt.

The three remaining younger kids jump up and down in front of the sensor until the doors open. They take off.

Tash grabs a towel and tries to wrap it around Mim's head.

I'm proud of her for moving when I can't. Can't move, can't speak.

Merrick brushes past me and picks up the phone in the kitchen. I hear him talking, but I can't make out what he's saying.

The doors burst open again.

This time we scatter. I find a wall to back up against, but it's the guy who always picks up Mim after her shift. He takes us all in, scoops up Mim like a broken doll and carries her outside, leaving behind dribbles of blood on the floor so bright it doesn't look real.

Tyres squeal in the car park, and somewhere too far away, an ambulance is coming.

It takes less than two minutes and everything is changed.

We go outside. I'm not sure whose idea it is.

Merrick, Tash and I are standing in a shell-shocked triangle.

'What just happened?' Tash says.

What do we do? Start cleaning up? Wait for the ambos? Wait for Macy? Run?

'Do we wait for the ambos?' Merrick. 'Or the police?'

'I'm kind of on probation.' Tash.

'For what?' Merrick.

She doesn't answer.

If I speak, my insides might come up. Not just my last meal, but other stuff too: liver, kidneys, intestines, gallbladder, pancreas. Like silly string.

'We should wait for Macy.' Tash.

'Do you think Mim's okay?' Merrick.

'I think she's pretty far from okay.' Tash.

Marsellus Wallace, I think.

'Marsellus Wallace.' Merrick.

'What are you on about?' Tash.

'*Pulp Fiction*.' Merrick.

'Right. I'd really be quoting *Pulp Fiction* when I had someone's brains on my hands.' She holds them out. They're shaking. Bloody.

'Well, you didn't do anything.' Merrick.

'I know.' Tash.

'I meant you didn't do anything wrong, so it doesn't matter

if you're on probation.' Merrick.

'I didn't do anything.' Tash. 'None of us did anything.'

None of us did anything. But what could we have done?

'What could we have done?' Merrick.

'I don't know. CPR? We should have checked if she was breathing. That guy shouldn't have moved her. What if her neck was broken? There's three of us—we should have pulled that crazy guy off her and held him down and, I don't know, hit him with something. Or something.'

'We should start cleaning up.' Merrick.

'We should go.' Tash.

I listen to Tash and Merrick, saying everything I'm thinking, out loud, trying to make sense of it all. The sound Mim made when she hit the floor—I'll never get it out of my head. Like meat. There's no coming back from that.

'Nate?' Merrick says.

What?

'Nate!'

'What?' I shout.

'He speaks,' Tash says.

Merrick does his best impression of a blind monkey. 'I'm just gonna tell them I didn't see nothing.'

All I say is, 'That's a double negative.'

'Two negatives make a positive,' he says. 'So you can suck my big one.'

Red, blue, red, blue, red, blue. The ambulance is coming. The police are, too.

We break our triangle to stand in a line, staring out at the street.

FOUR

Life goes on. I know because everything hurts.

I think it's nearly morning, but I'm scared to look at the clock in case I'm wrong and it's still the middle of the night. I suspect I'm going to have one of those days when you get angry if people are laughing about something. Worse, you get sad if they try to cheer you up. Worse still, you get angrier—at yourself—because you know they're just trying to be nice and you need people like that, but you can't be around them because currently your emotions are incompatible with theirs. So you shut them out and they get angry and they go away.

The world is ugly.

Otis makes a snuffling sound in his sleep, only when I look down he's not sleeping. He's lying on his side, turned away from Jake, one leg slung over the edge of the mattress, foot bouncing on the floor. It's weird—he's left space between him and Jake.

Slowly, he turns his head and peers up at me.

O's eyes sometimes switch between blue and green, like Dec's. They have the same blankness Nance's get when she's unhappy, only his are like that all the time—it's like he sees you, but there's something beyond that needs his attention, so they fix for a split second and slide past. Sometimes I wonder if his reality and mine are the same. Maybe red isn't red in his world, or dogs look like chickens.

Otis's lashes flutter and his eyes close. One fist uncurls and he stretches his arm, pointing one finger.

I reach down with my own. We're like that zoomed-in image of Michelangelo's on the ceiling of the Sistine Chapel when God created Adam, except we're touching, and neither of us will be around for that long.

When O opens his eyes again, they stay fixed. These moments never last, but when he's present like this we have wordless conversations.

Nate. It's you.

Hello, Otis.

The sun is up!

It's just the sensor light. Go back to sleep.

It's the sun! It's dark at night but the sun comes up every day.

Maybe you're right, O. Maybe it's the sun.

He takes his hand away and curls his fist again, tucking it to his chest like a broken wing.

I check the clock. It's five past six.

'Sun,' O says, clear as anything.

The world is beautiful.

For Otis,

They say

a piece of you is missing

and they don't know why

or where it went

or if it was ever there.

They say you might never walk

or use a full sentence.
You won't be able to tell us what you want
you can't live a full life
and you might never dance.
But you speak with your eyes
your fingers, your fists.
You'll never
steal cars
break laws
start wars.
What if you came to show us how to fly,
to teach us a new language?
What if the missing piece of you
is the broken thing in us?
What if natural selection
chose someone like you?
Who cares what
they say.

The next thing I know, it's after eight and someone is pounding on the front door. I'm already going to be late for school, but the knocking sounds like it means business.

Dec and Nance are scrabbling for their clothes in the next room, whisper-shouting at each other, feet slapping the floor. Dec hops into our bedroom, pulling on his shorts.

I sit up, and he grabs my arm and hauls me off the bunk.

Otis starts wailing, and Jake covers him with his body.

'Get the door. Don't let them in. Go out on the verandah, okay? Tell them it's just you and the boys.'

I'm only wearing boxers. I go to pick my jeans up from the floor, but he puts his hand between my shoulderblades and shoves me along the hallway, into the lounge room.

Nance is sitting on the edge of their bed, palms pressed to her cheeks. 'Who is it?'

'Cops,' Dec says. 'Just you and the boys, okay?'

I manage to nod, but getting to our front door when you're still half asleep is like playing hopscotch in a minefield: my eyelids are stuck together, I'm tripping over my feet and Jake's Lego blocks, which are scattered everywhere. I shove Dec's bong underneath the couch. The door shakes again.

'I'm coming.'

I turn the deadbolt slowly and stick my face between the gap. Two cops. A young one I recognise, standing behind an older one I don't.

The older one has his hand on the door. 'Nathaniel McKee?'

'Yeah.'

'Your parents home?'

'No. Just me and the kids. What's up?'

'You witnessed the incident at the youth centre last night?'

Incident. Sounds too much like 'accident'.

'I gave a statement.'

'You also gave a fake address,' the young cop says. 'So did your friend.' He checks his notebook. 'One Connor Wankridge. You know what his real name is and where we can find him?'

I didn't think to give a fake name. Too stunned.

'No.'

'You're not in any trouble.' Old cop.

'Then what do you want?' Dec exhales through his teeth

43

somewhere behind me. 'I told them everything I know.'

'A couple more questions. When you're accompanied by a parent we can go over your statement and sign it off.'

I shake my head. 'I'm already late for school. My parents aren't home. The kids are asleep. I don't have any clothes on.' My voice goes squeaky at the tail end.

Old cop breathes in. His nostrils flare.

My heart ratchets up a notch. If I open the door another few inches he'll see the mould stains on the ceiling outside my old room—it doesn't matter how hard Nance scrubs them with bleach, they come back like an incurable disease. One step inside and he'll get an absolute lungful; shortly after, he'll get out a warrant.

I push past him and close the door behind me. The deadbolt clicks. 'I can come to the station after school.' When he raises his eyebrows, I add, 'I've got a test this morning. I can't miss it.'

Inside, Otis is screaming like he's on fire.

'Who looks after the kids when you go to school?' Young cop.

'Babysitter's coming.'

Old cop's suspicious, but he lets it go. 'Righto. We'll see you this afternoon then.'

They saunter off.

'Wait.' I follow them out past Clancy's. 'Is she okay? Mim, I mean?'

'Serious but stable, last we heard.'

'Oh. That's good, right?'

I jog back to the verandah and bash on the glass panel.

Dec takes his sweet time. He hauls me inside by the elbow.

44

'The hell you been up to?'

'Nothing.'

'Didn't look like nothing.'

Nance calls from the kitchen. 'Coffee?'

'Someone got beat up at Youth last night.' I pull away. 'I saw it.'

'So you bring them around here?' He points at my old room. 'That's two years right there. What'll happen to all of you if I'm locked up, hey?'

'I gave a fake address.'

Dec pulls back his fist and growls.

He won't hit me. Never has. Doesn't stop me from flinching, though. The flinch gives me away every time.

'Coffee?' Nance says, louder.

'Hey.' Merrick jogs to catch up. 'You didn't wait.'

He looks as if he's just crawled out of bed too.

'Sorry. I thought you'd already gone.'

'We should ring Youth to see how Mim's doing.'

'Serious but stable,' I say.

'Cops give you a hard time?'

'Nuh. But they're looking for you, too.'

'We told them everything we saw.'

'I know.'

Merrick stops to pick up fifty cents from the gutter. 'Any point going?'

'To school? Probably not.' I wasn't lying about the test, but it doesn't matter now. By the time we get through security and sign in, it'll be all over. 'What do you want to do?'

'Dunno.'

I wish I'd taken the twenty-dollar note Dec left in the plant pot on the kitchen table, but it was too risky. It's impossible to tell if he's testing me, or he forgot he'd left it there.

Without speaking, we both take the next right down Harrington Street, heading in the opposite direction from school. It leads to concrete slopes beneath the underpass, the perfect place to go to think about where to go next. The bowling alley closed a month ago, and Merrick's on a six-week ban from Tunza Fun, the game parlour. We can't risk going to the shops for the free wi-fi—teachers have truant duty at lunchtime.

I want to ask Merrick how he's doing after last night. I wonder if he feels tainted somehow, like I do. No, that's not the right word—grubby, like I'm covered in something that won't wash off.

When we get to the underpass, we wait for a break in the traffic to get a decent run up the slopes. They're pretty steep, about forty-five degrees, but there's a ledge at the top where you can hide behind the girders and smoke, drink, make out, whatever, without anyone seeing.

Merrick and I don't do any of those things. We kick some cans down the slope and use a branch to sweep a clean space where we can sit on the ledge.

'Hey, remember when Isaac Renfrew lost his footing and rolled down onto the road? Car missed him by this much.' Merrick holds his fingers a few centimetres apart. He peers down the slope, plugging in his headphones, except he doesn't push the jack all the way in and I can hear heavy breathing and groaning coming from his phone in his pocket.

'Jesus. What are you listening to?' I push him away.

He laughs and offers me an earpiece. 'Zombies, Run!'

'No, thanks.'

'It's a sprint training app. You hear them coming up behind you and it makes you run faster.'

'Why do you bother? All you have to do is open your mouth and you've got the real thing.'

He flips me off.

Below, the empty cans clatter and roll in the gutter. The traffic goes *k-ch-k-ch-k-ch-k-ch* as cars pass overhead, the sound amplified in the echo chamber. In the white of a huge eye graffitied on the side of the bridge, someone has written *I sound my barbaric yawp over the roofs of the world* in black Texta.

I copy it into my notebook, do a search and discover it's a line from a Walt Whitman poem—another dead guy, but I like the sound of it anyway. I type *what is a barbaric yawp?* First up, I get a weird essay about Whitman being butt-naked in a forest, followed by a Rotten Tomatoes review of a Robin Williams movie about some rich kids at an all-boys' boarding school, then a Yahoo question from another kid—more clueless than me—who receives an answer from a random dude from another continent saying a barbaric yawp is your battle cry. Sounds reasonable. I assume the kid repeated said dude's opinion on yawps in his own essay, thus perpetuating the myth that there's a right answer—that a poem can be understood without asking Walt fucking Whitman Himself. What was Walt thinking? Who knows. It's all guesswork. That's the thing about teachers—they want you to tell them what a poem means, but they think they already have the answers. They're just waiting to catch you out. I reckon a poet could write something that felt true at the time, change his standpoint, then revisit his own work twenty years later, only to realise his most quotable quote doesn't mean what he thought it meant, or it isn't something he stands for anymore.

This is the main problem I have with art: art doesn't mean one thing. It can't. When Mr Reid asks us to tell him what a poem means, he's really asking us all to think the same.

I'll take my uneducated guess—I reckon it's as good as anything my search turned up:

Yawp.

A *barbaric* yawp.

A word, curling like smoke, slipping through the cracks in the same way darkness comes and light leaves, interrupting fights and fucks and family dinners, making everybody stop whatever they're doing, making them whisper—did you hear it, too?

I'm balancing on the ledge, my arms above my head, screaming, and the acoustics are incredible. As usual, Merrick doesn't wait for an invitation or an explanation. He just joins in.

For a change of scenery, we go to the skate park.

It's hidden behind Bunnings on the main north–south freeway, next to Jack Berry Dog Park. A couple of years ago it was a wasteland—now it's a 'People, Pooches 'n' Play' recreational space divided by the dog-park fence and a row of scraggly trees. The skate park has one shallow concrete track and a larger one about the depth of a swimming pool, a few ramps and rails, and a lean-to hut with a concrete bench. At night it's packed with guys who don't skate and girls dressed up for each other. Daytime is for the real skaters, and for waggers like us.

Merrick flops down on the bench and almost immediately bounces up again. 'I'm literally bored out of my brain.'

'You've literally been here for, like, two seconds.'

'Well, it's dead.'

D&G is the only one here.

We don't know his real name. He only ever wears the same black Dolce & Gabbana T-shirt and he's got to be thirty-something— an old guy with a mullet riding around on a kid's bike. He sticks out, but nobody pays him any attention. He rides past school every day at two, like one of those characters in an indie film who doesn't make it to the foreground and doesn't speak any lines, but you know he's somehow pivotal to the plot. It's like he has a force field around him, or possibly he's invisible to everyone but me. Most afternoons at about five, D&G cooks sausages on the community barbecue and feeds the leftovers to the ibises.

'Come on, let's go,' Merrick says.

'Go where?'

'KFC. I need food.'

'I've got no cash. Anyway, I want to watch for a bit,' I say.

'Poseur.' Merrick wanders off.

D&G tries a wheel spin, but the bike takes off over the rim without him and he lands on his side. He gets up, retrieves his bike and tries again.

I wonder what it must be like not to care what anyone thinks—to do your thing and take the hits and get straight back up again. I wonder what it's like to *have* a thing.

I watch for five more minutes and still catch up to Merrick, dragging his feet out on the main road.

'S'up,' he says, like we just met for the first time today.

49

'I've been thinking.'

'Does it hurt?' He places his palm on my forehead as if he's checking my temperature.

I slap his hand away. 'We should go see Mim. Take her flowers or something.'

'We hardly know her.'

'Yeah, I guess.'

Merrick pulls out a slingshot. It's lethal-looking, with an engraved metal handle shaped like a wishbone and a thick rubber sling. 'How about some target practice?'

'Where did you get that?'

'Traded it.'

'For what?'

'Gold Star card.'

I give a low whistle. 'A Gold Star is worth…what? A hundred bucks?'

'It was only worth what someone would pay for it.' He shrugs. 'Anyway, I wanted this. We could shoot some cans at the train station.'

In roughly fifteen minutes the station will be swarming with schoolkids. 'Nah.'

'Bin chickens at Macca's?'

'That's cruel.'

'They're feral, man. They eyeball me like they're plotting to eat my face.'

'And I suppose that puts you off your tasty burger.'

'Hell, yes.'

I shake my head. 'First, ibises are only feral because we built a McDonald's on their wetland—they have to adapt to survive. Second, don't you see the hypocrisy in sacrificing an ibis's natural environment to feed consumers of French fries and chicken nuggets, stripping it of its dignity and forcing it to resort to eating discarded pickles, and then calling it feral? The species faced extinction so you could have your cheeseburger. They adapted. There's the root of your repulsion.'

Merrick laughs. 'I hope you get this fired up the next time Brock Tuwy has my head in a toilet.'

'That's different. You always start it.'

We take the long way home through the alleyways to kill more time. In ten minutes school will be out and we'll be all clear to re-enter civilisation.

Merrick keeps turning the slingshot over in his hand. I wonder if he's starting to regret the trade.

'I still want to shoot something,' he says.

It comes to me. 'I really hate that sensor light.'

FIVE

Tuesday morning, double PE. Drought has baked the school oval hard enough to splinter our shinbones, but twenty-four of us are skidding around in an inch of black sludge.

Leaky sprinklers. I worry about that, too—thousands of litres, evaporating, wasted. If science is right, it'll turn into rain somewhere else, but screw that. We need it here. It's like watching Dec pump coins into the pokies, knowing we need them at home, but that they'll end up in government coffers, probably subsidising some mining magnate who has plans to frack all the way to China.

Teams have been picked, coloured bibs distributed. Merrick has played his third sick card this term and he's sitting on the bench, nursing his fake twisted ankle, keeping score. The sun is so bright my eyes are gritty and sore, like they were the time Ryley Peake yelled, 'Look, McKee!' and gave me a welding flash in Tech.

Ten minutes into the scrimmage game and I land on my arse. One semi-flat ball, courtesy of Brock Tuwy's left foot—*smack* on the bridge of my nose. I didn't see it coming. I don't see it leave, either.

The PE teacher, Mrs Davis, jogs over. 'What happened?'

Mrs Davis hates her job. She hates us. Why do teachers think we can't tell? She speaks like she has something caught in her throat—I worry whatever it is might dislodge one day and someone will lose an eye. I worry that my nose has spread across my entire face. I worry that worry, my constant companion, is trying to tell me something. I think worrying is a form of prayer for people who don't believe in god.

'McKee caught the ball with his face.'

'Nice catch.'

'*Bwahaha.*'

I stand up, clutching my nose with one hand, my arse with the other. 'May I go to the bathroom?'

'The *bathroom*,' someone sniggers.

Mrs Davis peels my fingers away. She gives a low whistle. 'Better ice that.'

She turns her attention to Liam Baker. He's on his hands and knees, lapping sprinkler water from a hole in the hose. Mrs Davis should warn Liam he could catch legionnaire's disease, but instead she points her finger at him and screeches, 'Nobody's laughing!' while everyone laughs.

'You are one ugly motherfucker,' Brock Tuwy says. 'And you just got uglier.'

Brock Tuwy is a year older than the rest of us. He was held back in Year Nine. He's big, nasty, always cashed up, and I think he only comes to school because he has broken everything in his own house and the school at least replaces the things he breaks. He's a destroyer, and I don't mean that as a compliment—he doesn't create anything, just tears things down. I wasn't even on his radar until late last year, when I was practising a smile (something Merrick suggested I do regularly and in secret; apparently I don't smile convincingly enough to pass for normal) right when Tuwy had to attempt a Physics equation on the whiteboard in front of the class, and failed. Anyway, freak convergence: Tuwy turned around, ready to kill anyone who dared to laugh at him, and there was me with a smile so wide my gums had dried.

I look down. The ball has landed right at my feet, probably because it's coated in muck, no longer ball-shaped, and weighs about three kilos more than a ball should.

Brock's eyes draw a straight line from my face to the ball. He makes a noise somewhere between a cough and a giggle. He toes the ball. It just misses my nuts and, when I cover them and lean over, he boots it again into my chest.

Oof. Down I go again. *Stay down.*

Merrick comes out of nowhere. I've seen videos of parachutists and that's what he looks like—mouth open, cheeks puffed, T-shirt sleeves billowing like sails. Or like a rabid flying fox. He launches himself onto Brock's back and digs his fingers into his eyeballs before I can remind him that we've talked about this: he has to control his temper, he's trapped in a body that can't back up his mouth.

Mrs Davis is about to intervene but her squat legs can't carry her fast enough. Brock peels Merrick from his back and flings him to the ground. Merrick's T-shirt is shucked, revealing his gleaming set of ribs—to Brock, they must look like a cabinet full of his grandmother's best china. He swings back his leg and takes aim.

I've already figured the odds—a short victory and long period of regret—but I still get to my feet, pick up the ball, wind back my right hand, and upper-cut-swing it like an orange in a sock. The ball smashes into Brock Tuwy's throat; his head snaps back and his legs fly out from under him—human motion in a graceful arc. Until he hits the mud.

Physics isn't my thing either but, if there's a sweet spot, I found it.

Mrs Davis screeches.

Merrick sits up, dazed.

I'm still half-winded, and Brock is clawing at his yeti-sized Adam's apple, wheezing, thrashing.

Mrs Davis bends over him. 'Get up. Shake it off.'

Brock rolls onto his side. His breaths are slowing.

I take a step back from the action. The circle closes me out. By now my nose has its own heartbeat. If Brock is dead, I'm dead. I can barely survive a life sentence in Bairstal, let alone prison.

'He's choking,' someone says.

'Who knows CPR?'

'That's when you've stopped breathing, dumbarse, not when you're trying to breathe.'

'Get up, Brock,' Mrs Davis says, white-faced. 'Everyone's laughing at you.'

Nobody laughs.

'I can't help you if you won't help yourself.'

That's what she says when she's out of ideas.

'Call an ambulance, Mrs Davis.'

'Roll him onto his back.'

'Let's carry him to the office.'

Merrick stands. He casually picks up his pen and note-pad and scribbles something. He holds it up so I can see.

Tuwy—1.

I grab the pen from him. 'You started it, you idiot,' I hiss.

Merrick's jaw drops, but he's laughing, and through the gap between somebody's legs I catch a glimpse of Brock Tuwy's face. He's on his side, still wheezing and clutching his throat, but he's staring at me, not a broken capillary in sight.

He's faking.

This is my chance to rewrite history:

Furious, I yank the ink tube from the pen, thinking of the countless number of disgusting spitballs Brock Tuwy has landed in my hair from the back of the classroom. I blow through the tube. It's clear.

'Let me through!'

Merrick stops laughing. So he should.

The crowd steps back.

Mrs Davis, useless as ever, is standing over Brock's writhing body with her phone to her ear. She covers it with one hand and says, 'What on earth are you doing?'

Her confusion is mirrored in Brock's expression. He's gone quiet and still.

Roughly, I roll him onto his back and rip his hands away from his throat. 'Emergency tracheotomy,' I say. 'Otherwise he'll be dead by the time an ambulance gets here.' I hold the pen just below his Adam's apple. 'It's okay. I've done this before to my brother's rabbit.'

Brock's eyes bulge.

Under my breath, I say, 'Your move, dickhead.'

What really happens:

Merrick says, 'Your move, dickhead.'

I excuse myself to go to the bathroom.

I'm seeking an alternative reality by taking a different route home. To avoid getting my head kicked in by Tuwy—and to dodge Merrick—I choose the track that runs behind the disused warehouses on Smith Street, past the abandoned jeans factory and the empty public swimming pool. There used to be a row of Norfolk pines that gave some shade, but recently the council cut them down to make way for more public housing.

I read about it. The soil is contaminated with oil. The buildings are cordoned off with temporary fencing. There's a rat plague, junkie squatters, asbestos in the walls, lead in the pipes. The site's still waiting for clearance from the EPA and could be vacant for decades.

Don't they know nobody cares? Offer people a roof over their heads today with a bonus terminal illness in twenty years' time—they'll choose the roof.

We live in the moment. The future is too far away.

It's stinking hot and my phone's dead. The skin on my face is swollen and tight. My clothes are crusted with dried mud and I have two days of afternoon detention, starting tomorrow. Brock's move, as it turns out, was to elbow Mrs Davis in the cheekbone, call me a choice four-letter word and take off across the school oval like Forrest Gump. He didn't come back to class. (When I was a kid, we used to have a German shepherd cross called Skitz who attacked you whenever you sneezed or laughed. Brock Tuwy reminds me of him.)

A short way along, I realise Merrick is following me about fifty steps behind, whistling 'Love Generation'. It's driving me crazy, even though he's a pretty good whistler.

'Stop following me!'

Anyone else would take that at face value, but not Merrick.

He thinks I'm talking to him again, even after I told him I was never talking to him again.

He closes the distance. 'Wait up.'

'Why?'

'Because. We're mates.'

'We've had this conversation.'

'What? About loyalty?'

'No, about including me in team Death Wish. I don't want your loyalty.'

He scratches his head. 'What *do* you want? Seriously, McKee. What do you *want*?'

Perfect scenario? 'I want to be a sixteen-year-old philanthropist.'

'What's that?'

'Someone who supports good causes.'

'Oh, yeah. Like a humanitarian.' He nods wisely.

'No, humanitarians are poor and they wear socks with sandals.'

'So you want to be rich.'

'Yes.' I really, really do.

'And then give it all away for a good cause.'

'Exactly.'

'What for?'

I squeeze through a gap between two sections of temporary fencing. 'Well, I could be a humanitarian and lay a thousand bricks per day for Habitats for Humanity, or I could pay a thousand people to build their own houses. I'm thinking big.'

He shakes his head. 'No way you'd give it all away if you got rich.'

'I would so.'

'*Nuh-uh*. If you were born rich, maybe. But if you're born poor and then get rich—maybe you'd blow it, but you'd never just give it all away.'

'How would you know?'

'I know you—all talk, no action.'

Merrick throws his bag over the fence and climbs up it like a spider monkey. At the top, he grips the bar with two hands and flips over backwards, wincing when he doesn't quite stick the landing and ends up eating dust.

'What is it with you and doorways?' I grumble. 'There's a bloody gap. Why do you have to do everything the hard way?'

'Stick to your philanthropism,' he says. 'I'd rather get my hands dirty.'

'Philanthropy.'

'What-*ever*. You talk different to the way you do at school.'

'What are you on about?' I know what he means, but I won't admit he has a point.

'I mean you act dumb and it makes me want to punch you in the face.'

'Well, you act smart and it makes me want to punch you in the face.'

Merrick stops and lifts his chin. 'Come on, then.'

'What? Hit you?'

'Yeah. Get it out of your system.'

'And then what?'

'And then I'll show you what I've got in my pocket.' He gives his version of an evil laugh, which sounds more like a squeaky dog toy.

'Keep it in your pants, paedo.'

'Fine. Look.' He holds up an iPhone.

'Is that an X? How'd you get that?'

'It's not mine. It's Tuwy's. I nicked it when I jumped him.'

My guts lurch. So that's what he meant by us being two-one up. 'He's gonna know it was you!'

'How?'

'Right. You don't think he might retrace his steps and come to the conclusion that the last time he had it was right before he discovered the Artful fucking Dodger on his back?'

Merrick looks so pleased with himself I think his face might split in two. With the amount of hindsight he has by now, his foresight should be improving.

'It has a password,' he says.

'No kidding.'

'It's two-seven-six-two-five-nine.'

'How'd you figure that out?'

'Der. B-R-O-C-K-Y.'

'Are you serious?'

'Deadly. Took me three guesses—Brock 1, Brocko, Brocky.'

We're about to come out behind the West Bairstal shops. If there's going to be an ambush, it'll be here. The Blockbuster on the corner has been empty for a few years. From experience, I know I can peek through the corner window and see along the concrete strip between the IGA, the deli and the laundromat. Chooks 'n' Chips on the opposite corner has an undercover outdoor eating area next to a block of public toilets—that's the only black spot.

I clean a patch on the window with my fist.

Merrick comes up behind me. 'All clear?'

'I can't see anyone.' The shops are deserted. 'You should go first since you got us into this mess.'

'Okay.'

I didn't really expect him to go. Merrick is impulsive, not brave. But he swaggers down the middle of the strip, kicking an empty can. He's cocky enough until he gets to the chip shop, but then he slows down, angling his body so he can see around the corner. Four more steps and he freezes.

I mutter, 'Shit—'

Merrick adopts his classic don't-beat-me-up stance. He's shaking his head, thumbing his chest and saying something that looks like, 'Who? Me?' He glances in my direction.

My heart slams against my ribs.

Merrick backs away slowly. Something makes him change his mind and he puts up his skinny fists. He disappears around the corner, into the blackspot.

'Shit, shit, shit.'

I wait for approximately two minutes. I know that's two minutes too long, but I can't get my feet to move.

Just when I figure out that I can probably enter the chip shop and check through the side window before I decide to take on whoever or whatever is around that corner, Merrick dawdles back without a scratch on him.

Typical.

'You had me for a minute.'

'You are such a disappointment,' he says. 'Where were you?'

I shove him, only I push him harder than I mean to and his feet get tangled up in his bag straps. He goes down hard and cracks his skull on the concrete. I wait for him to fight back, but he just sits up, rubbing the back of his head.

I'll tell you what you get when you combine relief, anger and shame: stupidity.

'There you go. More room for your brain.'

'Fuck you,' he says. 'I'd rather swing and miss than duck and run any day.'

I can't stand the look he's giving me, so I leave him there.

SIX

It's official—it took six years for Merrick to come to our front door.

When Dec got home late last night, he had to step over a pile of dog shit on the verandah. That's all he did: step over it. Then he woke Nance and told her she had a delivery, which was code for clean it up. Nance is adept at deciphering code, but I said I'd do it. When I went outside to borrow Clancy's shovel I found a Pokémon card next to the pile, which disproves our Art teacher's comments about Merrick lacking nuance in his artistic expression.

It's not like Merrick to hold a grudge, but his ban for Tunza Fun ticket fraud (his photo is currently displayed on their wall of shame) means he's supposed to complete community service, including running errands for the owner, Jack Berry, and doing poo patrol on Tuesdays and Saturdays at Jack Berry Dog Park. Otherwise Jack has threatened to ban him for life. (Jack Berry is a local who got rich and stayed here. He spends his money on community projects, so most of our parks and playgrounds are named after him.)

The card makes sense. The dog shit doesn't, but I'm sick of worrying about Merrick and whatever makes him tick.

I crawl out of bed at seven and tidy the kitchen instead.

'Hey, bub,' Nance says, sleepwalking to the table. 'Did you wet the bed?'

'No!'

She laughs at my red face. 'I didn't mean it. It's just something my mum used to say whenever I got up early.'

Nance is always telling me things her mum used to say. She misses her a lot. Her parents live in a small town somewhere north, and they must be nice people because Nance has that way about her. I reckon she was the kind of kid who had a pony.

Nance told me her parents don't think much of Dec: her mum once said he has the manner of a man just passing through. But they always send the boys presents on their birthday and at Christmas, and they send me twenty dollars because I'm technically their step-grandson, although I've never met them. Apparently they're waiting for Nance to come to her senses. It could be a long wait. And they're wrong about Dec. He would never leave us.

'Dec's taking Jake to the races,' Nance says.

'When?' If Nance said Dec was taking me to the races too, I reckon my jaw would dislocate. 'Why?'

'I told him he needed to do more things with the boys.' She lifts her chin. Like me, she's not sure yet if she has been brave or stupid. 'So he's taking Jake.'

'Not Otis?'

Her lips twist. 'You know O wouldn't settle.'

'Yeah.'

'It'll be fun for Jake.'

Fun? Dec will be at the bar all day with his mates while

Jake eats food off the floor and talks to strangers, and Nance will hold Otis until Jake comes home, because that's all she can do when they're separated—hold him tight while he thrashes, until he eventually falls asleep sucking on his bitten tongue. And Nance won't figure out until much later that asking Dec to do something that wasn't part of his plan costs all of us.

I know. I was once the kid who ate food off the floor.

I want to tell Nance all of this, but I don't. She's an optimist. She doesn't know Dec like I do. I make us instant coffee instead.

'You are ace, Nate McKee,' she says, and takes a sip.

There's a squawk from the bedroom. Otis is awake and hungry.

Dec yells, 'Nance!'

Nance puts down her mug, sighs, and pushes away from the table. I can count the hours of missed sleep by the lines around her mouth and eyes, and she makes the mistake of going to the toilet before she goes to pick up Otis. By the time she flushes, Otis has just about blown the roof off with his screaming.

Dec staggers into the kitchen wearing only jocks, looking for a fight.

'Fuck's sake!' he yells. He sees me, sitting with my hands wrapped around my mug, and no Nance. 'Do something.'

'Do what?'

Nance shoots down the hall behind him. Otis goes quiet.

Dec lights a smoke and repeatedly smacks his palm against his forehead, as if there's a thought in there he can't quite reach. 'Is that shit gone?' he says. 'That shit better be gone.'

I scurry off to make sure I cleaned up properly—and

there's a fresh pile on our verandah.

I'm about three seconds from scooping it up and flinging it at Merrick's window, when there's a snuffling sound from above.

I look up to see Kelly's snout. She's smiling.

Mystery solved. Looks like the old dog has a new trick, although how Kelly could fit her rump between the rails to back one out, I will never know.

Again, I borrow Clancy's shovel and spread the poo around the base of Nance's dying hydrangea. After that, I pick up Margie's butts from the bottom of the stairs so O doesn't eat them. I don't know how she misses the paint tin on her balcony; after about a hundred thousand cigarettes she should be a crack shot.

Inside the flat, Dec's still yelling, so I look around for something else to do to avoid going inside.

Merrick was right: I'm a pacifist. I'm not built to fight. I'm afraid all the time. If I was a few years older and she wasn't already married to my old man, I *would* marry Nance. Not because I want to get jiggy with her or any-thing—I just *love* love her. She's *good*. The boys are good. Nance and I deserve each other.

School without Merrick and Brock Tuwy is almost bearable. I find myself humming in Science and daydreaming in English; I know I'm at least partly responsible for Merrick's absence, but being hyper-vigilant takes energy and being invisible takes focus—it's kind of nice to just be. *Without* Merrick.

Forget safety in numbers. I'm safer on my own.

I stare out the window. The sky is full of dirt.

'If you know the answer, speak up,' Mr Reid is saying. 'Mr McKee? Thrill me with your acumen.'

I'm not sure what the question was, but I think I know the answer.

'Anthony Hopkins,' I say.

Mr Reid raises an eyebrow. That means he wants me to cite my references.

'Hannibal Lecter in *The Silence of the Lambs*.' I put on a Southern accent for a bonus point. '"Why do you think he removes their skins, Agent Starling? Thrill me with your acumen."'

The entire class laughs. My neck gets hot.

Across from me, Ruby Ames whispers to Takesha Phillips. I can read her lips: *He's so fucking weird.*

I wait for Mr Reid to detonate. Instead he shushes the class and seems to drift off into a catatonic state.

Ruby takes a chance and says it louder. 'You're weird, you know that?'

I cross my eyes and let a bit of spit dribble from the corner of my mouth. I lean forward. 'I *know*.'

Ruby recoils.

As a general rule, I try not to let the meanness in. It's in my blood, I know, but I can keep it dormant if I try. Unlike herpes simplex, which is fancy for cold sores. I have one coming; I can feel its tingle on my bottom lip.

It feels good to push back.

Mr Reid keeps me after class again.

'You like films?' he asks.

I shrug. 'They're all right.'

'But not poetry. Or essays.'

'I like essays.'

'Then what's your excuse? Let me have it.'

I'm drawing a massive blank.

'The mighty pen,' he prompts. 'The less mighty sword.'

Shit. All the stuff with Mim and Merrick and Brock Tuwy—I genuinely forgot this time.

'I like reading essays. I don't like *writing* essays.'

'Why not?'

Screw it. What would Merrick say?

'It takes time away from my personal development.'

I think he's going to ask me to elaborate, but he doesn't. He *laughs. At* me. I *hate* that.

'But you like films,' he says when he's finished laughing.

'I thought we covered that.'

'So you're not entirely prejudiced against the arts.'

'Art isn't real.'

'What is?'

'I dunno. Science. Politics.'

'You don't think art can be political? Isn't art the stuff of life? Truth? Reality? Doesn't art mirror, mimic, expose, question, illuminate—life? And you don't think it's real?'

He's wearing a self-satisfied expression. I'm his daily dose of validation.

'I see where you're going with this.' I laugh too.

'Where am I going?'

'I checked out a few scenes from *Dead Poets Society*. "But only in their dreams can man be truly free. 'Twas always thus, and always thus will be." Right?'

He leans back in his chair and interlocks his fingers. 'I think you've been flying under the radar for too long, Mr McKee.'

'No flying here.'

He nods slowly. 'Okay, Nate. I have to assume things are tough for you at home.'

Tough? *Tough*? He's got the vernacular. He's assimilated.

'I have to assume you wear a skirt on weekends.'

'Whenever the fancy takes me,' he says. 'Not only weekends. So, you owe me an essay.'

'You said any form I like.'

'Essay. You need the practice.'

He watches me go with his fingers laced together like a church and steeple.

I felt mean, pushed back and nobody died, *and* I've decided to blow off detention. This day just keeps getting better.

Nance and Dec are having dinner together in the kitchen while I play with the boys in the lounge room. Nance set candles on the table and everything, but Dec made her blow them out. He's just doing time until he can head to the pub.

Nance is disappointed—I can tell by the way she's scraping her fork back and forth against the plate.

We live in the dark most nights. Dec thinks the cops do flyovers in helicopters using heat sensors, so they can tell if there's an unusual amount of light and heat coming from one source. His grow-room—*my* bedroom—is bright enough to be taken for Christ's Second Coming if anyone should open the door. Green commerce, Dec calls it. He says his weed is for cannabis oil—medicine for people with MS and epilepsy and Parkinson's disease—because the government is dragging its arse on passing legislation and people are suffering.

Nance believes him. I'm not the only one who makes up alternative realities.

I'm half-watching the news, sitting cross-legged on the carpet while I hand O different toys to keep him busy. Jake has wandered off somewhere. The carpet is brown and tacky with old stains and it smells like bong water. Nance tries to keep it clean but the boys are way ahead of her. Jake can be cruel—I've seen him tip drinks over just to see if Nance will react. Otis is the worst offender, but he's just clumsy.

'Nate,' Otis says.

He's lying on his back, passing a plastic car from fist to fist.

'Nate.'

His hair is longer than Jake's because he freaks out if you come near him with scissors.

'Yeah, buddy.'

He's been saying my name for a few months now.

'Nate.'

'Yeah. It's me.'

It's gone quiet in the kitchen.

For some reason it pisses Dec off that Otis said my name before his. I've caught Nance repeating, 'Dadadadada,' trying to get him to say it, but he won't.

I catch hold of a slippery memory—my mum, whistling the theme from *The Muppets*, over and over. She's ironing, barefooted. I'm small, so short my legs dangle because I can't reach the footrest of the stool, and I'm blowing, making her laugh. There's a cockatiel in a cage in a corner and it's whistling back, off-key. She's trying to teach us both. 'Wet your lips and curl your tongue,' she says.

A chair scrapes in the kitchen and the image is gone.

70

Otis rolls onto his stomach. 'Nate!'

I want to clap my hand across his mouth, but Dec's standing in the doorway.

'Yeah. *Shh*, mate. Look—a car. *Car.*'

Dec grunts.

'Nate!'

Dec picks up his guitar, sits on the arm of a chair and plays a few riffs. Nance is doing the dishes, but she pauses to listen. Then he cuts to a familiar tune—one that makes the hair stand up on the back of my neck.

I used to think the beginning of 'Stairway to Heaven' was about the most perfect piece of music ever written, but a thousand of Dec's stoned renditions later, it makes me want to snip the strings with a pair of blunt scissors.

I get up.

Otis tries to flip over and can't. '*Naaaaate!*'

Dec closes his eyes and builds his tempo. We're ruining his vibe, man.

I scoop Otis up and carry him into the kitchen.

Nance takes him from me, stacks him on her hip and keeps washing one-handed.

'I can do the dishes,' I say.

'Nah, bub. You should go out.'

'Nate!' Dec's calling me.

'Go see Merrick,' Nance says. 'Go to Youth.' Her tone is low with warning. She shoves me towards the back door.

'Nate.' Dec's standing in the lounge-room doorway, holding a packed pipe and a lighter.

'How many times, Dec? Can you please not smoke that shit around the kids,' Nance says.

'S'not for me.' Dec holds out the pipe. 'It's for Nate.'

'No, thanks.'

'Leave him alone,' Nance says. 'He doesn't need it.'

'He wants it, though. Don't you, mate?'

'No, *thanks*.'

'Pussy.'

Nance sucks in her breath.

Dec points the lighter at her. 'Shut it, Nance.'

Nance gives Otis a biscuit, carries him back to the lounge room and plonks him in his high chair. She comes back to finish the washing-up.

'I don't smoke,' I say, looking at my feet. 'You know that.'

'It's a rite of passage. You need to chill the fuck out.' Dec pulls out a bar stool and pushes me into it. He flicks the lighter, sucks the flame into the bowl and blows smoke in my face. 'Got it going for ya, no worries.'

'Dec…'

'I said shut it.'

Dec's watching me the way a cat watches a mortally wounded mouse. The shaking starts at my toes and builds; my knees are knocking together, my fingers are drumming on the counter, my teeth are chattering even though I'm not cold.

'No.'

He slouches, pushing his groin forward. 'You think you're too good for home-grown?' He takes another toke and holds it in, speaking through wisps of smoke. 'Too good for your old man?'

'No.'

'This another one of my gifts you ain't gonna bother to open?' He smiles.

I hold his stare. I don't know how his teeth can be so white. Fight or flight—I can't decide; I'm as tall as him now, but twenty kilos lighter. I'm bones; he's ripped.

Mum left.

He stayed.

I look away.

Glass breaks.

Nance yelps and Dec's gaze slides over her. 'Shit. What've you done?'

She's standing with her hand raised to the ceiling. Blood dribbles from her thumb to her elbow. 'Cut myself.'

I try to move, but Dec beats me to it.

He grabs her hand, turning it over gently in his own. 'Needs a stitch.'

'It'll be fine,' Nance says. 'I'll wrap it tight.'

He kisses her nose. 'It's to the bone.'

I stare at a pair of Jake's sneakers sticking out from under the cupboard in the corner of the lounge room near the door to the kitchen.

'Watch the boys,' Dec says to me. He takes off his favourite Billabong singlet and uses it to bandage Nance's hand. He picks her up and carries her away. The door slams.

Underneath the cupboard, the sneakers move. Jake wriggles out. He comes to stand next to me and stares solemnly at the blood on the floor.

'Ouch.' Jake squats and runs his finger through a drop of blood. He looks up and rolls his eyes. 'Nance did something stupid. *Again.*'

SEVEN

Nance needed four stitches in her thumb, and I've been trying to stay away from the flat as much as possible. Dec has been making me do all the things Nance can't do one-handed, which is basically everything, because Dec is the man of the house and the man doesn't do drone work.

O's nappies are the worst.

Merrick is a ghost—I never see him. He's not answering my texts. He isn't at school, but that's not unusual. Point taken: I shouldn't have shoved him, but this is getting ridiculous.

I go to Youth on Saturday night after dinner. Nights are getting cooler; no one out on their verandahs, and the street-lights are misty. I know every crack in the pavement, every mean dog, every car in every driveway.

Deng and Cooper are standing under the spotlight in the car park, having a smoke. Deng and I cast the exact same shadow—long, lean, with pinheads. Cooper's is squat and lumpy.

'Hey.'

'Hey.'

'Hey.'

'Someone nicked the Goalrilla again,' Cooper says. 'Took the bike rack, too.' He's got his basketball jammed between his feet. He points to the space where the rack used to be. 'Looks like they used an angle grinder.'

I shrug. 'No one ever used the bike rack anyway.'

'Yeah, but a suit came and inspected. Macy must have reported it this time.'

We go quiet. Macy is supposed to report all theft and vandalism, but the last time it happened she secretly crowd-funded to replace the hoop. It was easier. She says it's hard enough to get funding without using the money to replace stolen stuff, or trying to justify why The Youth of Today continually Bite The Hands That Feed Us. As if the kids who come here and the ones who nick things are the same people. Well, sometimes they are, but mostly not.

I'm willing to bet the Goalrilla is already on eBay. A few hundred, at least.

Cooper pinches off his cigarette and flicks the butt into a bush, then has an attack of conscience and fishes it out. He puts it in the butt bin and sits on the kerb with his arms around his knees. 'You and Merrick on the outs?' he asks.

'Kind of. I think he's staying with his mum.'

'Nah. Saw him with Tuwy last night.'

My stomach drops. 'What?'

A police car does a slow cruise through the car park. Deng waves.

'They hate each other,' I say when the car's gone. 'Brock wants to kill him.'

'I know, right?'

Merrick is obviously alive and unhurt, but I can't imagine why he'd hang out with Brock Tuwy. Unless Tuwy's holding him hostage.

'Where were they?'

'Servo,' says Cooper. 'They bought slushies, then Brock and Merrick got in Toolio's car.'

Toolio is Brock's mate, older, dropped out of school two years ago. His real name is Shaun Fallon. Nobody calls him Shaun to his face. Beats me why he thinks Toolio is better.

Deng and Cooper are waiting for answers. 'I got nothing,' I tell them. I don't tell them what I did to Merrick. 'It's a mystery.'

We go inside.

The centre is pretty empty for a Saturday night, but it's still early. Tash is here, in her corner, headphones plugged in. She doesn't look up. Macy's cooking something in the kitchen. Whatever it is, it's on fire.

Things have been moved around: the couch and beanbags are in a different corner, along with the television, and there's a new green rug in the middle of the room.

Macy takes the saucepan off the stove and slams it down on the counter. She has a tattoo of Harry Potter's glasses on the back of her neck. Last week her hair was blonde, shoulder-length and frizzy; today it's black, shaved on one side and long on the other. She looks tired.

'Nice rug,' I tell her. 'It's the exact colour of your eyes.'

Her eyes are brown.

'I couldn't get the bloodstains out,' she says.

That shuts me up.

'Want some?' She slops burnt macaroni cheese into a paper bowl and pushes it towards me. 'Grub's up!' she yells.

No takers.

'How's Mim?'

'Home,' she says. 'They let her out yesterday. Thomas is covering her shifts for a couple of weeks.'

'She's coming back?'

'Of course.' She eyeballs me. 'This ain't a job, Nate. It's a calling.'

Macy always smirks after a serious statement, which means I never know what she really means.

'You were late.' I say it without thinking.

'I know.'

'Sorry.'

'I know.' She points to the bowl. 'Are you gonna eat that?'

'Not if it was the last food on earth and people were eating each other.'

'Fair enough.' She laughs. 'You're a funny guy. Help me get some boxes from the storeroom, would you?'

I follow her down the hallway.

'How long you been coming here, Nate?'

I shrug. 'Since I was about twelve?'

She reaches to the top shelf and levers a box up with her fingertips.

'I've got it,' I say, and reach past her to lift it down. 'This one too?'

Macy nods. 'What do you think would happen to these kids if this place wasn't here?'

'What do you mean?'

'I mean if they closed us down.'

I drop the second box. 'They threaten that all the time.' She doesn't say anything.

'For real?'

Still no answer.

'Is it because of what happened to Mim?'

'Yeah.'

'But what has that got to do with us?'

'Damage control,' she says. 'There's no money for security and someone has to be accountable.' Her face is red. 'I get it from both sides, you know. They make me cross every *i* and *t* and it's still not enough. I stay up nights filling out grant applications. I bust my arse for you guys and all I get is whingeing about how the PlayStation doesn't work properly. I'm tired of fighting for you little shits.'

She's almost in tears and it makes me uncomfortable.

'You dot an *i*. You don't cross it.'

'Did you hear what I said?'

'Yeah.'

She picks up the box and shoves it at me. 'Put these rolls in the toilet.' She storms off.

What does she want me to do? I'm a kid. Grown-ups are supposed to sort this stuff out. I've got the rest of my life to obsess about dotting and crossing things—geez, I've got high school to worry about, and my own dysfunctional family, as well as the shit I shouldn't be worrying about but can't help worrying about.

When I go back to the rec room, Macy is outside having a smoke. Tash is packing away her headphones. She still doesn't look up.

I grab two dessert spoons from the kitchen drawer, take the saucepan of macaroni from the counter and slump into the beanbag next to Tash. I hand her a spoon.

She looks at me as if I've grown an extra head. 'No way.'

'Trust me on this. We're taking one for the team.'

Tash sighs. She gets it. She scoops up one noodle.

When Macy comes back inside, I show her the pan: the saucepan is empty apart from the black crust on the bottom.

'Laptops,' Mr Reid says. 'Be quick about it.'

The whole class rushes the cart. There are twenty-nine of us and sixteen of them, and it's a mosh pit: laptops surfing above the crowd, pairs of hands in the air.

I don't bother. It wouldn't matter if I got there first—someone bigger always relieves me of my prize. Kobe Slater is the worst. He sits right next to the cart, and sometimes he grabs one for Andrew Brink and Seb Green too.

I slump in my seat and keep working at the hole I've made in the wooden desktop with the point of my compass. I happen to look up, and Mr Reid is watching me.

Up go the eyebrows.

I put the compass down. Mr Reid favours the hierarchal process: fight and ascend, or submit and sink. *Everyone finds the level they deserve*, he says. The man is a dinosaur.

We're supposed to be working on our book reports, but I figure I'll use the time to knock something up about the mighty pen instead, so Mr Reid will get off my case. I pull out my notebook and begin writing. When I zone out like this, I only hear crickets.

The sneeze arrives without warning. No delicate *at-choo* for me; mine bursts eardrums and scatters paper.

'McKee! I won't stand for your disruptions in this class.'

There's farting, burping, snickering, knee-jiggling, pen-tapping—and he picks on my *sneeze*?

I sneeze again, which sets off a chorus of fakes.

'Outside.'

I gather my stuff and move to the corridor. There's a chair by the door. I sit and wait for the talking-to. Fifteen minutes later I'm still waiting.

I open my notebook again, tear out a page and begin writing. This is the first time I've ripped a page from my book, the first time I've said exactly what I think, unfiltered, to anyone but myself or Merrick.

Mr Reid,

Did you know? Human muscles have grown weaker about eight times faster than the rest of our bodies; over the same time period, our brains have evolved four times faster. We're smarter, not stronger. We don't need to chase prey anymore. Recessive genes abound because we can fix shit; we breed hairless cats and mutant dogs because we're not happy with the painstaking job evolution has done over millions of years and unreal housewives need to colour-match their pets to their couches. We've got old, ugly, diseased men impregnating supermodels because the size of their eventual divorce settlement obvs outweighs the ick factor, and even a skinny kid like me has half a chance if I can prove I have a bigger bulge in my back pocket than my front. This is my time. I would have been unborn or dead early if these were Neolithic times. Supposedly the meek will inherit—one day, but not today, and not in your class. Not while we're still living at home with our parents, and surely not while we're wasting time sitting in a corridor anticipating an apology that doesn't come, for a punishment that wasn't deserved, for sneezing, which, by its very nature, is an involuntary reflex.

I know you're busy so I did some numbers for you: there are twenty-nine students in your class, and sixteen laptops. At least eleven students have their own devices. Granted, nine of these are alpha-people—por qué no los dos?—who fought and ascended and probably deserve two pieces of the pie. But if those students actually used their own devices, there would be just two without access to technology— not a perfect outcome, but I'm willing to stick with pen and paper and Benjamin Peros is always asleep anyway. Thoughts?

Regards.

Nate McKee

P.S. I got bored and wandered off.

When I'm finished, I leave the piece of paper on the chair and go to lunch.

Mr Reid doesn't bother coming to find me and there's no announcement over the loudspeaker. I figured he'd forgotten I exist until I got back to my locker ten minutes early to grab my books for the next class.

My note is taped to the door. Reid has graded it. And he's made comments:

B-. Rambling. Stay on topic and make the point, McKee. Take care not to allow sarcasm to undermine authoritative tone. 'Involuntary reflex' = tautology (a reflex is, by its very nature, involuntary).

P.S. Benjamin Peros doesn't go to this school.

I find him in the English room, still eating his lunch, shoes off, feet on the desk.

'You're smart enough, but your execution sucks,' he says.

I hold up my note. 'For real? Peros doesn't go here?'

He sighs and drops the crust of his sandwich into the bin. 'Keep it to yourself. If a seventeen-year-old dropout is that desperate to gate-crash my English class, I'm not going to stop him.'

'He's in my History class too.'

Mr Reid nods. 'The question is, what are *you* doing here?'

'Turning up. Trying to pass Year Eleven.'

'I meant right now.'

'It was a *sneeze*.'

'Your sneezes are full of disdain.'

I laugh.

'Your laughs, too.'

'Not intentionally.'

'Do you do anything with intent?'

There's something creepy about bare feet on a desk. Particularly a Morris dancer's feet.

Mr Reid made us read *The Life of Pi* in the last term of Year Ten. He talked about the difference between anthropomorphism and zoomorphism, and he made us assign an animal to each classmate based on their personality. And to ourselves. If Mr Reid was an animal, he'd be a marsupial mole. Dec is a jaguar—with a tan. Merrick: definitely a meerkat. Nance is something soft and shy, like a rabbit. The weird thing is, out of twenty-six classmates, twelve said I was an armadillo, which is an impressive stat considering half of them couldn't even spell it.

Mr Reid is doing his no-blinking thing again.

'I forgot the question,' I say. 'But I have one for you: if I was an animal, what would I be?'

'Why?'

'Enquiring minds want to know.'

'Enquiring minds should try being original once in a while.'

'Originality is undetected plagiarism.'

'You're a walking quote generator, McKee. I want to know what *you* think.' Blink.

'I think I'm not an armadillo.'

'Well,' he says. 'That's a start.'

EIGHT

I'm lying on the top bunk, lights off, window open, playing the waiting game. Usually I can call it: Dec won't be home, Nance will spend from seven until nine trying to get the boys to bed, Clancy will fire up some Elvis and start crooning, and Margie upstairs will begin her nightly smoking ceremony on the top step. And some time between nine and ten, when all is quiet, Merrick will come to my window.

Everyone does the same thing at the same time. Every night.

But tonight, Dec is home. Clancy's playing Bob Dylan super loud. Nance hasn't even started the two-hour wind-down ritual, the boys are still bouncing off the walls, Merrick won't be coming to my window, and I can't smell smoke. The only sure thing is O's screaming.

It's like the wind is blowing from a different direction: nothing is the same.

At ten-thirty the front door slams. Dec strides along the pathway between the flats, probably on his way to the pub.

A few minutes later, the bedroom door opens and Jake wanders in wearing pyjamas. 'Nance says tell Clancy to shut up.'

'Me?'

He nods and yawns.

'Is it bedtime?'

Jake rubs his crotch just like Dec does. 'Yeah.'

'Clancy, shut up!' I yell through the window. 'Happy?'

Across the way, the light in Merrick's room goes out. I squint. It's a black night. I've been watching for over an hour and my eyes feel as if somebody threw sand in my face. Of course he would choose to make his move now.

I make Jake squat next to me.

Merrick shimmies through the open window and shuffles on his butt to the edge of the gutter.

Jake tugs on my arm. 'What are you looking at?'

'Nothing. Go to bed.'

'Merri...!'

I clap my hand over his mouth. '*Shh.*'

'Why?' he mumbles against my palm.

Merrick does a commando drop 'n' roll and gets to his feet holding his hip. He limps a few steps, turns to look up at his window, then takes off the same way Dec did. He's up to something.

Otis is sob-hiccuping in the lounge.

'Tell Nance I've gone out,' I say, grabbing a jacket. 'Close the window when I've gone, okay?' I slip my arms through the sleeves and shove my phone in my back pocket.

'Where you going?'

'Out, I said.'

Merrick has a head start, and now Jake's hanging onto the back of my jeans.

'Let go.'

'No.'

I prise his fingers apart and he starts yelling.

Nance comes to the bedroom with Otis on her hip. 'Bed, mister,' she says to Jake. 'You going out?' Otis has thrown up on her shoulder, but she doesn't seem to have noticed. 'It's late.'

'Yeah. Just for a while.'

'Let go, Jake.' She takes his other hand and winces when he grips her bandaged thumb.

We're a human daisy chain: I'm hanging onto the window ledge, Jake has hold of my jeans, and Nance is pulling Jake.

Otis finds it all hilarious.

Now Merrick is almost out of sight. I reach behind me and slap Jake's hand hard enough to shock him into letting me go.

Nance stumbles back. Her shoulder slams into the corner of the bunk bed.

'Nate hit me!' Jake yells.

'I smacked you. That's different.'

Nance seems to fold in on herself. 'There's not a whole lot of difference, Nate,' she says quietly, and gathers Jake to her body with her spare arm.

'I have to go!'

'Then go.'

I throw my leg over the windowsill.

'You leave this house through the front door. You say goodbye, and you tell the people you love that you love them.' Nance is crying. '*If* you love them.'

I have no idea what I did to make her cry. I pull my leg back. 'What's wrong? Is it your hand?'

'Nothing.'

'Did Dec…'

'He didn't do anything. Go!' She lays Otis on the mattress

and gestures to Jake. 'In you get, mister.'

O has other ideas. Now that he has learned to roll over, it makes getting him into bed a wrestling match. In one slick move he flips onto the floor, and Jake bursts into giggles. But Otis has bumped his head—he lies there for a few seconds, stunned, until his mouth makes the shape that gave him his nickname and his uvula starts flapping and his scream could wake the dead.

'Help me get him up!' Nance shouts.

I manage to get my arms underneath his body, but he's thrashing and snapping at us. Nance cops a fist to her cheek and retreats. Jake has crawled to a corner. I pull Otis's arms and pin them against his body; he arches his back and throws his head from side to side, switches direction and delivers a head butt to my nose, which is still sore from Tuwy's kick.

'Fuck!' I groan and put him down.

He stops screaming.

'Shut those bloody kids up!' Clancy next door bellows.

'*Shh.*' Nance covers O with her body and plants soft kisses on his neck. 'You okay, bub?' she says to me between kisses. 'That was a good one.'

'This place is a circus!' I'm breathing heavily. I might be bleeding or it could be snot. '*Fuck!*'

It goes quiet until Otis says, 'Fuck,' clear as day.

Nance's body is shaking. I can't see Otis at all.

'Don't cry,' I say. 'I'm sorry.'

'Nance, don't cry,' Jake repeats.

She sits up with her legs tucked under her, hands on her knees. 'I'm not crying.' She's trying to catch her breath. 'Did you hear that?' She slips sideways, holding her stomach, and gives in to an attack of silent, helpless laughter. 'Did you hear what he said? It's a miracle.'

I'd have put money on 'fuck' being one of O's first five words. 'It's hardly a miracle,' I tell her as something warm and wet drips from my chin.

Otis reaches out a hand. 'Nate.'

I give him a death-stare. 'Thug baby.'

'Don't squeeze,' Jake tells me. 'He hates it when you squeeze.'

Otis grunts and wiggles his fingers.

I give in. I move closer but stay out of reach. 'What?'

Closer, his hand is telling me.

I close my eyes and lean in, ready for another hit, but all I feel is the lightest touch. When I pull away, Otis's lips are stained with blood—my nose is so numb I didn't even know I'd been bitten.

'You're bleeding.' Nance reaches for the ever-present tissue in her pocket.

'He bit me!'

'He kissed it better,' she says. 'Nate, do you know what that means?'

I nod. It means O is sorry. It means he feels guilt. He feels empathy. It means his world is bigger today.

And now Nance is crying again.

I'm lying on my stomach on the top bunk, again, trying to get started on the essay I owe Mr Reid. It's uncomfortable, but it's better than trying to work in the kitchen during feeding time at the zoo.

I tear out another page and crumple it into a ball.

After my nose took its second hit, I stayed awake for most of the night, waiting for Merrick to come home. That was two days ago. Maybe he got bored, or he's gone to his mum's. I've texted, but he doesn't answer, and he's blocked me on socials. I've even knocked on the door of the flat, but his old man just screeched something I couldn't understand and threw a plate. The only good thing to come out of this is Nance's hydrangea—it's sprouting green leaves and purple flowers.

I guess some things thrive on shit.

There's a light knock on the bedroom door, and it opens slowly. Nobody but Nance ever bothers to knock. I take aim for the basket in the corner of the room and land a three-pointer with the discarded page.

'Shot.'

My heart rate goes nuts. It's Dec.

'S'up.'

'Gotta talk to you about something. Between us.' Dec hoists himself onto the end of my bunk. The top of his head rubs the ceiling. 'I don't want Nance to hear.'

Shit. This is going to be like Dec's version of The Sex Talk. I wrote it all down.

Me: Jordan Brinkley grabbed my balls today.

Dec: In or out?

Me: In or out of what?

Dec: Your pants.

Me: What? Out.

Dec: Did you give a full salute?

Me: Huh?

Dec: A trouser tent.

Me: No! It hurt. I didn't know what to do.

Dec: [sighs] This is what you do. You gotta wait for her to come to you. Wait for her to ask for it, otherwise you'll be a dog on a leash. Is she pretty? She got tits yet? Wait. How old are you?

Me: Twelve.

Dec: Mate, wank it until you're old enough to bank it. Trust me on this.

Me: Huh?

Dec: No deposits until you can handle the withdrawal.

Me: Withdrawal?

Dec: It's an art form, mate. You've gotta time your exit. Leave it too late and you'll be changing nappies—one day you pull out your dipstick and there'll be a fucken foetus on the end of it. Or two, in my case. Look at Nance. Shit. Never thought I'd say this—look, tell this Jordan chick, no glove no love. If your swimmers are anything like mine it won't matter if you master the pull-out—these fuckers are egg-seeking missiles [grabs his groin].

Me: Dec...

Dec: Seriously, don't they teach you this shit at school?

Me: I know how babies are made. Dec...

Dec: So you want to know about the relationship stuff?

Me: [sighs]

Dec: I love Nance. Nance loves me. It's that simple. Nothin' we can't sort out when you've got love like that.

Me: Yeah, but...

Dec: Me and your mum were different. I felt it in here [grabs his groin again] but I didn't feel it in here [puts his hand on his heart]. Me and Nance have got a leash on each other. That's what a relationship is, mate. Y'know?

Me: Dec...

Dec: You'll know it when you feel it.

Me: Okay, but…

Dec: This Jordan is just practice. You gotta go in with full armour until you learn how to wave your sword without starting something you can't finish, okay?

Me: Dec!

Dec: What?

Me: Jordan Brinkley is a guy.

Dec: Whoah. Whoah. You let a guy grab your junk?

Me: I was trying to tell you. He wanted to rip them off.

Dec: Right. Well…

That was 'The Sex Talk'. Closely followed by the 'How to End a Guy Who Grabs Your Junk' talk. I wrote that one down, too. I haven't had the chance to put either into practice.

'Put the book away,' Dec says now.

I close my notebook and slide it under the pillow.

'Sit up.'

I do.

'Pay attention.'

I am.

'You listening?'

'Yeah.'

Dec clenches and unclenches his fist. 'Family Services sent a letter. Your mum tracked us down again.'

'Right.' My head is spinning. *Tracked us down…tracked us down…*were we hiding?

'She wants to see you.'

'Oh.'

'Anyway, I can't stop her. I tried. But you can—you're a man now. You're old enough to tell them you don't want to see her.'

Not *if* I don't want to see her. And he *tried* to stop it? What's up with that? But I have to be careful what I say. It's like Otis saying my name first—Dec can't handle being last.

'Why now? I haven't seen her for years.'

'I know, right?' He puts his heavy hand on my head. 'Mate. It's okay to be angry.'

I am.

'You just gotta put that big vocab into action and write a letter. Tell her to stay away.'

'I could do that in two words.' I'm saying all the right things, but already I'm leaning in the direction of *her*.

He nods. 'Make it at least a page. Like you put some thought into it.' He takes his hand away.

My head feels impossibly light. It's going to detach and float off like a hot-air balloon.

'What if I see her and I tell her? Then she'll leave us alone.'

Dec is already saying no. No—she's unstable. No—she'll tear our family apart and we're perfect the way we are. No—she'll fill my head with bullshit excuses. Change my mind, brainwash me.

And I'm telling him I can handle it—like he said, I'm a man now.

'She left us.'

'I know, but…'

'This is all about *her*. Not you. She'll hurt Nance and the boys.'

I hold up a hand. I just want him to give me space to breathe and think.

'Write the letter,' he says. 'You've got us. You don't need her back in your life.'

That's Dec. Always telling me what I need.

To whom it may concern,
Thank you for your visitation request. At this point in time it has been
disrespectfully declined.

To Ex-Mrs-McKee,
You owe maintenance. And an explanation.

Dear Angela,
It's been a while. How are you?

To Mum,
I don't need you. I don't want to see you. Things are fine without
you. I can't remember what you look like.

Dear Mum,
When you were packing your suitcase I asked you what you were doing.
I knew what you were doing. You had only packed your things, not mine.
Except for my baby photos—you took them, but not me. I can't remember
what I used to look like.

I can write letters to nobody like nobody's business—why is
the real stuff the hardest to write? In the end, I go with something simple but true:

Mum,
Here's my number. Btw, Dec can't know. I can't promise anything.

NINE

Six of us have been chosen to attend a careers expo at a school called Saint Monica's: me, Will Farnsworth, Lee Fortescu, Gurmeet Chambal, Leila Price and Zadie Zhang. In a surprise ambush, Mr Reid didn't tell us about it until this morning, probably so we couldn't get out of it.

I have several problems with this excursion: I'm sure it contravenes all kinds of laws to take us off premises without parental permission, and I have trouble believing there was ever a saint named Monica. It's as ridiculous as having a saint called Keith. Also, my underdeveloped frontal cortex can't compute how I'm supposed to decide what to do with the rest of my life when I can't even decide what do to tomorrow, or the day after that.

'Why us?' Leila says.

'We're geeks,' Gurmeet replies.

'Speak for yourself,' I mumble.

Zadie throws me a dirty look. 'Most likely to be employed one day?'

I point to my chest. 'Again, I offer Exhibit A.'

I don't know what I am. I'm not a geek. Geeks have no currency here. I don't count as sporty—basketball is a calling for Deng and an escape for someone like me. I'm not tough either, but I will be when I start growing out instead of up. When Dec's genes kick in.

'We're losers,' Lee says.

No one disagrees.

We're packed into Mr Reid's Audi Q7. Will keeps messing with the LED touch lights. I have the passenger-side kiddie seat in the back and my knees are touching my earlobes. Zadie Zhang is next to me, playing Tetris on her phone, trying her hardest not to make any kind of contact, and wearing her usual long-suffering expression. (Zadie suffers a lot because alphabetical order means she's last at everything.) She doesn't give me the slightest twinge in my reproductive organs, but Zadie's disgust upsets me more than most. She's my female equivalent, except she thinks she's better than me, and if Zadie Zhang would rather deliberately headbutt the window than accidentally let her knee brush mine, things are more dire than I thought. I'd give anything to be kissed by a girl—even Zadie. I don't fantasise about her—not exactly—but I do feel our futures are somehow intertwined.

Rowley Park's Class of 2020 High School Reunion—only about ten people have turned up because the rest either didn't graduate, or they died from drug overdoses or botched burglaries. I've filled out a bit. My acne has cleared up, but otherwise I look the same (no way am I getting a makeover in order to win friends and influence people). I don't recognise Zadie at first. I buy her a drink and she tells me she's an air traffic controller—all that Tetris has paid off. She's got amazing legs. She's impressed when I tell her I broke Wyatt Roy's record for becoming the youngest federal politician and she wants a ride home in my government car, but not before we have a surreal conversation about waxing versus shaving. She grabs my hand and runs it along her inner thigh. (I realise I'm a hypocrite for making Zadie hot, but I can't rewrite the scene when she's singing 'No Diggity' to me.) *'Oh, waxing, definitely,' I tell her, and she whispers, 'Pleeeease—'*

'—stop touching my leg!'

Okay, so I sometimes fantasise about her.

'I didn't mean to,' I stammer. 'We turned a corner.'

'What's going on back there?' Mr Reid eyeballs me in the rear-view mirror.

Zadie says, 'Are we there yet? Because if we're not I'd like to switch seats.'

'We're almost there.'

Saint Monica's is all girls. Not only that, it's a private school with a motto that sounds like a slogan advertising a deluxe Fiat or something. To get to the gym we have to walk along a long, paved path flanked by leafy trees and deadly rosebushes. Each brick on the path has a name engraved on it. Mr Reid tells us it's called Avenue of the Millions. At first I think he means a whole bunch of people donated a million bricks, but then I realise he's talking about dollars.

Millions.

A group of students passes us going in the opposite direction, and I'm guessing racquet sports and good nutrition must speed up evolution because the girls are terrifying in long socks and tartan skirts. They give us the side-eye—too polite to stare, but too curious not to look.

Whatever the opposite of slumming it is, that's what we're doing today.

Mr Reid leads us to a gym the size of four basketball

courts. I bet he's already wishing he hadn't brought us here. Our school 'uniform' consists of any item from the K-Mart or Big W black-and-maroon collection or anything you can get away with. I'm wearing my ripped Cleveland Cavs T-shirt and black jeans—I never show leg, even in forty-degree heat, not since Brock Tuwy pointed out I'm knock-kneed as well as ugly.

At the door, two girls hand us calico tote bags with the school emblem on one side. I'm dying to look inside (freebies are excellent) but I don't want to look like a kid with a show bag.

Lee Fortescu slips his hand into the bag and feels around. 'There's a pen,' he announces.

Mr Reid herds us into a foyer. 'The idea is, you chat to whoever piques your interest and take information if it's available. There are uni reps, too. Keep it short and to the point. Ask them whatever you like except how much money they make.'

'That's a fair question,' Will Farnsworth says.

'It's a rude question. And remember, you're representing me and the school. I chose you because I'm reasonably confident you won't let me down. This is the dreaming part of your plan. Remember?'

Dream—Goal—Plan—Action—Reality.

We all nod.

He checks his watch. 'We have one hour. Imagine anything is possible and keep telling yourselves that. Off you go.'

Anything is possible.

Anything *is* possible.

Anything is *possible.*

We peel off in different directions.

Saint Monica's Recreation Centre (it's not a gym) is packed, and the roof is high enough for another storey or a mezzanine floor.

Our gym has yellow asbestos warning signs all over the walls and the rafters are so low that there are more balls stuck in the rafters than there are in the equipment lockers. Our gym is also the best place to collect samples to grow weird things in agar.

I count around a hundred cubicles separated by carpeted partitions, with printed signs above each one, like Surgeon (Cardiothoracic), Veterinarian, Early Childhood Educator, Electrical Engineer, Human Rights Lawyer, Magistrate, Futures Trader, Member of Parliament, Geophysicist, Radiologist, Pathologist…lots of -ists and -ologists and -arians. It's professional and intimidating, except they've used Bradley Hand font on the signs, and I find it hard to believe a school with a coat of arms and a Latin motto doesn't have a policy to prevent font-based judgements.

One line stretches from half-court to the baseline of Court 3; I join the queue, only to realise they're all waiting for a uni rep. Zadie, I notice, is interested in teaching. (I'm not sure playing Tetris and avoiding human contact is the best preparation for that.) Gurmeet is still loitering by the entrance, and Will is helping himself to the coffee machine.

I leave the line.

There's one guy by himself in the far corner. Franchisee. The only -ee in the room and I figure it's a good omen: one day I'd quite like to be an employee. 'Bob' is obese, bald and unshaven, and he's doodling cubes and arrows on a notepad.

I sit down. 'Nate,' I say, offering my hand.

'Bob.' We shake and he leans back in his chair. 'You're my first. What are we supposed to do now?'

'I dunno. Analyse your doodles?'

He shrugs, tears the top sheet off, and screws it into a ball. 'Ask me anything you want to know, I guess.'

Fifty-three minutes to go—still almost a whole hour of feeling like one of Merrick's bin chickens.

On our way out, a grey-haired woman wearing a Saint Monica's blazer hugs Mr Reid, tells him everyone misses him and says she hopes he has found what he was looking for.

He takes a long time to answer. 'Thank you for letting my students come today. It's not an experience they'll forget.'

'It's a *fabulous* learning opportunity,' she says, beaming. 'We're *always* happy to share resources.'

Mr Reid pats his comb-over all the way to the car park. 'So what did you all think?' he asks when we're seated.

Leila smirks. 'There was an opera singer.'

'Oh, do you sing, Leila?'

'No. Just thought it was pretty unhelpful. All of it, really.'

'Gurmeet?'

'It was okay.' Gurmeet stuffs his bag under the seat. 'Just pamphlets and stuff.'

'Oh yeah, I found my vocation,' Zadie says, sneering. 'What about you, Will?'

Will shrugs. 'The surgeon makes around four hundred grand a year. I asked and he told me, and then he said if I worked hard and studied for about ten years and paid hundreds of thousands of dollars, I could be one too.' He frowns and gazes out the window. 'Jobs are expensive.'

'Such a great *learning opportunity*.' Zadie reaches across and taps my shoulder. 'What did you think, Nate?'

I've got a hot spot just under my heart. It was there before Zadie touched me voluntarily, and it's spreading. I don't think I've ever seen so many perfectly good sandwiches in a single rubbish bin.

I mutter, 'Options.'

'What about options?' Mr Reid says.

'There were so many.'

'And none appealed to you?'

'Some did. I spent most of the time talking to a franchisee called Bob.'

Leila laughs. 'The lawnmower guy?'

'The whole *hour*?' Mr Reid says.

'I felt sorry for him—nobody was lining up.'

'Probably not the best use of your time, Mr McKee.'

'I learned a lot. Twenty-five thousand bucks will buy me in. I'd have to mow about seven hundred lawns to recoup my investment—actually, more like eight hundred because fifteen per cent are write-offs. Once I pay tax and expenses I guess it's more like a thousand lawns, plus franchise fees—so around twelve hundred lawns should do it.'

'You've done your sums. Is mowing lawns a new life goal?' Mr Reid is amused.

'Nobody in Bairstal even has a lawn,' I tell him. 'And you have to *have* money to make money.'

He frowns.

'Forget it.'

'No. Tell me.'

I turn around in my seat. 'Hey, Will? How much cash is in your pocket right now?'

'None,' he says. 'I spent my last four bucks on their shit coffee.'

'Leila?'

'About fifty cents.'

'Gurmeet?'

He shrugs. 'Twenty dollars. But that's to buy nappies for my mum on my way home.'

Will cracks up. 'Your mum wears nappies?'

'All right, all right. Your point, McKee?' Mr Reid says.

'Some girl was complaining because she needed change to buy a shit coffee and she only had a twenty, so I offered her my four bucks change. She really *really* wanted a coffee.'

'And?' Mr Reid looks nervous. 'What did you do?'

'Don't worry, I didn't mug her or anything. I just—' I rub my temples. I've got a massive headache. 'If she'd given me the twenty, I would have split it with you guys. She'd have her coffee and we'd all be better off.'

'But she didn't want to trade?'

'That's the thing—she did.'

'So? Did you take it?'

'No.'

Will whistles through his teeth. 'Dickhead.'

'She said, "Say please," and when I took it she said, "Now say thank you." Screw that. I don't get why she was so surprised when I gave it back.'

'A reasonable reaction would be to show gratitude,' Mr Reid says.

'It wasn't worth twenty bucks to kiss her arse.'

'Fair enough, McKee. Fair enough.'

'I still think you're a dickhead,' Will says.

But Zadie mutters under her breath, 'Screw that.'

It goes quiet inside the car. Mr Reid adjusts the rear-view mirror and starts the engine.

I blurt, 'You want to know what I think? I think we're helpless, and being helpless is about the worst thing you can be—except maybe a psychopath, but anyway—there should be people who help us navigate this shit so we're not helpless. So we have options. *Real* options. That's what I think.'

Mr Reid is doing his no-blinking again.

'I chose the only option I thought I could choose, except it turned out to be just as unlikely as Will ever making four hundred grand a year.'

'Hey!'

'Sorry, Will. I'm pissed off.'

Nothing from Mr Reid.

I punch the door. '*Fuck*! Why'd you bring us here anyway?'

With the exception of Lee, who's rummaging through his show bag, we're all hunched in, arms crossed. This is what it takes to bring us together.

I used to like school. I liked it when my teachers praised me in class or shared my work. I don't know exactly when I decided school was pointless, and I don't know if school did it to me or the other way around, but now it feels like taking a long train ride in the dark—nothing to see, nowhere to go but straight ahead, no place to disembark because the train never, ever stops. I've been waiting for my time like it's some kind of inevitable destination. I'm starting to think you have to close your eyes and jump.

Mr Reid puts the car into reverse and looks over his left shoulder, even though it has a reversing camera. 'I'm glad you're all pissed off,' he says slowly, as he pulls out of the car park, narrowly missing the heavy wrought-iron gate. 'It means you're thinking.'

I shake my head. 'What good is that? It's not like we can do anything.'

He nods as if I've scored a point. But then he says, 'Of course you can. This is about life. It's easy to choose the path of least resistance—it's much more difficult to *be* the resistance.'

Gurmeet huffs. 'Who has time for that? We're all just trying not to get our heads kicked in.'

'This is how I see it,' continues Mr Reid. 'First you fight your allies—it's just human nature. Then you fight your enemies. They're beatable because they're willing to engage.'

'Then what?' My rage has gone off the boil already. 'What if you beat them?'

Straightaway, I regret it. We're trapped for the next hour in a car with a guy who probably practises his speeches on his fifteen cats. I don't want to give him a platform.

Reid makes eye contact in the rear-view mirror. 'Then you fight apathy. Apathy is the true enemy because it just doesn't care.'

I reach across the console. 'Is this the part where you say we can do anything or be anything we want—all we have to do is work hard and follow our dreams?'

'No,' Mr Reid says. 'This is the part where I ask you to put your seatbelt on and stop waving your fist in my face. I'm not your enemy.'

—

When I get home, Nance is napping on the couch, curled up with her arms tucked under her legs. She looks as if she's tied in a knot. The boys are asleep too.

I throw my bag in a corner and forage in the kitchen for something quick to eat, but all I can find is a half-empty packet of plastic cheese slices and a dozen snack-sized packets of the barbecue chips nobody likes, including me.

I'm still angry, mostly with myself. Apart from the girl who needed change, the Saint Monica's students were nice: well-mannered, friendly, welcoming.

They're free to save the world. The rest of us have to find our way out of the jungle first.

I pull out a chair at the kitchen table and take my books out of my backpack as quietly as possible. I have Geography homework and Chem revision to finish. Usually I try to get homework done during lunch because it's quieter in the school library than at home, but today's unexpected excursion means I didn't have the chance.

I get fifteen minutes of pre-procrastination done before Jake wanders in. He stares at Nance until she sits up, blinking, and Otis lets us know he's awake too. A moment later, there's the jingle of Dec's keys. He staggers in with red eyes and a bleeding foot, which makes me simultaneously pleased that he does in fact bleed and worried he's so far gone he doesn't feel it.

'You're drunk,' Nance says. 'It's not even five o'clock.'

Dec falls onto the couch and pulls Nance close. Her knots unwind and she turns liquid. When O starts yelling from the bedroom, Dec pulls her closer and whispers something that makes her smile, and I wonder how long before they disappear into their bedroom and close the door.

Like Dec said, he loves Nance, and Nance loves him. But it's not simple like he said—it's complicated in a way that makes my brain hurt, and it makes me worry I'm not normal because I don't think about sex a million times a day like Merrick does, and when I do think about it, it feels like something I don't want to do because of all the responsibilities that come from doing it. I suspect, if it's true there's nothing they can't sort out with love like theirs, Nance wouldn't cry as often as she does.

'What're you doing?' Dec asks over his shoulder.

'Me?'

'Yeah.'

'Homework.'

He snorts. 'Right.'

Nance shifts.

Dec hauls her back. 'Go see to O,' he says.

'I'm doing homework,' I repeat. 'This assignment is due tomorrow.'

Nance tries to get up, but he catches hold of the straps of her top. One day I might tell him he looks like Jabba the Hut yanking Leia's neck chain. But not today.

'What's for dinner?' Dec asks.

Nance says, 'Chips?'

Dec looks at me.

I know what's coming next—I'll have to pick up extra-large chips and ninety-nine cent Vietnamese bread. Cheapest meal you don't have to cook yourself, because Dec keeps his weed money for betting.

Otis screams and Nance squawks.

'Okay, I'm going.' I close my textbook.

The slap is loud and Dec's head whips around. 'You giving me attitude?'

'No.'

'I reckon you are.'

Nance's eyes: she's pleading with me.

'I'm not. I'm going, all right?' I make it halfway across the room before Jake appears in the doorway, holding something in his fist. Otis is quiet now. 'What have you got? Where's O?' I ask him, but he presses his lips together.

'Leave him alone,' Dec slurs. 'He's just a kid.'

Jake pushes Nance out of the way and crawls onto his lap.

In the bedroom, Otis is lying on his side. It's like he fell asleep on the floor halfway through a tantrum, except his eyes are open. One of his Barbies has been beheaded. I assume Jake has it in his fist, until I notice a raw patch of skin on O's head, a chunk of his hair missing, and the Barbie's head under the bed.

There's no way I'll be finishing my homework tonight.

I sit on the floor next to O, stroking his face, wondering why he's not crying, worrying about whether eating chips four nights a week can cause adolescent heart disease and if bread that doesn't grow mould after a month in a sweaty plastic bag is carcinogenic.

Most of all I worry about Nance's reaction when I tell her Jake has taken another piece of Otis, only this time he did it on purpose.

TEN

Full moon lunacy is an actual phenomenon. So are Friday Night Fights at Youth.

By the time I roll in, three people have already been ejected and Macy and Thomas look as if they need full riot gear. It's as if everyone has been on their best behaviour all week and Youth is the place to where it all spills over: an argument starts over nothing, others pile on for something to do, the fight ends up in the car park and the cops come to break it up. When the paras arrive for an OD, you know the party's over.

Deng's hanging around the Rage Cage, bouncing his Spalding between his legs. Someone has cable-tied a rusty ring to the fence. There's no backboard but I guess it's better than nothing.

'Shootout?' he says.

I nod. 'I'll get the lights.'

'They're not working.'

'Unfair advantage.'

He bounce-passes me the ball. 'It's okay.'

'Where's Coop?'

He shrugs. 'Where's Merrick?'

'Gone to the dark side.'

A few younger kids gather to watch.

Deng wants to practise his post moves, so I'm stuck in D. His advantages are many: he's faster, more athletic, and his standing jump is almost double mine. When it's one-on-one, we play no-charge rules in the key. Just about anything goes, except elbows and knees. His drives are pretty brutal, but I manage to put him off a few shots and box him out for some rebounds off the fence.

After ten minutes, I've used all my oxygen.

Deng beats his chest. 'I am the beast in the paint!'

I'm dripping with sweat. Deng's not even breathing hard.

'I quit. I'm going inside.'

'One more,' he says. 'Fast feet. Like this.'

He jabs left and drives right, leaving me flat-footed. His shoulder catches mine on the way through, and I land hard on my wrists and arse, hissing through my teeth as the asphalt shreds a layer of skin from my arm. The kids at the fence *oooooh*.

Deng offers his hand, but I slap it away and get up by myself.

'It's okay,' he says. 'You were in my way.'

Deng always says things are okay, even when they're not.

'Charge.' I punch my palm.

He bangs his fists against his hips. 'Block.'

'It was a charge.'

'Block. Your feet move. You flap your wings. You should be like a statue—no move, no fear.' Deng spins the ball on his index finger, making clucking sounds, and the kids egg him on.

It's all right for him. He's only fifteen but he's already

playing Under 23s. He doesn't have to feel around for a way out. His exit has a big red flashing sign: *This way to the NBA*.

I punch his precious Spalding like a speedball—it shoots through the cage entrance, ricochets off the car park light post and bounces across the car park towards the road.

Deng chases after it.

Cooper has finally turned up. 'What was all that about?' he says, staring after him.

We still have an audience. My face burns. 'He dropped his shoulder.'

'No-charge rule counts.' Coop catches Deng's pass in one huge hand. 'Can't leave you two alone for a second. You've got anger issues, man.' He shakes his head and lays the ball up.

My temper can get me in just as much trouble as Merrick's mouth.

'Sorry,' I say to Deng when he comes back. 'I'm having a bad day.'

Deng gives me knuckles. 'It's only one day.'

'I'm having a bad life, then.'

He throws his arm around my shoulders. 'It's okay.'

Everything inside the centre is occupied: TV, pool table, laptops, beanbags. Someone's playing music too loud and I can hear the thump of the ball as Cooper and Deng carry on scrimmage without me. Trent Povey, Youth's resident spaceman, is taking up the whole couch. Povey can sleep through anything.

Macy was here a moment ago, but now she isn't. With Mim away, it just leaves Thomas and that makes me nervous.

I'm still having flashbacks. I jump every time I hear the door.

There's been a new wave of kids in the past few months, some as young as eight. I've been coming here so long I'm starting to feel like staff, but Macy says she won't know the new kids for half their lives the way she knows Merrick and me. These days she has to report everything. The system will swallow up these kids.

According to the Book of Macy, the best people in youth services were once the worst human beings, or they've at least been up close and personal with some Very Bad Things. She says you shouldn't judge others until you've sat down, shut the fuck up and listened to their story—and not just the parts you want to hear. Macy is straight up about recovering from domestic violence, meth addiction and homelessness. When she talks, we do as she says—we sit down and shut up. Macy can be scary, but she's real.

Thomas is ex-army. He lived on the streets for fifteen years. There was a rumour he served time for attempted murder, but Macy told us that's not his whole story either. Some drunk idiots pinched his shopping trolley and rolled it into the river, so Thomas gave the idiot he caught a couple of busted ribs and made him dive repeatedly until he'd recovered Thomas's worldly possessions—including the trolley. The guy had a bit of trouble swimming.

And Mim—is just Mim. I can't imagine her doing anything bad. I'm not sure she even *has* a story.

Macy used to try to get things happening, like workshops and short courses, but I think she's given up. The workshops are supposed to inspire us, but mostly they remind us that our ambitions are too ambitious. Bit like a careers expo. In the last year, we've had basic computer courses, basic cooking classes, basic origami. How to Write a Résumé. Painting to Relieve Stress.

Most kids could teach the teachers a thing or two about programming or hacking, and we've got nothing to put in a résumé. Basic cooking? Yeah, most of us have mastered that in the spirit of not starving and dying, and learning to make an origami ninja star is only useful for the prototype—the real fun would be to make a working stainless-steel version in Tech.

'Time's up,' I say to a kid of about twelve who just sneakily reset the laptop egg timer.

'Fuck off,' he says, not bothering to turn around.

I can't be arsed having a fight about it, so I flip through the DVDs in the rack. Merrick and I were up to L—*The Last Airbender* to be precise—before our friendship went on hiatus.

The stack wobbles. I put up my hands, but it's too late. The DVDs fly off the shelf as if I've cast a spell with an invisible wand. Out of a hundred, I catch maybe five.

'Here, I'll help you.' It's Mim. She kneels and scoops up a handful of cases.

'You're back.'

'Macy had a call-out, so she asked me to come in for an hour.'

Her hair is pulled back in a messy ponytail. She has a thin red scar across her nose, and she speaks through her teeth, as if her jaw is wired shut.

She notices me staring. 'It wasn't as bad as it looked.'

'How are you feeling?'

'Fine, thank you.'

'That could mean you're fine, or you want everyone to

think you're fine, or you're absolutely not fine.'

'I pretty much say what I mean and mean what I say. I'm *fine*.' She puts the DVDs back on the shelf and straightens the stack. 'I don't remember much about what happened, but thank you. I appreciate what you and your friends did.'

'It was nothing.'

She frowns. 'It wasn't nothing.'

'No, I mean we really didn't do anything. We didn't stop him.'

'It wasn't up to you to stop him. You stayed, and that's more than enough.' She motions the kid with the music to turn it down. 'It's getting cold out.'

'Yeah. Feels like summer is finally over.'

For the first time since that night, I think I might cry. I don't know why—it happened weeks ago, but things haven't been the same. Or maybe I'm not the same. I hardly know Mim, but it feels as if I do—something about witnessing a person's worst moment makes talking about the weather seem ridiculous. The scary part is, it might not have been her worst moment. More than anything, I want to ask her if there's a crack in her life now, too. And, if there isn't, if she's no more afraid than she was before, how did she stop it?

The front door swishes open.

We both jump.

Mim's hands fly up. She presses them flat to her chest and breathes out.

I guess that answers my question.

'Tash,' Mim says. She crosses the room and pulls her into a hug.

Tash is blank-faced and stiff as a mannequin. She's wearing

her dad's coat again, her hands stuffed deep in the pockets. 'Is it true?'

'What?' Mim says.

'Cranky said the centre's closing.'

I assume she's talking about Thomas.

'We don't know for sure.' Mim's expression isn't giving much away. 'I can't really say anything more.'

Tash snaps out of her trance and starts pacing around the perimeter of the rec room, weirdly agitated, like she's high on something.

'Some of these kids are going to take it hard,' Mim says, watching her.

'So it is true.'

'It's a rumour.'

'I was going to stop coming here, anyway.' It's how I feel, but it's probably not helpful right now.

'Why?'

'I don't really fit in.'

'Well, that's kind of the point,' she snaps.

'I've aged out, then.'

'You're not too old, Nate.' She points to the notebook in my pocket. 'What's in your little black book? I've always wanted to ask. Is it like a diary? Coming-of-age stuff?'

'Coming-of-rage. I purge so I don't explode, that's all.'

She laughs. 'I exploded once. I sat on the kerb one day and decided to stop making excuses and blaming everyone else.'

Tash is hovering nearby as if she wants to talk to Mim privately. I go to leave them alone, but Tash grabs my elbow and pulls me in.

'We have to do something,' she says. 'Youth can't close.'

Mim tries to change the subject. 'I'm going to make coffee if anyone's interested?'

'You don't understand.' Tash shrugs off her coat and ties it around her waist. 'What if we raised enough money so they couldn't shut it down?'

'I don't think it's just about the money, Tash,' Mim says, shaking her head. 'It's many things—' She stops and gives a helpless shrug.

I think about what Macy said. Maybe Mim blames herself.

An argument has broken out at the pool table. Mim squeezes Tash's shoulder before going to sort it out, and Tash glares at me for no apparent reason. She flounces off in the direction of the toilets.

I take the distraction as an opportunity to claim a recently vacated beanbag. I flip through my notebook, searching for empty pages; they're so loose I have to keep them together with a rubber band. I'm still not ready to start a new one. Earlier, I was itching to write something about the careers expo, but now I'm not feeling it.

Tash is back, circling like a bird of prey. 'Do you know Banksy?' she barks.

'Umm...'

'Loner graffiti artist. Girl with a balloon? Kissing coppers? Don't forget to eat your lunch and make some trouble?'

She looks like she has a fever.

'Are you sick?'

'No,' she says.

'Okay. Let's have a completely random conversation.' I pat the spare beanbag.

She ignores it. 'You've heard of Banksy, though, right?'

113

I nod. 'There's no way he's a loner. I bet he has a stencil cutter and someone to carry his spray cans and a PR man. He probably has a tea lady.'

Tash regards me carefully. 'What—exactly—does the tea lady do?'

'Makes his tea.'

She puffs out her cheeks. 'I've got a theory for you. Banksy—is a woman.'

'No way. Impossible.'

'Think about it. No guy would be able to put his art above his ego. He would want the whole world to know who he is.'

'I'm not buying.'

'I'm right,' she says, smirking. 'It's the perfect cover.'

I pull too hard on the rubber band and it snaps, scattering pages. 'That artist DOT DOT DOT is better. Art that's mass-consumed and printed on greeting cards has peaked— it's tipped over the edge into a bottomless well of uncool.'

Tash watches me sort the pages. 'Ever done it?'

'Done what?'

Slowly, she rolls her sleeve to reveal a tattoo of a girl hugging a nuclear bomb on the inside of her forearm.

I whisper, 'Holy shit! *You're* Banksy?'

A fast-moving rash is spreading from her collarbone to her neck. She rolls her sleeve back down. 'I knew I couldn't trust you.'

'I was going to stop coming here, anyway,' I repeat.

'What do *you* stand for?' She points her fist at the centre's rule chart and pops up three fingers, one by one. 'Fuck. The. Establishment.'

A few nearby kids clap and punch the air even though they have zero context.

I feel bad. But not bad enough to follow Tash when she leaves.

Mim appears next to me. 'What was that?'

'A difference of opinion.'

'She needs this place more than most.'

'More than me?'

'You'd have to ask her about that.'

I try to push myself out of the beanbag, but beanbags are designed to make you look like a three-legged giraffe stuck in a tar pit.

Mim offers her hand and hauls me out. 'We get why you all act so tough, you know.'

'I'm not tough. That's the problem.'

She says through her teeth, 'The willingness to expose wounds is a sign of privilege. Vulnerability is a survival risk, so you don't show it.'

'Is that a quote?'

'It's a fact.' She bends down to pick something up. 'Don't forget your rage book.'

ELEVEN

I'm sitting outside a noisy cafe called Celestial Beans, drinking my second glass of complimentary tap water, waiting for Mum. It's fancy. The food's weird. The couple at the next table are sucking greasy beans from a shared bowl and slurping from cups without handles. We have cups at home with no handles.

Mum is twenty minutes late.

Her text came through last night, three days after I sent her my number. No explanation, just the time and the place. I caught two buses to get here. I keep checking my phone and waiting for a message to say she isn't coming. I'm nervous, but not the kind that twists your guts—it's more like a slow-moving feeling that something bad is about to happen. I read somewhere that people feel like this after they've been transfused with the wrong type of blood.

Science says it's impossible for us to recall a memory without altering it in some way—that's my first thought when I realise the woman with her back to me, just inside the door of the cafe, is her. I wouldn't have known if she hadn't lifted her ponytail and wound it around her finger. Something about the action was familiar.

Memories are made when groups of neurons are primed

to fire together, and the brain has around a hundred billion neurons, each capable of making tens of thousands of connections. But the human mind is susceptible to glitches and failed saves and data corruption, just like a computer, except science also tells us it's nothing like a computer and making a memory isn't as simple as entering the correct data.

So much can go wrong.

But my memories must be faulty: now that I can see her profile she looks nothing like the mum I remember. One neuron must have misfired, and I filed the skinny zombie edition away in my memory box. Nobody I know has ever transformed this dramatically—at least, not in a positive way.

It's her.

She picks up her phone and plays with it. I watch her hands. They're steady, and that's the only reason I sit down at her table. I can almost hear her counting to ten in her mind before she takes a shuddering breath, and speaks.

'Nate?'

'Yeah.'

'Hello!' She's almost shouting. 'It's good to see you!'

She has shiny hair. Her fingernails are polished.

'I didn't recognise you.'

She smooths her hair, then her skirt. 'I'm glad you came. Are you hungry?'

'Not really.'

'You should try the ancient grains with yoghurt and raspberries. Delicious.'

Does she have a brain injury or something? What the hell are ancient grains? Mummified oats they discovered in the bottom of a sarcophagus? Should be, at eighteen bucks for a bowl of cereal. There's a patch of flaking white paint on the wall, near her head—I know that if I go over there and start picking at it, I won't stop until the whole wall is grey.

I glance down at the menu.

'I look different, huh?' she says. 'You haven't mentioned it. I'm vegetarian now.'

'I did mention it. I said I didn't recognise you.'

She spoons a mouthful of mush and swallows without chewing. 'I know it must be a shock. Look, are you sure you're not hungry?'

'Yes.'

'Coffee?'

'No. So you're clean?'

'Three years,' she says. 'I have a sponsor.'

Three years? Three. *Years*? Almost four since I saw her last.

'I have a job. It's not much—four days a week selling gym memberships. I get cheap gear and—' She stops when she sees my expression. Her lips flatten. '*Gym* gear.'

There she is. I can still see the zombie underneath. The last time I saw her, I was pushing thirteen and she was a skeleton with a full repertoire of tics and two missing teeth. (I want to ask how she fixed them. Teeth are expensive.) She could barely hold a conversation; she kept fixating on random details, like the way my voice sounded so much like Dec's when it started to break, and how my arms were too long and my feet too big. Puberty seemed to terrify her—a sign of something sinister.

But this is also the same mother who patiently dug up my dead pet rat three times in three days because I was terrified we'd made a mistake and buried him alive.

'That's great. Good for you.'

'I signed up thirty-two memberships last week,' she says. 'My boss says I could sell sunglasses to a blind person. I think I've found my superpower.'

'Convincing people to buy something they don't need is your superpower?'

She flicks her hand. 'Building muscle makes you live longer.'

She needs to see the stats on the number of deaths caused by barbells.

'Blind people *do* need sunglasses. Just because they can't see doesn't mean they don't need sun protection.'

'I s'pose. And so they don't get freaked out by people looking at them.'

I'm not sure if I sigh out loud or just in my head. 'I think I might have discovered my superpower too.'

'Oh, yeah? What is it?'

'Invisibility.'

'Everyone says that. I'd want to fly or move things with my mind. There's a childcare centre right next to my apartment complex. I'd move that.'

'So you've got an apartment?'

She swipes through some photos on her phone. A sixth-floor one-bedroom, she says. Just big enough to swing a cat. It has a balcony. She grows succulents because they're hard to kill even if you forget about them for a long time. They're tough.

If I bite my tongue any harder the tip will fly off and land in her bowl. She'll be a lapsed vegetarian.

'What does the sponsor do?'

She tells me his name is John. He saved her life. He drops

in every day. I stop listening after that. I can tell he does more than drop in—it doesn't really matter because she's done worse. She's still smiling and her mouth is still talking. She looks good. John might be a magician.

'—still with that girl?' She's asking about Dec.

'Nance is all right,' I snap. 'And she's not a girl. She's twenty-*four*.'

'And the kid? The one with—?' She twirls a finger. 'Is he still only half there?'

'Otis. My brother.'

'*Half*-brother.'

My half-there half-brother. She says it like he's not a full person.

'And how *is* Declan?'

'Dec is Dec.'

'You're angry.' She slumps back in her chair.

I nod. 'A bit. How did you find us?'

She frowns. 'What do you mean? I always knew where you were.' It's the wrong thing to say and she knows it. 'Look, I knew this was a bad idea. My sponsor said this would be tough for me.'

Tough? *Tough*?

'I'm hungry. I think I'll order something now.' I choose a tasting plate with goat's cheese and other stuff I can't pronounce, because it's the most expensive thing on the menu. After I've ordered I tell her I don't have any money.

'That's fine.' She pulls a credit card from a zippered pocket in her purse, separate from the rest of her cards. She scrapes underneath her fingernails with a corner, chewing her lip. 'For emergencies,' she says.

'I'm starving.'

'Well, that counts as an emergency.' She laughs. 'You're getting so tall. I bet you eat a lot.'

'*All* the time.' I roll my eyes. 'Never stop eating. Seven or eight meals a day. Nance says I have the metabolism of a racehorse. She had to put a padlock on the fridge because I sleepwalk and she'd get up in the night and I would be, like—' I make grunting noises and mime stuffing handfuls of food into my mouth. Mum leans back in alarm. 'She's a great cook. Nance says soon they'll have to make the doorways bigger so I can fit through them.'

Nance never said or did any of this. Nance can't cook for shit, but every time I say 'Nance says', Mum flinches like I've flicked her wrist with a rubber band.

'Nance says I'll need both bunks soon, so I have somewhere to put my legs.'

She did say that.

'I want to know about *you*,' she says, slapping my hand harder than she needs to. 'What's been happening? Give me the good stuff.'

The tasting plate arrives. The joke's on me—it has about eight foods I can't identify, and everything smells like dirty socks boiled in vinegar. I store a yellow cherry tomato in my cheek and cut the cheese into isosceles triangles. If this isn't going to be a sentimental reunion I might as well embark on a full reconnaissance mission.

'Do I still have grandparents?'

'I haven't seen them since before you were born.'

'Why not?' I bite down on the tomato accidentally. I'm forced to swallow it.

'They kicked me out when I got pregnant with you. I never want to see them again.'

'What about on Dec's side?'

She laughs. It's an ugly sound. 'I met his old man once. His mum was really young—she ran off with someone else when he was four. Dec always said he hated his old man but then he went and turned out just like him.'

'Like how?'

I know how he turned out—I want to hear her say it. I'm not sure why I'm asking. Maybe I want to know where I come from. I would like to be a throwback, but it doesn't exactly sound as if I'm a direct blood descendant of royalty or genius.

Right now I think I'd prefer to turn out like Dec.

She turns to stare at that patch of flaking paint on the wall. 'Drunk and mean and not around.' She looks back at me. 'He was never there when I needed him.'

I push the plate away. 'He's mostly there.'

'He must really love her, huh?' She looks sad. 'And you. I mean, he kept you. I used to think he only did that to hurt me.'

'He didn't have a choice, did he? You left me behind.' My voice is too loud.

'John says we have to become a monster to defeat a monster,' she says. 'One day you'll understand.'

When I was younger, I wished she'd come back, be different—better. I thought I wanted a new beginning, but I'm not a kid anymore and now I'm not so sure. I think I want an ending.

I leave the flat as soon as Nance and Dec start arguing about money, or the lack of it. Dec's complaining about O still using nappies, and Nance is furious because he spent three hundred bucks on a second-hand kayak.

I don't want to run into Merrick or Tuwy, so my options are limited. No Youth, no underpass. No money, no shops. All that time it took me to master the saunter—now I realise it doesn't work when you're on your own. Move too fast and it looks like you're nervous; walk too slow and you're too easy to catch. Only make brief, heavy-lidded eye contact with other humans (ignoring them altogether is a further sign of submission) and make like the clock's ticking, like you have somewhere to be. Except I have nowhere to be.

Can't walk forever, so I turn around and head home.

One street over from the flats I run into Nance, pushing Otis in the pram, half-dragging an unwilling Jake behind her. Both are screaming.

'I'm trying to get O to sleep,' she says.

I don't mention she's still wearing pyjama bottoms. 'I can take Jake.'

'Where've you been? Somewhere exciting?'

I think of Mum. Maybe she's still sitting in the cafe, eating my leftovers. I left before the conversation turned to Dec for the hundredth time. Told her I'd miss my bus.

'Just catching up with someone I used to know.'

'Oh. That sounds like fun.'

She says 'fun' with her tongue poking the inside of her cheek, like she's trying to recall the flavour of something without actually tasting it, and it hits me—Nance has no friends, unless you count Margie upstairs, and Margie only ever drops in when she wants to borrow eggs or milk or money, so the entire relationship is based on Nance serving black coffee and being embarrassed that we don't have enough of whatever it is Margie wants to borrow.

Nance hands over Jake and takes off, cornering the pram like a rally car. One broken wheel is spinning. O is still yelling.

'Skate,' Jake says.

He has short legs and an even shorter attention span—it takes us twice as long as it should to walk to the park. When we get there he's tired and thirsty and he wants to go home again. It's a mild day but the concrete is sizzling. D&G is here, as usual, but instead of pulling tricks he's pedalling figure-eights in the shallow track. A couple of boys around ten are writing swear words in chalk around the edge.

Jake grabs his crotch, and for a second he looks like a mini-Dec. At least he's toilet-trained. I tell him to piss behind the shelter because the toilets are filthy. I check my phone.

Jake's only out of my sight for half a minute. When I look up he's climbing down the side of the shallow track, and by the time I get there he has walked straight in front of the bike.

D&G growls and drops his BMX to avoid hitting him.

I grab Jake by the waist and swing him over my shoulder. 'Sorry about that.'

D&G just stands there with his thumbs hooked in his back pockets, staring at the bike as if Jake almost ran over it, instead of the other way around. I can't see any major damage and it was already a bit banged up anyway.

'Is everything okay?'

He doesn't reply, so I carry Jake away.

'I want to talk to the man.'

'No. You don't talk to strangers.'

'Can I ride his bike?'

'You can't. It's too big. And don't go on the track—you could have been hurt.' I plonk him down. His eyes are filling with tears. 'What's up?'

'No!'

'No, what?'

'No crying.'

'*I'm* not crying. *You* are.'

'Don't cry,' he says, sticking out his bottom lip. 'No! *No* crying. Pussy.'

'That's not a nice word,' I tell him, and he follows up with, 'Fuck. *Fuuuuuuuck!*'

My first instinct is to smack him. I turn my back instead. Nance says if you don't pay a screamer any attention he'll stop screaming, but that doesn't work either. I walk ahead without him, and he throws himself at my legs and punches me behind the kneecap. I turn and raise my fist and he backs away. There's snot dangling from his nose and a graze on his cheek.

I'm out of options—except for the hardest thing. I don't know why it's so hard.

I scoop him up and hold him until he stops fighting.

TWELVE

Wednesday afternoon, double English. Mr Reid has handed us each a pad of miniature fluoro Post-its, a Faber-Castell HB pencil, and an A2 photocopy of a Snakes 'n' Ladders game board.

'Where's the dice?' Lee says.

Reid shakes his head. 'There will be no rolling of dice yet, Fortescu.'

A2-sized photocopies are the unicorns of the classroom. These, plus the legit Post-its and the deadly-sharp Faber-Castells, make me think Mr Reid has financed this exercise, which further leads me to believe that he's committed to having himself a teaching moment.

I commit to staring out the window. D&G is early today—it's only 1.45 and he's already on his way to the skate park. His rear tyre pressure is low.

'For the whole double lesson, you'll be working in complete silence.'

Groans.

'I'd like you to think of your moves on your game board as a series of steps towards a personal goal. Whether that's something short-term, such as buying your first car, or long-term, like becoming an astronaut, is up to you. You need to consider possible obstacles or setbacks, and also positive steps that take you closer to your goal. Nobody can inherit a large sum of money from a mysterious benefactor, win the lotto or achieve anything without doing the work. Okay? Use the ladders. Do the work.'

Kobe asks, 'What has this got to do with English?'

'Everything and nothing,' Mr Reid says. 'We're deviating today.'

'What about the dice?' Lee says again.

'Pay attention. There must be a minimum of three black squares on each game board. The black squares are like the longest snakes. They're your biggest obstacles—they take you right back to the beginning of the game. But you all have *something* that will give you a serious advantage, whether that's your work ethic or a particular talent or simply the focus you need to achieve. *Use* that advantage.'

The only way I can think to swing an advantage is to be more like Dec: tough, stubborn, single-minded in the pursuit of winning, and afraid of nothing. It would be really helpful if his genes kicked in soon.

'What's the aim?' Gurmeet asks.

'The aim is to win, of course, but you need to counteract the setbacks.' Mr Reid looks at the clock above his desk. 'You have the full double lesson to finish the task. If that's not long enough, you should complete it in your own time.'

Gurmeet releases a deep sigh that ruffles my paper and sends it floating to the floor. 'Sorry,' he whispers. 'What's your goal? I can't think of anything.'

'Me neither.' I reach down to pick up the game board.

'I wonder if getting Netflix counts,' Gurmeet mutters, chewing his pencil.

I glance over my shoulder. Leila has already written something in the first and last squares.

I put up my hand.

'McKee?'

'What if I have no immediate or long-term goals?'

'Then you can take the second option.'

'What's that?'

He gives me a cold smile. 'You can design a board game based on an aspect of contemporary Australian society instead.'

I tear off a Post-it.

The last time Macy checked my job log at Youth was over four months ago. I'd applied for over a hundred part-time and casual jobs, received rejections for six, 'we'll keep your application on file' emails from nine, and I didn't hear from the others at all. Even Macca's knocked me back. I haven't applied for a single position since Christmas.

I stick the Post-it in the last square and stare at the blank space for most of the first lesson. All I can see is the jungle.

When the bell rings at the end of the day, I take the usual route via the path running next to the train line.

A kid who looks uncannily like Merrick pushes past me at the oval gate, breathing hard. He's trying not to look over his shoulder, walking exactly like Merrick used to when someone bigger was on his tail.

I glance back. Two Year Tens are about thirty metres behind me, whipping at the weeds with sticks.

Merrick and I have taken this detour for the past year without incident. We know the blind spots: behind the junk heap, inside the old shed full of paint tins, under the drooping pepper tree where, years ago, someone set up an outdoor lounge room complete with sofa, lamp, coffee table, bookcase and a massive old TV, as thick as it was wide. We could always tell when there were signs we were being followed, or if the birds were too quiet, and we made adjustments: turn right, cut across the train line and double back, or seek safety in numbers, hop the train and ride for two stops until we were in the clear.

This route has its advantages and disadvantages. It's a longer, sweatier, dustier walk, and it loops around junk food corner, so there's no chance to stop for a frozen Coke on the way home. But it's also safer—anyone who heads home this way is either running for the first train, in which case they don't have time to start anything, or they're already trying to avoid confrontation.

The council still hasn't cut the summer weeds—now there are five or six different tracks and nobody can find the original way through anymore.

The Merrick look-alike kid makes a rookie mistake and turns left. Now there's nowhere for him to go except along a kilometre of train line until he reaches the next stop.

My phone pings. I stop to check it and the two Year Tens pass me about fifty metres along the track. One is a decent size, with sloping shoulders and a pushed-in face; the other is much shorter, with white-blond hair and teeth like a rat. I've seen them around but I don't know them.

Ahead, I can see the other kid, darting erratically, trying

to find the most direct route in a crazy warren. He breaks into a run and disappears around the next bend.

They follow.

I think about turning around, but I'm almost halfway home—my bag weighs a tonne, it's hot, I'm thirsty and I'm a *fucking senior*. I'm tired of making adjustments.

I round the bend.

Here's the blind spot: the pepper tree and the lounge room, just off the path, just out of sight. I used to find it funny that someone could be bothered installing an entire lounge room, but now it's overgrown, covered in graffiti and other foul things I don't want to think about.

If I look straight ahead I could almost pretend I don't know it's there, but the kid's schoolbag is lying in the middle of the path.

Pug has pinned him to the couch. He has one hand on the kid's head, pressing his cheek onto the broken inner springs, and Rat is making a documentary on his phone.

'S'up?' Rat says, unfazed.

'Hey.' I wave.

The kid on the couch yelps something, but I can't make it out.

Rat films me as I walk past.

I know I should have said something. I'm not a complete arsehole. Just scared. It's not as if I don't have the words—I've been filling these notebooks with words for years and at least three are dedicated to writing down things I should have said at a particular time, but only thought about later. L'esprit d'escalier. Staircase wit. I'm packing a full arsenal of comebacks and takedowns. But here's the thing about high-school social currency: you only increase your own by backing someone who's already loaded. Doesn't matter if you don't think they're a nice person (generally, people guarding the mother lode aren't, because currency begets currency and, at their core, winners are capitalists). Or, you can accept that your pile will be depleted by giving it to a person who has none; you might have a moment of self-congratulation before you check your pile and find it gone, but it's an act of sacrifice and, ultimately, self-sabotage. There might be nothing wrong with the kid on the couch. He's probably smart and funny. It's not his fault he was once on the losing end of a whole string of transactions—now it's a legacy he has to carry all through high school. I bet he's a regular visitor to the school counsellor. She says all the right things, but deep down she suspects he deserves the negative attention; she has no proof, but for some reason he is repulsive to his peers, so his claims must be treated with scepticism. They talk about him in the teachers' lounge. He's a strange kid. There's something off about him. Maybe he doesn't have the right shoes or clothes, or maybe he doesn't say thank you when someone is kind. So she'll counsel him, she'll mediate, she'll give him coping strategies and encourage him to work on his resilience, but she won't give him what he really needs. He needs her to believe him. He needs another person to back him, to say he's telling the truth and he isn't to blame, because pretty soon it will be too late. He's starting to think he's repulsive, too. But it won't happen. We're all protecting our currency. Even if I had stepped in, together we'd make a black hole that would suck anyone standing nearby into its vortex. Merrick was a master at spending currency he never had. Sorry, kid. Sorry I kept walking. Saying something means I have to do something, and that's the part I don't have written down.

If I was told the only way to guarantee my survival was to eat chip sandwiches for the rest of my life, I'd opt to die.

The boys don't care—they'd eat chips every night of the week if they could—but Nance knows. She's been staring at me staring at my plate. Hers is clean, Jake has been back for seconds, and Dec ate the chips but left the bread. He's watching *Goodfellas*, which means Jake is watching by default, O is watching but *no comprende*, and I'm totally tuned out because I've seen it about thirty times in the last ten years. Each time someone gets shot, Nance covers her face with her hand and watches through her fingers.

It would make a great drinking game.

'I'm going to bed,' I say to no one in particular.

It's eight o'clock.

Nance mumbles, 'Good night.'

On my way past, Otis grabs for my ankle and misses. 'Nate!'

'Shut up.' Dec nudges him with his foot. 'Get me a beer,' he says to me.

I grab a Heineken from the fridge. Dec sends me back for a Miller. I offer the Heineken to Nance, but she shakes her head.

'Top's off. You gotta drink it,' Dec says.

'I don't like beer.'

'You'll get to like it. It's a required taste.'

I sit back down. It takes me ten minutes to drink the beer. When I say goodnight for the second time, Dec points to my plate resting on the arm of the couch. To get a few moves ahead, I collect Nance's and Jake's too.

'Come here.' Dec snaps his fingers. 'Forget something?' He takes a cold chip from my plate and flicks it at my head. 'Finish your chips.'

Acquired. Beer is an *acquired* taste.

'I don't want any *fucking chips*!' I drop the plates. They don't smash—they bounce.

Jake and Otis freeze.

Nance says, 'It's okay. It's okay.' Her eyes are like glass.

Dec tells her to shut up. He cocks his head and smiles before he tips the last of his beer down his throat. He stands, grabs his wallet and keys from the table, and tells Nance he's going to the pub.

On his way out, he slips me a wink.

When he's gone, I run to the bedroom and slam the door. A minute later Nance knocks gently, but I ignore her until she gives up.

I put on my shoes and leave through the window so I don't have to see Nance cleaning up the mess I made.

Nance thinks Dec is getting worse, but he's always been like this. She thinks it's the beer and the gambling, but I know it comes from way back—maybe it was his dad, or his dad's dad, or his dad's dad's dad. Maybe it was his mum. And the reason I know is because it's in me too, and someone like Nance will always make excuses for me if I let her.

Gunshots are still coming from the TV when I'm outside on the street. It's getting harder to tell what's real. I keep walking until I can't hear them anymore.

I'm not sure what the wink meant—it could mean Dec was sorry, but it felt more like a welcome to the club. He knows he's winning. There comes a point in a script when you're too familiar with the characters and you know all their lines, and all you can see is how fucked up everyone is.

That goes for life, too.

THIRTEEN

I need new exercise books, so I go to administration at lunch. There's a full house for detention seated on the row of chairs outside the Acting Principal's office. Year Nines. All staring at the box on the shelf containing their phones.

'I need two ninety-six lined and one graph, please.'

Mrs Gough, the admin lady, looks uncomfortable. 'You can't put that on account today, Nate.'

'Why not? I always do.'

'The account's been closed. I'm sorry.' She turns away to straighten a perfectly straight stack of paper.

'Didn't we pay?' This has never happened before. 'I'll try to fix it up next week.'

'It's not that. Off you go. Have your lunch.'

'But I don't get it.'

She comes back and leans close to my ear. 'I'm not supposed to say. The account you used—it was a school account. It was just for some of you. The teachers used to chip in every week to pay it off, but the Acting Principal has shut the account down. I'm sorry.'

'Oh.'

She sighs and reaches under the counter. 'Look, just take

them. I'll do some creative stocktaking at the end of the month.' She hands me the books.

Mortified doesn't begin to cover it. I'm trying to control the early symptoms of spontaneous combustion. It's polite to advise people if they've been granted honorary membership to the Charity Club, so their humiliation doesn't play out in front of the entire lunchtime detention crowd.

'Don't worry about it.' I push the books harder than I mean to. They skid off the counter and onto the floor.

Mrs Gough tilts her head. She's disappointed in me. She can have honorary membership to *that* club.

'Can you wait for one moment, please?' She leaves the admin area and strides to the end of the hallway to knock on the school counsellor's door.

Oh, fuck no. Counselling? I brace myself on the counter and pretend to bash my head on it.

'Nate? Can you come in?' She's holding the door open. 'Miss DeVries would like a word. It won't take a minute.'

It takes longer.

Miss DeVries looks like an ugly beautician. She does all the things—hair, make-up, nails—but the overall effect isn't a fine endorsement for the beauty industry.

She tells me to have a seat, proceeds to click madly with her mouse, prints a bunch of pages that she shuffles into some kind of order, and reads through them. Twice. When she finally speaks, it's not about me.

'Connor Merrick,' she drones. 'It says here that you live at the same address.'

'No. Same block of flats, that's all.'

'Oh.' She picks up another piece of paper. 'My mistake.'

She circles something. 'Do you know the flat number?'

'No,' I lie.

Up goes a wonky eyebrow. 'Phone number?'

'No idea.'

'Really? Because I'm having trouble contacting his parents, and I thought you might have some idea why he hasn't been at school.'

'I don't know. He just stopped coming.' It's not unusual—the drop-out rate almost doubles here in Year Eleven. 'He can leave, right?'

I suppose they need a form filled out or something. Dec's proud of the fact he set a maintenance shed on fire the day he left school. I'm only here because the thought of being at home for six more hours a day does my head in.

'Well, yes, but he was doing so well.'

I try to get a glimpse of the piece of paper she's waving around now, but she whisks it away. Merrick? Doing well?

'Like, *passing*?'

'*Excelling.*'

Excel. Excellence. Merrick? She must have mixed up her pieces of paper.

'Could you ask him to come and see me?' she says. 'Tell him if he comes back soon he'll catch up in no time.'

'I'll tell him if I see him.'

'Thank you.' She looks at the clock on the wall. 'And how about you? How are you going?'

It sounds like an afterthought because it probably is one. 'Fine.'

Without looking up, she puts a diagonal slash through an entire paragraph of Merrick's notes and slips the page into a tray marked 'Outbox'.

Did she just make him disappear?

'Okay, then,' she says brightly. 'You can go back to lunch.'

I'm present and invisible.

Merrick is absent and excellent.

Don't try too hard. Make fun of people who do.

Fuck.

On my way home from school, two undercover cop cars shoot past me on Dorrington Street. They don't have their lights on, but you can always tell—Commodores, plain rims, a CB aerial and two blokes in the front who check you out without turning their heads.

When I get home the same cars are parked under the visitors' carport, and I remember I never turned up to sign that statement.

Shit.

I sneak around past the bins. Nance and the boys are on the verandah, O lying on a grubby cot blanket, Jake playing with his cars in the dirt, staging crashes and making siren sounds under his breath.

'It's not us,' Nance says. 'It's Barry in the middle.'

'What's happening?'

'I'm not sure yet,' she says. She grabs Otis by the leg to stop him rolling off the step.

The cops are definitely in unit twelve. Barry Pierce's place. Merrick and I used to nick food from his Woolworths home deliveries—he'd leave the stuff sitting outside for so long, it seemed like a waste. He's quiet and keeps to himself, but I suppose that description has appeared on every mass murderer's psychiatric evaluation.

'What do you reckon?' she asks. 'Drugs? Credit card fraud?'

'Child exploitation material, for sure.'

Nance pulls O closer.

'Where's Dec?'

She jerks her head. 'Inside. You'll have to stay here. We're locked out. He's paranoid.'

That doesn't sound like Nance; she always defends Dec. But she's right about Dec being paranoid. He's worse when the buds are ready and he smokes too much. He thinks everyone's out to get him.

'But why do you have to stay out—'

'Because he thinks they'll think we're just an ordinary happy family.' She picks up O and holds him in her lap. 'Wave to the nice policeman. Hello, Mr Policeman.' She grabs O's hand and flops it around.

'Are you okay?'

'I wonder what would happen if I told them about what's in your old bedroom?'

It's warm in the sun, but I have goosebumps all along my arms. I've been conditioned to believe the cops are the enemy since I could walk.

'Prior record. Two years, minimum. Dec won't make it inside—he's too pretty.'

Nance cracks a smile. 'He is pretty. But he'd better let us in soon—I'm getting sunburnt.' Her smile disappears. 'What prior record?'

'Assault,' I say. Dec will kill me for telling her. 'It's okay, it was just a brawl with some mates. It was way before you. Stuff this. I'm going in.' I knock lightly on the front door.

Nance hisses, 'Wait—they're coming out.'

One officer makes his way down the steps carrying an ancient computer.

'Child exploitation,' Nance and I say at the same time.

I know she's thinking about the times Jake runs around outside without any clothes on.

'I hate this place.' As she says it, the sun slips behind a cloud.

I laugh because the cloud has perfect timing, but Nance's expression only gets darker.

I grew up here. I don't know any different. I hate it too, but some part of me has always believed I'd turn eighteen and that would be it: I'd be free to go to a better place. It would be as simple as closing a door and stepping through another— everything would be cleaner, brighter, more predictable and more controllable. I never realised an expectation so ordinary might be out of reach.

Or that you could go to a worse place, like Nance did.

The cops take more things. Barry doesn't make an appearance. Whatever they've pinched him for, it can't be too bad.

When the cops drive away, Nance bashes on the window and Dec unlocks the door.

Nance opens it and shoves him hard with both hands. 'Don't ever do that again.' She pushes past him. 'I need a shower.'

Dec clutches his chest in mock horror. 'I love it when she's angry.'

He still looks like an ex-MMA cage fighter when he's not wearing a shirt, but the layer of fat around his middle is growing. Too many beers and parmigianas with chips, hold the salad.

Jake marches in and swings a limp punch at Dec's thigh. 'I'm angry, Dad,' he says, and Dec pretends it's a knockout and falls to the floor.

The scene would be heartwarming if it wasn't so screwed up.

Dec opens one eye. 'All right, Nate?'

'Yeah.'

I go to put my bag in the bedroom. Nance brushes past me on her way to get a towel from the hall cupboard. I feel like giving her a high-five for balls but I know that'll tip the balance—her small victory was only because Dec let her win.

Ten minutes pass before we remember we left O on the verandah. Luckily he never gets far.

Merrick has new kicks—a pair of Yeezy Boost 350 V2 in semi-frozen yellow. I know because I've just seen him take them out of his backpack and put them on outside our place. Then he tied the laces on his old ones together, raised them to the sky, one in each hand (giving thanks to the God of sneakers?), wound up and let go. Hooked them over the power lines.

People think a pair of shoes hanging from the power lines indicates a drug house. It's an urban legend—more likely it's just that a kid got new shoes and wants to commemorate the occasion—but people still believe it.

This is a major breach of protocol.

It's nearly ten o'clock. Dec went out earlier and he still isn't home. Nance and the boys are sleeping.

I pull on a black hoodie and climb out the window, into the shadows. I'm starting to think shooting out the sensor light was not one of our greatest ideas.

The Yeezys looked legit. If they are, it means Merrick has crossed off number two on his current wish list (last time I checked, the Evo was still at number one). If he's confident enough to wear three-hundred-dollar shoes without worrying someone will boost them—and suddenly successful at wish fulfilment—it means he's up to something.

It's not hard to catch up. First, I don't have Jake hanging off me, and second, those shoes are positively radioactive. I pull my hoodie over my face and keep out of sight by walking on the opposite footpath.

Merrick's heading towards Rowley Park. It's been two weeks since he's come to school, and this is only the second time I've seen him. Either he's avoiding me and the places we usually hang out, or he's turned nocturnal.

We're at the main road. He stops briefly to check his phone before darting between two cars, jogging along the median strip, and crossing the lanes on the other side. He looks back once, but I wait behind a huge commercial For Sale sign until I know which direction he's going to take.

When he darts down a side street, I cross the main road and jog to catch up. Half the street lights aren't working and the road is riddled with potholes. He must be heading for the warehouses on Smith—there's nothing else out here— unless he's cutting through to the estate on the other side.

Just when I think I've lost him, I spot movement behind a section of temporary fencing near the end of the road. Merrick checks both ways and enters a narrow, cobbled driveway between two warehouses.

I tiptoe around broken glass and turn the corner.

Merrick is facing me, in the middle of the driveway, legs

apart, thumbs hooked in his front pockets, like he's ready to draw pistols.

'Nice Yeezys,' I say. 'Do they make those for men?'

'Stop following me.'

'That's my line.'

'Seriously, Nate. Fuck off.' He hoists himself onto the top of an industrial waste bin. 'I'm not going any further until you do.'

'And I'm okay with that.' I lean against the bin. 'You could have chucked your shoes somewhere else. I mean, come on—anywhere but our place.'

He shrugs and checks his phone again. 'I gotta go.'

'Did you know Youth might be closing?'

'That sucks. We had some good times there.'

'Yeah. We did.' I point to my chin. 'Look, give me one for free and we're even.'

'Not even close.'

'I just snapped, okay? Come on. We're mates.'

'We *were*. You treat me like I'm your annoying little brother.'

'You *are* annoying.' I climb up next to him. The bin stinks like cabbages and dead rodents. 'Barry Pierce got raided today.'

Silence.

'Is it true? You're rolling with Tuwy and Fallon? Tuwy stopped coming to school the same time as you.'

Nothing, but his mouth twitches.

'DeVries wants to see you.'

He picks a grass seed from his shoelaces.

'Why did you make out you were barely passing at school?'

He snorts. 'Why do you reckon?'

'Since when do you ever listen to anything I say?'

'All. The. Time.' He jumps off the bin. 'But that's all you

do. Talk. So I got a few A pluses in a row. So what? What good are they? They don't make my old man talk to me any nicer. They don't put money in my pocket. They sure as hell don't impress you.'

'I *am* impressed.'

'No way. You say that now, but you're full of shit. You know what the best part of my day is? It's when I crawl out my window and remember I don't have to knock on yours out of loyalty anymore. You did me a favour, man—I'm flying solo. You'll be fifty years old, still ranting and raving and telling everyone what's wrong with the world, but doing nothing to fix your shit.'

I laugh. 'You're freestyling now? You totally just flipped the Chuckie scene.'

He shakes his head. 'Whatever. I'm offski.' He digs around in his pockets for a cigarette.

'Where are you going? To fix your shit?'

He turns. Slowly, he reaches behind his back—I think he's about to pull out his slingshot and use my face for a target, but he's twisting something around to the front. A tool belt.

I crack up. 'You're *seriously* fixing shit? I didn't think you meant it *literally*.'

His ears are bright red. 'It's my shift. I'm going to work.'

'Here?'

He gives a vague wave in the direction he's headed. 'Look, I'll see ya. I'm gonna be late.'

'What about the shoes?'

'Work it out. You know everything.'

'What about school?'

'You go.' He gives me a wave. 'But don't bother trying too hard. You were right about that.'

FOURTEEN

Many species have evolved to form social groups and hierarchies. This structure affords group protection against predators and allows animals to pool resources, share territory and divide labour, such as finding food and raising young. Some species live alone, guarding a territory and only coming together to reproduce. Predators often make successful solitary animals—they're able to claim a food source as their own and defend their territory. Prey animals, however, increase their chances of survival by clustering together and keeping their predators on the fringes, often sacrificing the weaker animals for the good of the group.

See, this is where the evolution of *Homo sapiens* is messed up. Our predators are the *same species*. They look the same, exhibit similar social behaviours, move through our clusterfuck of a social group undetected and, as long as their big reveal doesn't involve being strapped to a backpack full of nails, they're guaranteed promotion within its ranks. *Leader!*

Left to itself, I reckon evolution would have sorted this problem out. Then again, I may already have been picked off. Merrick, too, except it's possible he's now masquerading as a predator.

I guess that makes me a solitary prey animal, in which case I'm dead.

Nance has asked me to watch Jake and Otis while she's outside taking the washing off the line. She said she smelled rain. She set them up on the kitchen floor with a packet of bow tie pasta, a saucepan each and two spoons.

O is lying on his stomach, passing his spoon from fist to fist, staring at it like it isn't the same implement he just saw at breakfast. Jake has already filled his saucepan and now he's topping it up with O's pasta.

This Biology assignment is due in two days. I have the information in my head, but making sense of it all on paper is near impossible when I'm trying to pretend O hasn't just loaded his pants. If I had a laptop I could copy, paste and camouflage the syntax by adding unnecessary conjunctions and adjectives, like everyone else does.

I don't mind Biology. Facts are facts—hardly any original thought required—and we all present the same information, more or less. We're only being tested on our ability to parrot information, and I could do that in the middle of a tornado with cows flying past. Writing or typing in peace is my problem. If I can just prepare these notes, I'll type them up on a laptop at Youth later and scrounge some coin for printing from Nance's jar on the windowsill.

Nance's head pops through the back door. 'All right, bub?'

I give her the thumbs-up.

What I really want to do is tell her no, it's not all right, and this is why I plan never to have sex with anyone other than myself.

'I might dash to the shops and grab some milk and bread. Pass me the jar?'

Thanks, universe.

Jake helps himself to something from the fridge. I have

some sentences ready, so I don't bother to tell him off. O is still quiet; I'm good to go.

Some species are known to invest heavily in trying to give their young the best chance of survival.

The Sumatran orangutan carries her baby on her back for several years, and infants aren't fully weaned until around eight years of age. After weaning, young orangutans remain part of the social group, often visiting their mothers, who continue their education even when there's a new sibling on board.

Meerkats are considered one of the true teachers of the animal kingdom. Meerkat parents have been documented killing scorpions before showing their infants how to feed. As the infants progress they're given live scorpions, but mortally wounded and with the stingers removed. Finally, when they've passed their apprenticeship, the young meerkats are ready to kill and eat their dangerous prey without falling victim to the scorpion's lethal sting...

'No, O!'

Otis has rolled as far as the hallway, and now he's trying to eat pasta off the dirty carpet.

'You'll choke and die.'

I hook some pieces from his mouth with my finger and roll him back.

'Don't let him get that far,' I tell Jake, who's still sitting on the floor, chewing whatever he found in the fridge.

Typically, animal mothers are the primary caregivers, however there are several examples of exemplary fathers. The male emperor penguin is the sole incubator of the egg, withstanding a harsh Antarctic winter and shedding up to half his body weight to protect the chick and ensure his progeny lives long enough to leave the nest. (The female penguin takes off on a leisurely cruise, returning to regurgitate food for the chick only when the male is weak from fasting and exposure.)

Animal parents who raise a single infant have lower mortality rates, and their progeny are proven to be longer-lived and more successful in continuing the lineage. But there's more than one way to pass on genes successfully. Some species don't educate or care for their offspring at all—they simply procreate in large numbers, leaving the strongest to survive and the weakest to die.

I look up just in time to see Jake scoop a spoonful of pasta and shove it in O's mouth.

'Hey! You little—'

I flip O over and smack him between his shoulderblades to make him spit it out. Then I whack the back of Jake's legs with one of the spoons and yell at him to go to his room. I pick up O and try to calm him down by whizzing him in circles. I'll keep going until he shuts up, or one of us throws up.

He's finally quiet. I stop spinning. O's eyes are flickering from side to side as if he's watching a tennis match. I worry I've shaken more loose.

Jake peers around the kitchen door.

'Get back in your room!'

O's eyes fix on mine and slide past. He recommences screaming.

The last specialist told Nance that the reason Otis screams all the time is because his mind wants to go places his body can't take him, so we should work on his fine motor skills. I'm not so sure. I think the sooner we teach him to speak, the sooner he can tell us what he needs himself. But the problem is the words we give him are names for things he already has. We need to give him the words for the things he wants—except what he wants is one of life's great mysteries.

147

I sit down and bounce him on my knee, holding his stiff body with one hand, trying to write with the other, yelling the words as I write them down so I can hear my thoughts above the noise.

Cannibalism and infanticide are common among many species. Perhaps less well known is the practice of fratricide—animals who kill their siblings to ensure their own survival. Most predatory animals, such as cats and dogs, are born without teeth; no matter how strong the instinct for survival, the infant cannot establish dominance until its teeth have developed. However, some baby animals seek to eliminate competition from birth: hatchling birds will eject siblings from the nest, a baby mantis's first meal is often a sibling, and the embryos of the grey nurse shark begin killing other embryos and unfertilised eggs until there is only one survivor left in the womb.

I think of Jake's bump and O's dent. Maybe they weren't joined at all and it was an epic battle for supremacy.

I seem to have strayed off-topic.

When Nance gets back the boys are playing happily again, but that's because Jake knows I'm watching. I tell her I'm going to Youth and ask if she has any spare change for printing.

She disappears into the bathroom and comes back holding a ten-dollar note. 'You can have this.'

I know it probably came from her secret stash for medical emergencies. If there's one thing we never go without in this house, it's pain relief.

'No, it's okay. They might let me pay later.'

'Bub, take it.'

I do, but I feel guilty. It gets worse when Nance has a close look at the spoon-shaped mark on Jake's leg and makes no comment.

'I'll pay you back.'

'You don't have to.'

'But I will.'

'It's *our* money,' she says, pointing at me, then herself. 'Us.'

Like Nance predicted, it's starting to rain. First rain + hot tar + dry grass = the memory of running through the neighbour's sprinkler, and lining up for Jerry's Ice Cream van with fifty other kids, a few dollars in my pocket, trying to decide between sprinkles or Flake. Good times.

Or were they? Here's what really happened.

The neighbour's kids didn't want to play with me because I kept turning the sprinkler off. I was worried it was wasting water. I had enough money for a plain cone, not sprinkles, Flakes weren't even a thing, and the ice cream had a gritty texture as if it had been melted and re-frozen a hundred times.

Nance thinks I write things down because I want them to be different. It's not only that—I write them down because I want to remember exactly how it feels to be me, right now. Otherwise my brain plays tricks—it changes things, normalises things that aren't normal. I don't have the data, but I'm willing to bet nostalgia is the brain's way of protecting itself, making sure you only remember the good stuff. By the time we're eighty, our entire memory bank is probably some kind of utopian alternate reality. That's why old people only tell you stories about the good old days.

Not me. I'll remember everything.

I stop at the main road to wait for traffic.

I cross roads all the time and I've never been hit. Crossing a road safely is probably survival instinct, but I had to learn how, the same way a meerkat has to learn not to mess around with a live scorpion. And I'm trying to remember who taught me: Mum, Dec or neither. I decide it was more likely a few near misses and a school excursion to the Road Safety Centre in Grade Two.

Look right, left, right again. I cross.

Something about Youth is different. It's pretty obvious when I finally figure it out: the graffiti mural on the wall has been painted over.

I step off the kerb without looking, and a car swerves and beeps. I jump back.

White noise in my head. The mural looks messy, blurred at the edges, as if it's been painted in the dark, in a hurry.

There are words on it. The words belong to me.

When they've burned all our houses
the streets will inherit.

They're my words—I wrote them in my notebook and now they're on the wall. And the odds of a person from the same suburb, who goes to the same youth centre, coming up with the exact same combination of words have to be statistically improbable.

Tash. The thief.

I lunge for a gap between a trailer and a truck and somehow make it to the other side.

I hope she gets arrested. I have no idea where Tash lives, but if she isn't here at the centre now, I'll find out. I'm trying to think of a time when she could have stolen my notebook, or at least copied the lines. Maybe she has a photographic memory. Maybe she took a photo. But—if Tash has a page from my notebook, she could implicate me.

150

I'm staring at the wall, trying to decide whether to salute it or spit on it, when a news van pulls up in one of the wheelchair parks. A woman wearing a tight grey suit gets out first, followed by a bearded guy carrying a camera the size of a suitcase.

I duck my head and slouch off towards the entrance.

The woman spots me and rushes over. 'Excuse me?' She fumbles in her pockets. 'Are you a member of the centre?' She flashes an ID card.

I nod. 'Yeah, but—'

'We're almost ready. Could you answer a few questions about the vandalism?'

'Sorry. I don't know anything about it.'

The guy hoists his camera onto his shoulder and aims it me.

'Look, I don't—'

'Just a quick sound bite? We'll blur your face.'

I put up my hand, say, 'No comment,' and run off like a guilty kid.

Inside, Povey is dozing on one of the couches. Tash isn't here.

I nudge him awake. 'Hey. What happened to the wall?' He blinks and tries to focus. 'Are you all right?'

He groans and closes his eyes again. 'Headache. Been nanging, hey.'

I find Macy in the storeroom putting labels on filing boxes.

'There's a Channel Nine news crew outside. They tried to interview me.'

She sighs. 'I thought this might happen.'

'You've seen the wall?'

'The Hubble Space Telescope has seen the bloody wall.'

'Do you know who did it?'

'Well, if I knew, you would have noticed them strung up and disembowelled on your way in,' she says, but she doesn't seem that upset. 'They used to do that, you know, to deter crime and dickheadedness.'

'When did it happen?'

'Sometime last night.'

Macy goes to the bathroom and comes back a minute later with her hair semi-brushed and her name tag pinned to her T-shirt. She grabs my hand and drags me behind her to the rec room.

'Stay here.' She nods at Povey. 'Make sure he does, too. The last thing we need is Mr Whip-It representing the clientele.'

Povey's already asleep again. He doesn't look well.

Dec says I shouldn't touch anything but booze and home-grown. Nitrous is bad. Pingers are bad. Psychs are bad. He told me if he ever catches me doing anything that God didn't put on this earth, he'll kill me himself. I raised my doubts about God and alcohol with him, but he said booze is just barley, wheat and potatoes. Whatever. Seems to me Dec and Povey head for the same planet, only on different spaceships.

Macy is back, sweating, flustered, looking like she didn't just brush her hair five minutes ago.

'What did you say to them?'

'Nothing that did you, me or the centre any favours.' She looks pretty pleased with herself.

FIFTEEN

We're all glued to the Channel Nine news. Every available chair, beanbag, box, table—even a stack of Mim's magazines—has been dragged in front of the TV. I count around twenty kids, not including Macy, Mim and Thomas.

No Tash. Guilty by dissociation.

'Shut up! Everybody sit down and shut up!' Macy leans so far forward her chin is almost on her knees.

The reporter I ran into a couple of hours ago is on the TV, standing near the end of the wall outside Youth.

'Rumours of the closure of YouthWorks, a popular youth centre in Rowley Park, have prompted teens to protest by vandalising a local landmark.'

A photo of the original mural is displayed on the screen.

'Sometime last night this mural, designed by a well-known artist, was defaced.'

Then it switches to a shot of the wall as it is now.

'Locals are at a loss to explain how this could have happened near a busy main road without any witnesses. We asked youth worker Macy Blair to comment on the vandalism.'

Macy appears. With her shaved head and tatts, she looks like a member, not the director.

'*This is their centre. If they want to use it to protest something that directly affects them, then I call that a good use of space.*'

'*Do you know who's responsible?*'

'*No, I don't.*'

We all cheer and clap.

The camera shows Macy heading back inside the centre. As she closes the door on the camera-person, she sticks out her pierced tongue.

'God, they made me look like I did it,' Macy says, holding her head in her hands.

'*Agnes Butcher, a Rowley Park resident for over forty years, disagrees.*'

We groan. Agnes lives across the road and every week she lodges a complaint about noise. It's probably her who throws stones at the court lights. She's clutching her hand-bag in front of her. Her voice is low and quivery, nothing like the razor-blades-on-glass pitch she saves for us when we're scrimmaging.

'*It's disgusting. They've fouled their own nest. My taxes pay for this and all those entitled brats do is destroy it. If they don't paint over it soon, I'll do it myself.*'

'Fuck, Agnes, we're not gonna steal your pension,' I say.

'Two sides, remember?' Macy cautions. 'She's old and alone and probably scared.'

'*The local member of parliament, Robert Down, has responded by saying: "Peaceful protest is a basic right of democracy, but destructive, violent behaviour only damages their cause. I suggest these young persons find a way to get their message across without upsetting the people who hold this decision in their hands. It could be argued these methods invite condemnation, rather than support."*'

'Robert Down,' someone says. 'Bob Down. Get it?'

'What violence?' Mim cuts in. 'I didn't see anyone throwing punches. They don't even mention why the centre is being closed—because an adult with no affiliation was violent, and there's no funding for security. It's one-sided reporting.'

'The council says the vandalism will be cleaned up in the coming days. The teens affected are noticeably silent on the matter.'

The camera pans to me as I put my hand up and walk away, muttering, 'No comment.' It doesn't show my face, but we all know it's me.

Cooper groans. 'Nice one, Nate. You had a chance to say something. Why didn't you?'

I don't have an answer.

The reporter signs off. An ad for furniture polish comes on.

'That's it?' I say.

'Looks like it. Well, I might as well go out with a bang.' Macy stands and turns off the TV. 'Maybe they care so little they won't even bother to replace me. I guess the cat's out of the bag, guys.'

'Can we put a line through that no-shouting rule now?' Mim says. 'I feel the need to scream.'

Macy doesn't just put a line through it—she tears the entire chart from the wall. 'Doesn't mean you can't respect each other,' she says, waving her finger. 'Common rules of decency still apply. Or *I'll* be the one throwing punches.'

'Tell us how long we've got.'

'Three months, give or take,' Macy says. 'Now, who did it?'

I say nothing—technically, I didn't.

'Someone knows something. Come on. I've got nothing on the cameras, but you all know where the cameras are, right?'

She's right. We do.

'Nobody knows anything?'

I shake my head along with everyone else.

'We could picket the wall. Stop them painting over it,' Cooper says. 'That might get some attention.'

'But if nobody ends up giving a shit, it'll just prove their theory about the lack of support for the centre,' I say.

'Just because you don't give a shit doesn't mean nobody else does.'

Who is the 'they' we're talking about anyway? The government? The entire system? Or is it one guy, sitting behind a desk, who put a tick in a box because he felt like it and sent it down the line? It feels like we're swinging at an enemy without a face. Even our mysterious activist isn't showing hers. What's the point?

'What does it mean—about the houses?'

It takes me a few seconds to realise Deng is talking about my words on the wall.

'It means if they don't want us on the streets, then they shouldn't shut our youth centre. Are they so stupid they didn't think of that?' Cooper says.

'It's powerful,' Mim says. 'But ambiguous. I think it's about displacement. It's the backfire effect. Instead of causing division they're creating an army. Anger unites people. That's what it means when it says the streets will inherit.'

'Only if people can be bothered doing something,' I say.

She rolls her eyes. 'Anyway, it doesn't tell us what it means. It just makes us think.'

My words were taken and used out of context, but I'm never sure what they mean when I write them anyway. They always seem foreign to me. Macy will suspect I'm involved if I speak up. Even if I could explain, I can't.

Now I know how a dead poet would feel if a dead poet could feel.

'Do you know anything about all this, Nate?' Macy asks.

I shake my head. I want to give Tash a chance to explain. If I drop her name now, she could drag me into it, and then she might never return my pages.

Mim gives me a sharp look. 'It wasn't Nate.'

It pisses me off that she can dismiss me so easily. 'How would you know?' I say.

'I just know.'

Thomas, who hardly ever speaks except to bark orders, clears his throat. 'I agree with the message, if not the method. "If you are neutral in situations of injustice, you have chosen the side of the oppressor." Desmond TuTu.'

Macy nods. 'Okay, listen up. I don't want anyone going all vigilante and causing trouble. Off the record, I think we should decide if it's worth organising a petition. Remember, we need the local residents onside, so nobody is allowed to upset Agnes.' She shoos kids from chairs and starts cleaning up.

I go outside. I need a picture of the wall before Agnes gets slap-happy with a paint brush and my fifteen minutes' of anonymous fame are over.

I stand back and snap a pic, then move closer. From a distance, it looks as if the mural has been painted. Now I see it's a large poster, like the gig flyers on empty shop windows. It's made from separate sheets of A4 paper, pasted with glue and spray-painted around the edges to blend with the background of the original mural. That explains why it's slightly blurred, and how Tash could have done it so quickly without anyone seeing. But it's only temporary. Any more rain and the whole thing will disintegrate.

I could claim some responsibility and take the credit, or the blame. I could deny everything and let Tash take the fall. Or I can stay quiet and see how things play out.

So many emotions. So many *options*. I don't know what to do with that.

I have my notebooks spread out on my bunk. I started filling notebooks because it was the only way to quieten my mind—there were too many things I couldn't say out loud. Still can't. Eleven, total, written over a period of about seven years. I thought there were more. It's not much for a life's work.

The first notebook is still blank apart from a single sentence:

If I could go back in time I would shoot the goat.

After that I started collecting random thoughts and questions, like:

Can you feel a cloud?

Who invented Pokémon?

Where do flies go to sleep?

A few pages later I seem to have solved these mysteries, which proves what I already know: I have always been good at research. I like facts. Facts resolve questions, and a question with an answer is a worry that has lost its power.

I wrote down scientific discoveries:

- *the deadliest flu virus in the world was created in a university lab*
- *microbes are evolving faster than we can develop methods to fight them*

• *we are probably in the middle of a mass extinction event right now* and floated conspiracy theories:

McDonald's/government-owned/Happy Meal toys are bugged and burgers contain mind-control drugs

Later, I seemed to be preoccupied with documenting conversations between me and Dec:

How to Foil a Home Invasion (keep a machete under the bed)

Why Marijuana Should Be Legalised (stoned people are chill)

And lately I've regressed to making cryptic statements:

• *religion is the root of evil*
• *slam poets are the new evangelists*
• *no one left without an agenda to tell the truth*

Reading through, the first thing I notice is how often I change my mind. And the common thread between the early notebooks and the last one, the one I can't seem to finish, is that I only seem to write about my worries, never the things that make me feel happy, or proud, or valued, like:

Nance

Otis

Jake (ish)

Merrick

There are so many worries left unresolved. And so I conclude:

I'm a pessimist

I have a conflicting set of beliefs

I don't stand for anything

One person can't possibly make a difference

It's safer to keep yelling down the well

One thing is sure: I've been through my latest notebook twice and the page with the sentence from the wall is definitely missing, and that worries me because I can't remember what else is on that page. I don't usually re-read what I write. It serves a purpose at the time but it's like exhaling vapour. Was there anything personal? Did I mention names?

It's possible Tash has no intention of using any more words from the missing page. I don't know her well enough to guess. I do know it's bad manners to drag someone you hardly know into a pointless war.

SIXTEEN

Owen Kleinig. That's his name—the kid who got his face smushed by Pug and Rat.

He has a stainless-steel stackable lunchbox with about eight compartments. It's filled with food cut into heart shapes and smiley faces, and his name is written on the lid in huge letters. The compartments are arranged in a semi-circle on the table in front of him and, if I'm not mistaken, he's sorting the foods into complementary colours: strawberries with cucumber, carrots with blueberries, cabbage with corn.

I've never seen this many pieces of fruit and vegetables in a lunchbox before. Come to think of it, this is my first sighting of purple cabbage.

Owen Kleinig is the sole occupant of the senior study room in the school library. I'm sitting at the end of the magazine aisle, watching him through the glass. We're not allowed to eat in here, but Miss Sheridan has walked past twice and she hasn't said anything. Year Eights aren't supposed to be in the senior study room, either.

I'm trying to decide whether I should mention what happened the other day—apologise to him, or at least acknowledge his existence—when he suddenly tips the contents of each compartment into the lid. With a look of furious concentration, he uses his fork to make a pulp, and scrapes the mess into a sandwich bag. Once he has carefully sealed the bag, he stands, slips it into the pocket of his shorts and re-stacks the lunchbox.

Miss Sheridan makes another pass. She stops and says, 'If you're finished now, Owen, you can make your way outside.'

He nods, but when she's gone he lets out a sigh. He wipes the table, pushes the chair underneath, picks up a stray piece of carrot from the floor, and drops it in the bin. He turns off the light and closes the door behind him. When he passes he throws me a backwards glance. It makes me think he knew I was there the whole time, but his expression is blank. There's something about his entire methodical process, broken by an act of violence against fruit and vegetables, that makes me add Owen Kleinig to the top of my worry list. This is a kid who looks like he's ready to break, and not in a shoot-up-the-school kind of way—more like he's about to walk into a river with pockets full of mashed vegies. And I feel like it's partly my fault.

I stuff my phone in my bag and get up to follow. My bag catches on the rack, bringing down a whole folder of *Science Illustrated*.

'Shit.'

I stuff them back in the folder as quickly as I can, but Miss Sheridan has eyes in the back of her head and ears like a Fennec fox.

'I know you're going to put those back in date order, Nathaniel. Am I right?'

I nod and sigh and get to work.

By the time I've sorted and replaced the folder, Owen is long gone.

I spend another ten minutes checking the benches by the hardcourts, behind the A-frame shed (out of bounds), and in the alcove under the middle-school stairs. Being a senior has granted me some invisibility, if not invincibility or an all ac cess pass, and usually I'd be able to guess where someone like Owen Kleinig would go to be left alone. They're all places Merrick and I used to hide too.

It's not until five minutes before the bell that I see him step from behind the partition concealing the walkway between the music block and the library. I walked past the opening at least twice. He must have been there all along. There's noise and movement all around, but Owen Kleinig is unnaturally still, as if he's waiting for something to happen.

I stop in front of him. 'Are you all right?'

'Go away,' he says.

His voice is deeper than I expected. He stares past me and makes a half turn.

'Look, I didn't—'

His eyes flicker my way. 'I'm all good.'

'Okay. Whatever.'

Jesus. The kid is as stubborn as Merrick, and with the same masochistic tendencies. I wander back to the bench near the library entrance. He's still standing there looking at his feet when I see his nemeses approaching.

Rat grabs him by the arm. Pug points to the walkway, and Owen goes along with it.

I get the feeling he has done this before.

I back up to the partition and lean against it, so I can see through the slats. Owen puts his bag down. He stands facing the wall, hands behind his head, legs apart, as if he's about to be frisked. It's so B-grade. They're stealing his money.

I check if there's a duty teacher within range, but they're probably all on their way back to class.

'Hurry up. Bell's about to go,' Rat says.

Owen just shrugs, his hands still interlocked on top of his head. Pug gives him a shove, then plunges a hand into the left pocket of Owen's pants. He comes up empty and jabs the back of Owen's neck with his elbow. Then he goes for the right pocket—and I know what's coming.

Pug pulls his hand back like he's been bitten.

'What?' Rat says.

And while the sneer is still on Rat's face, Owen turns, reaches into his pocket, grabs a handful of pulp and rubs it in his face.

Rat staggers back, spitting chunks of mashed fruit, and Pug leans down to help him up.

The bell goes. Owen grabs his bag and takes off, darting between students and disappearing faster than the other two can gather their wits.

His timing is magnificent.

One small act of defiance that will probably cost him for the rest of his school days.

When I get home from school Nance and the boys aren't there. Dec's out in the yard and the back door is wide open. I can hear the whine of a whipper-snipper and the flat reeks of petrol.

This has only ever happened once before. Dec's so paranoid about getting busted, our flat looks like nobody lives here most of the time. It can only mean the Housing Trust is forcing an inspection. This is a catastrophe.

Our backyard measures about nine by six metres. It's the biggest one in the block—just enough room for a washing line, a metre-wide strip of broken concrete, and a patch of weeds. The flat backs onto the alley. Our rear fence has been buckled by a thousand kickings, so Dec made it higher by screwing extra panels around the top. There's still no privacy because Margie upstairs can see straight into the yard from her kitchen and bedroom windows, but Nance won't let the boys play in the yard anyway. The weeds haven't been cut for as long as I can remember, and there's a deadly carpet of three-corner jacks underneath. Nance thinks she once saw a brown snake.

I drop my bag on the kitchen table and go outside.

Dec's hacking the weeds. He's only wearing jocks and his shoulders are sunburnt, his massive muscles slick with sweat and dirt. The eagle wings tattooed across his lats seem to flap when he flexes.

He cuts the motor. 'Don't you ever check your fucken phone?'

I pull it out of my pocket. I've missed three calls and two texts. 'I was at school. It was on silent.' And nobody ever calls me, least of all my old man. 'What's up?'

'We're fixing up the yard. Nance won't be back for another few hours.' He points to two large rolls of what looks like carpet near the door. 'Get your skates on.'

'Have we got an inspection?'

He winks. 'Nah. I just wanted to surprise my girl.'

Now this is an alternate reality: Dec, sober, industrious, planning a surprise.

'Where's she gone?'

'Appointment for O. In the city.'

I get changed into shorts and a tank and fill up a water bottle. It's not too hot outside, but the sun's brutal. I have a roll-on sunscreen in my bag that I got from school (which I now know was a charitable donation). When I twist off the cap I discover it's dried up, so I pull on a Cavs cap instead.

Dec's doing pull-ups on the washing line. He drops down and points to the piles of hacked weeds. 'Pick them up and chuck them over the fence.'

'You can't just dump it.'

'Hey, Greenpeace!' He taps his finger on his temple. 'It's organic—it'll break down.' He goes inside and returns with two open beers. 'Get that into you.'

I take one swig and stand the bottle in the shade. If he makes me drink it all now I'll probably spew. But he hasn't noticed—he's checking out my legs.

'We've gotta get you on the protein, mate. I weighed ninety at your age. Shit, I was benching a hundred.'

'I'm built for speed and grace,' I say.

'You're built like a fucken whippet. Like your old lady.'

'You say that like it's a bad thing.' I grab an armful of weeds and haul them to the fence. He watches as I try to launch them over the top, but the breeze brings them back down on my head. I sneeze. Now I'm itchy as hell.

'Has she called you?'

'No,' I lie.

Dec is lengthening the string on the whipper-snipper.

'What're those birds that lay eggs in other birds' nests, then fuck off and the other birds have to bring them up?'

'Cuckoos.'

'I knew you'd know,' he says.

Wait for it.

'What good does learning stuff like that do you? Nothin'.'

'It means we get to have this fascinating conversation.'

'You've got a mouth like hers, too.'

I scrape together another armful. This time I kick an old milk crate over to the fence, upend it with my foot, and stand on top so I can get some leverage. I do this five times until most of the cut weeds are gone, while Dec finishes his beer in silence.

He has no idea how to connect with me. None. I think of Owen Kleinig and his pathetic attempt to fight back today. That's kind of what I do, too—score enough points that I don't feel completely hopeless, but not enough to stop it happening. My mouth versus Dec's muscle—no contest. That blows Edward Bulwer-Lytton's theory. At least Owen Kleinig wasn't afraid to get physical.

Dec's still watching me.

'Are we gonna finish this?' I say.

He snaps to attention. 'Yeah.'

He revs the whipper-snipper and gets to work on the last section of weeds. I use a broken plastic rake to scrape them into a pile and ditch them over the fence.

On the final round, my foot goes through the rotten crate and Dec has to smash it with a hammer to get it off. My eyes are red and swollen and I have a gash on my shin. Dec looks like he's burned a couple of kilos off his gut already. We're both running with sweat.

'Right. Give me a hand with this.' He heaves one of the rolls near the door into the middle of the yard.

'What's that?'

'Fake turf.'

'Where'd you get it?'

'From The Man.'

The Man is a mythical figure, like the grandparents—we never see him, but occasionally he provides us with bountiful gifts. I think The Man is closely related to the truck that always has things falling off it.

I wrap my arms around the second roll of turf, but I can only drag it a few inches at a time before I have to stop and shake the deadness out of my biceps.

'Jesus Christ on a fucken bike,' Dec mutters. He pushes me aside, squats and jerks the roll of turf onto his shoulder.

I thought we'd have to do something about the uneven ground, but he just puts the turf down at one end of the yard, kicks it and rolls it out like a carpet, right on top of the stalks and divots and stones. We stomp it down. I guess it'll stop the weeds from coming back. I have to admit it looks pretty good, like a bumpy indoor cricket pitch.

Dec gets himself another beer. He stares pointedly at mine, gone warm where the sun has overtaken the shade.

I pick it up and take a sip. It's foul.

'Are you gonna throw another plate at me?' I wouldn't call it a smile, but he shows his teeth.

'I didn't throw them. I dropped them.'

'Right.' He shakes his head. 'You never did appreciate anything I gave you, did you?'

I find a cool spot on the steps and sit down to keep my legs from shaking. 'I do. I do appreciate everything.'

'Entitled little shit.'

'I'll be out of your hair in another couple of years.'

I wait for the explosion, but it doesn't come. Unpredictability is one of his many talents.

'See this?' Dec lifts his arm and points to the dagger-and-snake tattoo on his ribs. 'Look close.'

I've always wondered about it. But if it means sticking my face in his armpit, I'll pass.

'See the dagger?'

'Yes.'

'That used to be your mum's name. Angela. It was a bastard to cover up. And these—'he points to our names, one by one—'hurt like a bitch. Now, you're gonna grow up and leave home like we all do, but I'll tell you, if you're fixing to never come back for a beer with your old man after I've put food in your belly and kept a roof over your head your whole life, I'll come after you and put you out of your fucking misery myself. I'll erase you. You got that?'

I nod because there's nothing else to do.

'I did ten times better than my old man and don't you forget it. I *love* my kids.'

I nod again.

He grabs me in a headlock, putting just enough pressure on my windpipe to make my eyes water.

'Let go.' I pretend I'm laughing. I give him a limp slap on his chest.

'Come on, kid.' The pressure increases. 'You can do better than that.'

'Dec, let go,' I wheeze, and he does let go. Blood rushes in my ears. I reel away and bash my head on the metal handrail.

He gives the top of my head a rub and says, 'You're all right. Come on, I want to show you something.' He gets up and opens the screen door. 'Move your arse. Before Nance gets back.'

I follow him inside, still hyped and dizzy.

Dec's kneeling on the kitchen floor beside the cupboard under the sink. He jerks his head. 'Come here. Look at this.'

I kneel next to him. He pushes my head down and twists my neck. There's a bundle of something wrapped in newspaper and taped to the underside of the sink. I can only see it if I put my head and shoulders inside the cupboard.

'That's insurance,' he says. 'I'm showing you because you're blood, and I trust you. Blood is *everything*. If someone comes through that door and I'm not here—'he points—'this is the first thing you take. Okay?'

'But—'

'The first thing.'

'Okay.'

Before he closes the cupboard, he grabs my chin between his thumb and forefinger. Whatever he sees in my expression must reassure him. He gives me a light punch on the arm and winks.

It's a test. There's always a test.

SEVENTEEN

Double English, part two. Mr Reid allows snacks during double lessons, and I'm enjoying a half-decent coffee from the seniors' kitchen and the extraordinary sense of wellbeing that comes from finishing an assignment on time.

I won't be in his firing line today.

Mr Reid is walking around the classroom rattling a bag of dice. 'I hope you all remembered to bring your board games. For the second half of our exercise you'll be working in pairs. Find a partner, please.'

I thought we were just handing them in, not sharing them. It's one thing to spar with Mr Reid privately—it's another to do it in front of the whole class.

I feel instantly sick.

Everyone else has had their default pairings sorted since the beginning of the year. There's an odd number in the class, so I usually wait for Mr Reid to direct me to make up a three-some. That way I can avoid choosing, or acknowledging I have not been chosen.

'Three absent today,' Reid says. 'Hurry up, McKee.'

I look around. Three absentees means we're at even numbers. The rest of the class are already seated in pairs, which leaves me and Benjamin Peros, who has never spoken a word to me in his life.

He is, thankfully, awake.

I pick up my stuff and shift to Peros's desk at the back.

Peros has only two distinct body languages—slumped and asleep, or dazed and confused—but he seems about as thrilled to be working with me as I am about working with him. He has nothing on his desk apart from a water bottle and a pencil case.

'What are we supposed to be doing?' he says.

'He's going to make us play our board games.' I unroll my piece of paper and use his bottle and pencil case to hold it down. 'You don't even go here. I don't think it matters if you do the work or not.'

He frowns. 'Of course it matters.' He pulls a cylinder from under the desk and pops off the cap. His board game is laminated.

Mr Reid drops two dice on Peros's desk and continues. 'You'll play each other's game to see if it's winnable. At the end you'll use your extra Post-its to add notes if you believe there's an obstacle or pathway your partner has overlooked. Consider anything about your own circumstances—past, present and future—that you would change to improve your chances of success.'

What would I change? Shit, I don't even need three wishes. I'd change *me*. Circumstances are too complicated.

I still can't believe Peros laminated his work. 'But you're always *asleep*.'

He speaks slowly, as if I might not be very smart. 'I work afternoons. I'm tired. So what?'

'Where?'

'The wool plant.'

'I just don't get why you're even here.'

Peros rolls his eyes so hard I think he's having a seizure.

'And I don't get why we're playing with dice either.'

'So?' he says.

'So, if this is supposed to be a realistic goal, there should be no element of chance.'

He slaps his forehead. 'Look, let's get this over with. Do you want to play yours or mine first?'

'Yours.'

'Fine.'

He unrolls his board game and lays it on top of mine. He has printed labels, and he's coloured them to match the squares on the board. That's an A for presentation right there, but the most impressive thing is his goal: Benjamin Peros wants to work for Aerospace.

'Hey, that's cool,' I say. 'What do we use as a game piece?'

He sighs and pulls a twenty-cent piece from his pocket. 'Go.'

I roll the dice.

A six and a five. I skip past *pass Year Eleven, obtain school leaving certificate,* and *apply to the RAAF.* Then I roll a double six, and with the next roll I hit the longest ladder and shoot straight up to *complete degree in Engineering.* After that it's pretty much all over. I didn't land on a single snake.

'Congratulations! You're an aeronautical engineer.' I hold up my hand for a high five.

'You were just lucky,' he says, ignoring it.

'Precisely.' I write a Post-It and stick it to his game board.

'You forgot to *enrol in high school*. Other than that it's fail-proof.'

'I *am* enrolled. They haven't decided whether I need to go back and finish Year Ten, so for now I'm just turning up. I don't want to fall even further behind.'

'Why'd you drop out?'

'I was expelled.'

'For what?'

'Making a ninja star in Tech.'

I slap the table. 'I've always wanted to do that.'

'Yeah. I pushed for them to drop the expulsion—technically I smuggled a weapon *out*, not in, and at the time there was no rule against it.' He points to my creased game board. 'My turn to play.'

I know what's about to happen and I'm already embarrassed. For him and for me.

'That's your goal? A job?' he says.

'I was gonna put driver's licence but I need a job first.'

'What kind?'

'Any kind.'

Peros rolls the dice. Two fours. He moves eight spaces. 'Wait. Where are the ladders?'

'There aren't any.'

He rolls a two and a three, hits a snake and goes back to the beginning. 'I see where this is going.'

'Yeah. Like I said, I didn't know we were going to play for real.'

He says nothing—just keeps rolling the dice, moving the coin, and making *wheeeee* noises each time the game piece has to go back to the start. He makes no comment about my obstacles and setbacks, even when he lands on *missed email, no*

174

wi-fi, or *couldn't get to interview, no bus fare* or *I don't own a shirt*.

'There has to be a way to win.'

'There is. But it'll take a while.'

He rolls again. 'But why do you want to fail?' He seems genuinely interested.

'I don't *want* to. This is just how it is. He said it had to be a realistic goal—I've just added realistic obstacles.'

'No, I mean why not just do the assignment the way he asked you to, and take the pass?'

'Because it wouldn't be real.'

Mr Reid clicks his fingers. 'All right. Let's get to know some of our peers' goals.'

I stare out the window. I didn't see D&G ride past today. I need to pee. I'm still having trouble believing Benjamin Peros *laminated* his work. I wonder what happened to his ninja star. Anything to avoid having to think about what I'll say if Mr Reid asks me to explain myself in front of the whole class. It's not the objective that's embarrassing—it's the stuff that prevents me reaching my goal.

'Raise your hand if you have achieved the objective.'

Everyone. Except Peros.

'Did you all complete your critiques?'

Everyone except Peros. Again.

Mr Reid checks a few games, asks some questions, makes several comments, then heads over to our desk. 'What's the problem here?'

Peros hesitates. Then he says, 'I can't win.'

Reid leans over, studying my board. He scratches his head. He tugs on his beard. 'Mr Peros, how many times did you play the game?'

'I'm still playing. I haven't won yet,' Peros says.

'Where are the ladders?'

Peros looks at me for help.

'My game is called "Snakes",' I say.

'So it's not possible to win?'

'It's not *im*possible—you can win if you avoid all the snakes.'

'And what are the chances of that?'

I think. 'Probably around one in a hundred.'

'So Mr Peros has to play your game around a hundred times to reach the objective, which is—?'

'To get a job.'

'What kind of job?'

'Any job,' I repeat.

'Why those odds?'

'Because I've applied for over a hundred positions in a year. I think that's a realistic probability.'

His eyes narrow. 'Perhaps you could share a self-evaluation with the class?'

I hate it when he makes us to do this. It's not possible that nobody has noticed how red my face is, or how shaky my hands are, or how I have to keep swallowing in case the burn in my throat turns into a pile of vomit on the carpet. This is exactly why it's always better to keep my mouth shut.

Peros says, 'Breathe, before you pass out.'

I'm embarrassed, but I'm pissed off too. I completed the task. I nominated a goal, counteracted the element of luck and chance, included realistic setbacks, *and* I focused on an aspect of Australian contemporary society. I achieved the objectives he set—just not my own.

I take a deep breath. 'I killed it. Sir.'

Mr Reid walks slowly to the front of the class. I've challenged him. He'll have to put me in my place, otherwise there'll be anarchy.

But Mr Reid says, 'Okay.'

Okay? That's it? Is that a fail?

'Start packing up. If you can do that quietly you can all leave a few minutes early.'

Peros is just about in stitches.

Who needs good looks, talent or ambition when you can open a can of instant popularity by uttering four dumb words?

'I killed it. Sir.'

Ruby Ames says she's going to have T-shirts made. Will Farnsworth coaches me through a complicated bro handshake. Lee Fortescu tells me I'm a legend. Gurmeet Chambal offers to partner up for the next exercise, and Zadie Zhang says she wishes she was quick enough to take a photo of the expression on Kobe Slater's face.

It turns out Benjamin Peros lives with his older sister Amelia just a couple of streets away from our flat. We end up walking halfway home together along the main road. He says he needs to catch the 3.30 to his afternoon shift at four.

'How come we never run into each other on the way home?' he says.

'I usually walk behind the tracks.'

'That must take three times longer.'

It's true. Normally I wouldn't be home until after four, but coming this way means I'll be there half an hour sooner.

'I try to put off getting there for as long as I can,' I say.

It's possible Peros was never the kind of kid who had to take the long way home.

'Fair enough,' he says. 'Hey, you know how you said you've applied for over a hundred jobs?'

'Yeah.'

'Does that mean you've stopped looking?'

'I guess. Why?'

'Technically you gave up just before your luck turned. If you apply your own logic,' he says.

'I *said* luck has nothing to do with it.'

'Probability, then. Because I could put in a word for you at the plant. I'm not sure if they need any juniors at the moment, but I could ask.'

'Hey, thanks.'

'That's how it works—who you know and all that.' He takes his bus pass out of his bag. 'Reid went easy on you. I was waiting for him to blow his stack.'

'Me too.'

He stops at the bus shelter and slings his bag on the bench. 'You made some fans, that's for sure.'

'They hardly ever said a word to me before today.'

He frowns. 'Did you ever talk to *them*?'

'Not really.'

'Man is no island,' he says mysteriously. 'Except me. I'm an island.'

I sit next to him on the bench. 'What happened with the ninja star?'

'Confiscated.'

'Did it work?'

'Don't know. Never got to try it.'

There's a break in traffic, and Peros leaves a long enough silence that I blurt the first thing that comes into my head.

'Do you ever think it doesn't matter who you want to be—that other people decide for you? Like, there's a whole lot of shit you have to carry and it's part of you even if you don't want it, and there's nothing you can do to change that?'

'Fuck, no. You have to offload the shit. Nobody can *make* you carry it,' he says.

'Okay. Thanks, I think.'

He gives me a two-finger salute and waves down a bus. 'This is me. See ya tomorrow.'

'Later.'

Once the bus pulls away, I turn down a side street and cut through the alleyways. Being on the main road makes me feel exposed, like any minute someone could chuck a can at the back of my head.

When I get home, a removalist's pod is sitting in the middle of the residents' driveway. A guy and a girl, probably in their early twenties, are shifting furniture into the empty unit at the far end of the block.

I hope they don't turn their backs or half their stuff will go missing.

I'm still replaying the scene in the classroom and it feels off, like it was staged. Mr Reid let me get away with something he wouldn't ordinarily excuse. Peros knew it too. It reminds me of the night Nance cut her hand—as if things were going bad and suddenly turned, but it was nothing I did to turn it around.

I try to shrug it off, but the feeling won't go away. Nance says I care too much what people think of me, and half the time they're probably not—thinking of me, that is. But it's my modus operandi—blurt something, regret it, overanalyse and obsess about it for the next hundred years.

EIGHTEEN

The young couple who moved into the empty unit are having a housewarming party. Their guests have spilled out onto the residents' driveway, and they're cooking a whole pig on a spit under the visitors' carport.

Dec has been pacing and whining for hours. He says if he hears fifty smashed idiots singing 'Copperhead Road' one more time, he's going to get punchy. I can tell he's torn between calling the cops (too risky), breaking it up himself (riskier) or going out until it's all over (too paranoid).

Nance is sitting on the couch. Otis is fast asleep with his head in her lap.

'They're young,' she says. 'It's not even midnight. Let them have fun.'

Dec's pacing and whining has been winding me up, too, but Nance always sounds so reasonable. She calms me down.

She has the opposite effect on Dec.

'They only put the pig on three hours ago. Use your brain, Nance.' He taps his head.

'What?' she says. 'Does it take longer than that?'

'*Does it take longer than that?*' he mimics. 'They'll be lucky if it's cooked by fucken breakfast.' He stands.

'Dec, no,' Nance says. 'Don't start anything.' She tries to get up, then remembers O. 'Don't wake him up. Please.'

I know what she means. O could sleep through a hurricane, but when Dec raises his voice it cuts through his coma like an adrenaline shot.

The noise can't go on forever. O and Jake are sleeping through it—I decide to just go to bed.

'Me wake him?' Dec thumbs his chest. 'Not *them* with their raw pig and crap music?'

I wonder if he knows his pectorals twitch when he's having a tantrum.

I can tell Nance wants me to do something. I hate confrontation, but the alternative is to let Dec loose and that's a no-win situation for everybody.

'All right, I'll go. I'll ask them to turn it down a bit.'

Dec laughs. 'Right.'

'He can handle it,' Nance says. 'Hopefully without punching anyone.'

I pull on a T-shirt and slip my feet into a pair of Dec's slides. On second thought, I pull on a pair of jeans so I don't look as scrawny as I do in boxers.

Dec's standing by the door, ready to let me through. 'Don't be soft.'

'Yeah. I got this.'

I squeeze through the gap.

There's no wind and a layer of smoke hangs like a dirty blanket. The pig smells good. I can hear the smooth tones of Elvis coming from Clancy's, but Eminem soon drowns him out. It's impossible to spot the hosts in this crowd after seeing them only once, so I push past a group of people and head for the side gate leading to their yard.

'Hey.'

Merrick is sitting at the top of the fire escape on the side of the building, smoking. His Yeezys are fading.

I climb the stairs and sit next to him. 'What's up?'

'Not much.'

'So you haven't quit yet?'

He clicks his jaw and sends a smoke ring my way. 'I'm trying to make my body an inhospitable environment. I strongly suspect I have a parasite in my brain. What is the most resilient parasite? Bacteria? A virus? An intestinal worm?'

Years of riffing off Merrick's prompts means I'm perfectly aware he's quoting *Inception*. But I don't feel like playing.

'Definitely the worm.'

'The *worm*?'

'Yeah. The Guinea worm. Up to eighty centimetres long, and her only job is to burrow through your subcutaneous flesh until she causes a blister on your foot. It's so painful you have to cool your foot in water, but that's what she wants because she's carrying three million embryos and—'

'Wrong,' he cuts in. 'It's an *idea*. Resilient. Highly contagious. Once an idea has taken hold of the brain it's almost impossible to eradicate.' He shakes his head. 'You're off your game.'

'I'm trying to be more original.'

'Are you serious?' He flicks his cigarette onto his butt graveyard on the roof outside his bedroom window.

The gutter is full of them. I worry about the fire hazard.

'I'm working on my own material. So should you.'

'I meant about the worm.'

'It's real. It can take *weeks* to extract this thing, and we're talking a millimetre at a time, otherwise it can break off and start decomposing inside your body, causing a massive infection.'

'*Shit*,' he says.

'I know. And you think Pokémon designers are creative—they've got nothing on the animal kingdom.'

He grabs my shoulder and points. 'Your old man's looking for someone.'

Dec's out on the verandah.

'I'm supposed to be asking the new neighbours to turn the music down.'

'Me too,' he says.

We watch as Dec paces a few times and goes back inside.

Merrick lights another cigarette. 'I'm not staying at Mum's anymore.'

'Why not?'

'It's pretty crowded with the new baby. At least Senior doesn't freak out if I roll in at 2 am.'

Things must be bad if he's willing to stay with his old man full-time. But where does he go? Youth isn't open that late. We were always home soon after twelve because there was nowhere else to go.

'What baby? You mean, like, a brother? I didn't know there was a new baby.'

'Sister. I told you.'

'No, you didn't.'

'I'm sure I did,' he says. 'I tell you everything.' He looks cagey, and more than a bit upset.

I take his cigarette away and butt it out on the step.

'Hey! That's worth a buck.'

'Seriously, your lungs must be like popcorn by now. Anyway, you're loaded, aren't you? You can afford it.' I point to his feet.

He sighs.

'What's going on?'

'I've been thinking,' he says eventually. 'I've decided it's really, really hard to be good. Like, being a decent person is hard work. Do you know what I'm saying?'

I know exactly what he means.

'Do you mean going to work and stuff? Being responsible? Cos I don't think that's what you should be doing just yet. I think our job is to be kids for as long as we can before the law says we're not anymore.'

'Yeah, but...' He gets up.

'Where are you going?'

'Look, if I say anything you'll just tell me I sold out.'

'Did you?'

He holds out his hands. His palms are covered in tiny scratches and cuts. I notice a ridge of calluses and a couple of raw blisters inside the thumb on his right hand.

'Extreme wanking injury? I thought you were a leftie.'

He snorts. 'I wish.'

'What's it from?'

'Cable stripper. For cleaning copper wire.'

'Your new job?'

'Not exactly.'

I'm beginning to get the picture. 'Merrick? Where does the copper come from?'

He shoves his hands in his pockets. 'It's not just copper, it's brass, stainless steel, aluminium. You get it from pipe, offcuts, swarf—'

'*Specifically*, where does it come from?'

He won't look at me. 'Houses, factories, warehouses. Swarf bins. Air-conditioning units and water meters. Clean copper gets about five or six bucks a kilo, sometimes a bit less, and there's about two hundred kilos of pipe and wiring in a house. There's twenty kilos of brass in a meter.'

This is like pulling teeth. '*Whose* houses, Merrick?'

'The new ones they're building at Hedge Grove Estate, mostly. It's too hard to get to once the interior walls go up.'

'You steal it,' I say.

Now the party is cranking 'In Da Club'. Dec must be climbing out of his skin. He hates that track.

'I don't do the stealing. I just strip the wire for them.'

'Who? Tuwy and Fallon?'

He nods.

'Dude, you sold out for a pair of Yeezys.'

'I knew you'd say that.' He looks miserable. 'It's not that simple.'

'You have to stop.'

'Maybe I can't.'

'Yeah, you can. Drop them. Come back to school.'

'Okay, so maybe I *don't want to*.'

He seems very small and young, sitting next to me. It's like he hasn't changed in six years, except instead of chewing my ear off about Pokémon, he's casually talking about organised crime.

'How did you even get mixed up with them?'

'Brock said I owed him for jacking his phone.' He shrugs.

'Anyway, he's not that bad. Fallon's weird but he's actually an okay guy.'

'You're dead to me.' I smile to show I'm joking, but he jumps up and bounds down the steps three at a time. 'I'm kidding!'

'Maybe you can do this on your own, but I can't.'

'Do what?'

'*Life!*' He starts ticking off his fingers. 'I've got money in my pocket. I've got ambition. And maybe those two don't really count as friends, but do you have any idea how good it feels to stop looking over my shoulder?'

'You're delusional. Your glow-in-the-dark shoes must be leaching toxins into your blood.'

'They think I'm funny!'

'You're not that funny.'

He throws his hands in the air and starts pacing along the path with an exaggerated swagger. 'Welcome to Bairstal! What's your dream? Some dreams come true, some don't; but keep on dreamin'—this is Bairstal.'

I give him a blank look. 'Original?'

'*Pretty Woman*,' he says. 'The whacked dude at the end.'

'We were only up to *L*.'

He shoves his hands in his pockets. 'I've moved on. I'm getting out of this shithole, with or without you. Why don't you try hanging out with us sometime instead of judging.'

'This is a tragic development.' I get up and slide down the railing. 'You can do ridiculous sums in your head. You have a superpower.'

'Well, fuck living in a place where your superpower is considered a defect.' He clears his throat and spits on the ground. 'I hate this song. It's like the soundtrack to a disaster movie.'

I assume he's going back to his place, but he disappears down the driveway. I look across at our flat—in darkness, as usual—to see the silhouette of a couple standing right near our verandah. I'd better go. Dec'll be losing it and Nance will be worried.

As I get closer, the couple break apart. They mutter an apology and stumble back to the party, leaving two empty plastic cups on our step. I pick them up, toss them into Nance's hydrangea and knock lightly on the door.

No answer.

I knock again until my knuckles burn, but nobody comes.

I go to let myself in at the window—but at the last second, I stop. Dec has locked me out. Every instinct is warning me that, even if the door *was* open, I'd be crazy to walk through it.

I can picture Nance, lying awake, listening, Dec's arm slung over her body like a steel band. I hate that she has to choose between standing up to him and leaving me outside. She has fewer options than I do.

I walk along the driveway to the street. Cold sweat has left a damp ring around my neckline. So many streetlights are out along Whittlesea Road, it's almost completely dark. Dogs bark and curtains twitch, and I can't get the soundtrack to a disaster movie out of my head. Dec's slides slap a beat on the pavement: *help-less-ness, hope-less-ness, home-less-ness. Gut-less-ness.*

Less is never more. Only a person who has enough could say that and mean it.

My mind is so busy calculating risks and working through

possible solutions, it feels as if there was a logjam in my brain and now that one thought has worked its way loose, the rest are tumbling after it.

Youth will be open for another hour—after that I don't know what I'll do. It's against the rules for anyone to sleep at the centre, but if Macy's staying there tonight she might let me curl up in a corner until morning.

I can't believe it has taken me this long to work out why Dec locks Nance out of the flat. His rule is: real men don't hit women or children, but I think he's afraid. Not of Nance—of himself. The only way he can stop himself is to put the door, with its steel mesh plate and triple lock, between him and the thing he wants to hit.

Merrick was right: once ideas have taken hold, they're impossible to let go. For so long I've told myself everything would be okay because Dec won't hit me.

But I'm sixteen. According to Dec, I'm a man now. It's probably safer out here.

When I reach the main road, it's drizzling and Youth is in darkness. Macy probably has the outside lights switched off so Agnes won't be offended by the wall.

I cross and trudge up the footpath. As I pass the Rage Cage, I hear the scuff of shoes on the asphalt. It's Deng—not shooting, just sitting there with his back to the mesh.

'You can't play in slippers,' he says. 'I will break your ankles.'

He's talking about his crossover—he changes direction so fast anyone would trip over their own feet in sneakers, let alone slides.

'Hey.' I push through the gate. 'Where's Coop?'

'No Coop.'

'Why is it so quiet?'

'No lights.'

'I can see that. So why are you sitting out here on your own?'

'There are others,' he says. 'It's okay.'

I peer through the mesh. In the undercover space behind the wall there are a few kids sitting on the concrete. It's dark there, too.

'We're locked out?'

Deng nods. He lights a cigarette. 'Yes.'

He'll have to quit soon if he wants to play NBA.

I leave the cage and head to the entrance. The roller door is down. As well as the four kids huddled behind the wall, there's a solitary figure at the far end. 'What's going on? Why is it closed?'

'We don't know,' a boy says. 'Macy isn't here.'

'Then why are you all sitting here?'

Stupid question. They probably have nowhere else to go. Like me. Nobody says anything.

The rain gets heavier and Deng takes cover with the rest of us. His phone screen lights up. The four are all boys, around twelve or thirteen. I don't know their names, but the figure at the far end is a girl.

Tash. She ducks her head but I can tell it's her.

I wander over, slide my back down the wall and take the space next to her. She ignores me. This isn't the time or place to pick a fight, but I'm having trouble believing she hasn't got *something* to say. She always does.

'Do you have any idea what's going on?'

She sniffs and wipes her nose on the back of her hand. 'Macy's sick, maybe?'

'But they'd call in Thomas or Mim, wouldn't they?'

'Nobody knows anything.' She hits the home button on her phone. 'It's almost closing time anyway.'

'Where are you gonna go?'

She shrugs. 'Stay here till the rain stops.'

'Then what?'

She half turns. 'Why are you here?'

'Looking for you,' I lie. The cold concrete is already making my arse numb. If Nance was here she'd warn me about haemorrhoids.

'Why?'

'You know why.'

She reaches into her bag, unzips a compartment and pulls out my two missing pages from my notebook. 'I didn't take them. I found them on the floor.'

I grab the papers. 'You used my words, though.'

'I like your poems.' She zips her bag and tosses it aside. 'I'm shit at poetry. I'm much better at pictures.'

'They're not *poems*.'

'They sound like poems.'

'Well, they're not. They're mine and they're *private*.'

The rain eases. One by one, Deng and the other kids leave.

'So what will you do with them?' Tash asks.

'Nothing.'

'We could team up.'

'And do what?'

She gestures at the wall behind us. 'Make a statement.

Every bloody day if that's what it takes.'

'They'll be watching now.'

'Yeah. I know.' She looks up at the camera near the entrance, pulls a selfie face and waves. 'Anyway, you should take credit for the wall. You might be famous.'

'I don't want to be famous. Why don't you take the credit?'

'I can't. I've already been busted three times—two clean-up orders and a two-thousand-five-hundred-dollar fine.'

'Shit.'

One last burst and the rain stops altogether.

'The rain's stopped,' I say.

She gathers her things and stands. 'Come on—I want to show you something.'

NINETEEN

Tash lives in a block of flats in Rowley Park West. Merrick and I have always had an unspoken agreement not to come here—we keep to Bairstal, or the Rowley Park side, where our enemies are known and we know all the exits. We made Rowley Park West out to be the slum of all slums, but even in the dark I can tell it's pretty much identical to Bairstal.

If I had known Tash lived this far from my place I wouldn't have walked all the way with her. And she insisted on taking the side streets because someone she knew might spot her, so it took us forty minutes to get here.

'Why do you always wear the same clothes?' She plucks at the sleeve of my hoodie.

I shrug. 'Why do you always wear *different* clothes?'

She doesn't answer—just frowns at her socks as if she doesn't agree they're mismatched. She keeps asking rude questions. *Why am I so skinny? Have I tried Roaccutane for acne? Am I as pussy as I look?*

I don't know. Genes? No. Maybe.

'This is where I live.' She waves at the flats across the street. Exactly like ours, but painted green. 'I'm not going in yet.'

We sit on a low brick wall outside a weatherboard house

with boarded-up windows.

'So why aren't you supposed to be out? Grounded?'

She shakes her head. 'No. Not really.'

She asks a lot of questions, but she sure doesn't like answering them.

'Who do you live with?'

'My mum and sister and my stepbrother and stepdad.'

'Oh. Right.' I must say it with the wrong inflection or something because she shoves me. 'What's that for? Why are you so angry?'

'Girls aren't allowed to be angry?'

'Of course they are.' I move further away from her. 'But you are a bit full on.'

'See?'

'Yeah, but it's not a gender thing. It's a *you* thing.'

'The fuck it's not.'

'You're the one who used the word pussy.' Again, she doesn't reply. 'Look, you're home safe. I should go.'

'Go where? And I haven't shown you my piece.'

'So show me.'

A car passes slowly, only its parking lights switched on, and she tenses. 'It's not safe,' she says. 'Youth was safe, but now they're closing it down, there's nowhere safe.'

'What about school? Where do you go?'

'I don't.' She smirks. 'They stop looking for you after a while.'

'But what are you going to do?'

'Run away,' she says. 'I don't know where to yet. I'm still working on a plan.' She jumps off the wall and strides across the street. 'Come on.'

I follow her into a laneway, dodging an orange-striped cat that shoots from behind a row of bins and tries to wind between our legs.

'That's Monty.'

'Yours?'

'He's a stray.' She presses a finger to her lips. 'Keep your voice down. It echoes in here.'

The laneway is paved with cracked, uneven bricks, scooped like a drain in the middle and wide enough for two cars. An arched canopy hangs over crumpled iron fences on both sides, and the rear brick walls of the flats—three storeys high and without any windows—make the laneway feel like a tunnel. Tash leads me to a gap in the fence and slips through. On the other side is a flattened path winding through a tangle of weeds.

Monty darts ahead and disappears.

I can barely see my own feet; I'm wondering how I'll be able to see whatever she wants to show me, when I realise she's heading towards a faint greenish glow.

'What's that?'

'Through here,' Tash whispers. 'It's the only one left.' She ducks under a branch and pulls it back to let me pass. 'Luminous paint. It's expensive, so I only use it for accents.'

'Wow.'

The mural is painted on the side of the flats. It's about the size of our lounge-room wall: an army of children with empty eyes, wearing hoodies, some holding a brain and others a heart in their outstretched hands. The colours are ghostly greys and misty blues, apart from the phosphorescent green coming from their hollow eye sockets. Only the figures in the front row have any detail, but it's obvious there are thousands of children in receding lines, all marching behind a taller, cloaked figure beating an enormous drum.

'They made me clean up the others.' She stands back, hands on hips. 'Nobody knows about this one. I didn't tag it.'

'It's amazing. What does it mean?'

'What do you think?'

'Who's the guy with the drum?'

She rolls her eyes. 'Who is he to *you*?'

Dec. No question.

'You're really good,' I say instead.

She turns away. 'I know.'

'But why hide it? Why don't you make art that's legal? What if you got permission to paint the wall at Youth? Macy's the director. Like she said, it's our space.'

She sneers. 'I want to *stay* angry. I don't want *permission*.'

'Why?'

'Because discontented people are the ones who effect change. Happy people don't—they just keep the status quo to protect whatever makes them *content*.' She puts air quotes around the word. 'The very fact that I graffitied the wall is what makes it newsworthy. If I was allowed, nobody would care.'

I take a deep breath. 'I meant why are you angry?'

'Aren't you?'

'Yeah, but the things I'm angry about I can't change. They're personal. You appear to be angry with the whole world.'

'Personal, how?'

'Small stuff. Family stuff.'

'That's where it starts,' she says. 'We should go.'

She heads back the way we came, this time letting the branch go to whip my face, and we exit the laneway.

'You took a big risk with the wall.'

'I stuck up a few posters. It's only temporary, so it's a lesser penalty.' She pauses under the streetlight. 'So are you in or out?'

'Huh?'

'Are you going to fight or what?'

For a moment I'm not sure what she's talking about. 'For Youth?'

'Yeah.'

When I take too long to answer, she changes the subject again.

'What words would you put there?' she says. 'Caption it—whatever. My mural.'

'I don't know. I have heaps of stuff. I just don't know if I want anyone to see it.'

She considers for a moment. 'You're scared people will laugh at you.'

'Maybe.'

'The right people don't.'

'You're pretty smart.' I smile. 'For a high-school drop-out, I mean.'

I wait for a comeback, but she just looks sad.

The last time I pulled an all-nighter was when Merrick wanted to sit outside the FOMO Festival and we missed the last train. I can hardly keep my eyes open.

I go in through the window. Ditch my bag in the kitchen.

There are dinner plates still on the table and the air inside the flat smells like it's been locked in for days. No sign of Nance or the boys.

Dec and Jarrod are sitting in the backyard on our freshly laid turf, drinking. Jarrod always comes over on Sundays so they can pre-load on the cheap before they go to the greyhound track for some live action. I thought they'd be gone by now.

Nance opens the bedroom door. Her eyes are puffy. 'Where have you been? I was so worried.'

'What are they still doing here?'

Her nostrils flare. I half expect smoke to shoot through them. 'What do you think?' She slips through the gap and closes the door. 'O's asleep. He kept me up half the night. Are you okay?'

'Fine. Where's Jake?'

'He's upstairs with Margie. Where did you stay? Youth?'

I shake my head. I don't bother telling her it was closed for the first time I can remember. 'It's not a hotel. You can't stay there.'

'Oh. Merrick's?'

'No.'

'Who?'

'Tash.'

'A *girl*?' Nance is delighted. 'Did you meet her at school? Is she your girlfriend? Is she *nice*?'

Aside from not wanting to have this conversation with my eight-years-older stepmother, I also don't want to have to admit that I didn't exactly *stay* at Tash's house. More like sat outside, in the dark, for hours, after Tash went inside to bed.

Partly because I hooked into some random's wi-fi, but mostly because I couldn't think of anywhere else to go.

'She's not my girlfriend,' I say to cut her short. 'Not even a friend, really.'

Nance gives me a look she reserves for Dec when he says something disgusting. 'Don't be that guy.'

'You cohabitate with that guy. You *procreate* with that guy.'

She follows me to the kitchen.

I open the fridge and check inside.

Dec is saying something to Jarrod that I can't make out, and sneering at me through the window while he talks. He breaks eye contact and they both burst out laughing.

'He feels bad for locking you out,' Nance says. 'Don't make a big deal out of it, okay?'

I want to make something of it, but Jarrod gives me the creeps. Ever since I missed the goat he likes to sneak up behind me, cup my balls and pass judgement on their progress south.

'There's nothing edible in here.' I show Nance the expiry date on the milk carton. 'The milk's off. So's the pineapple juice.'

Her pupils shrink. She grabs her handbag, takes out a few dollar coins and slaps them on the table. 'Go get some chips.'

'No, thanks.'

Nance regards me from the doorway. 'They bring you up to do like your daddy done,' she says. 'It's from a song. I can't remember which.'

I know it. It's holding spot 99 in my Top 100.

I'm working on Plan B. Well, staring at the ceiling and thinking about Plan B.

I can't live with my current situation. Merrick's hanging with Tuwy and Fallon; Nance is so fixated on keeping the peace that she has forgotten about justice; Jake is turning into a mini-Dec with his crotch-grabbing and bad language, and Otis hardly says my name anymore. Jake has left Otis so far behind he'll probably never catch up.

But maybe it's true that each time a door slams another one creaks open. Or I could frame it a different way: since my allies are dropping off, maybe it's time to engage the enemy.

Mum has texted six times in the past two days. She wants me to see her apartment.

I lie awake for ages, listening for the sound of Dec's keys in the lock. Upstairs, Margie sings to Kelly on the steps. Next door, Clancy sings to Elvis on the record player. In the room next door, Nance sings Otis to sleep. On the bottom bunk, Jake is spread out on his back like a starfish.

Dec comes home at 2 am, stumbling drunk and fumbling for light switches. He stays up for another hour playing his guitar, and I have to bite the corner of my pillow to keep from screaming like Otis.

When the flat is finally dark and everyone's asleep, I sneak into the kitchen—I take the twenty-dollar note from the empty plant pot on the kitchen table.

So what if it's a test?

I fold it into a tight square and put it in my wallet. It feels more honest to steal from my own blood than it does to beg from a stranger.

TWENTY

Mum meets me downstairs in the lobby of her apartment building, a huge concrete block with lots of greenish glass and weathered timber and rusted metal panels. I don't know why they try to make something brand new look old—it's like when rich kids get new kicks and they dirty them up before they wear them.

She shows me how you have to put a card into a slot to be able to press the buttons in the lift. 'Security,' she says. 'So nobody who doesn't live here can go past the ground level.'

We zoom up to the sixth floor and she uses the same card to open a heavy door with 614 on it in brass numbers. Before I step inside, I make a pact with myself: I am one hundred per cent committed to being nice, positive, helpful.

Dream—Goal—Plan—Action—Reality.

I'll be good.

Mum's apartment looks like it came fully furnished by IKEA—everything is white, brown or beige, apart from three flamingo cushions on the couch and a fluffy white carpet with pinkish streaks. It looks like a polar bear carcass. I brush against a coffee table and it squeaks. I run my hand across the spines of books on the bookshelf, and the whole thing sways.

John the Sponsor might be a magician, but he's not so handy with an Allen key.

'It's only one bedroom, one bath,' Mum says. 'There are two-bedroom apartments on the upper floors, but there was just me, so...' She flips the flamingo cushions onto the floor. 'The lounge is a sofa bed. This is where you'll sleep when you come to stay.'

When I come to stay?

She pulls on a metal handle. 'It's stuck. Help me out.'

I throw my weight behind her and the mattress unfolds, still covered with plastic.

She lies on the side next to the window. 'Try it.'

I take the other side. My feet hang off the end. I can feel every spring. 'Perfect.'

'There's a gym,' she says, smiling at the ceiling. 'It's on the third floor, and there's a lap pool, too. You could work out.' She sits up. 'What do you reckon?'

I reckon both my parents are fixated on the idea of me lifting weights, and I'll most likely never have a bedroom to myself.

'It's great. When should I come and stay?'

She waves her hand. 'Let's get used to the idea of each other first. Come on. I'll make you a smoothie, then we can sit on the balcony. I'll show you my plants and my view.'

Getting used to the idea of each other involves watching her bustle around the extremely white kitchen, wearing skin-tight yoga pants and a T-shirt that reads *Inhale, Exhale, Repeat,* and mowing a clump of grass on the windowsill with a pair of scissors. She throws the grass into a blender along with a frozen banana, a pear, a handful of leaves, a few ice cubes and something called almond milk.

Over the racket, she says, 'Do you like the place?'

I nod. It isn't as far from home as I thought. Only three buses. The apartment block is near the port, a few hundred metres from a stinky beach where the tide goes out so far the water is a mirage.

'Here you go.' She puts a straw in my glass but she gulps straight from hers. A pale green moustache sticks to her upper lip.

I take a mouthful. The smoothie tastes like grass clippings with a slight banana-ey aftertaste. Watching her, I feel almost optimistic. She's happy. Over-hyped and possibly nervous, but *happy*. I'm not really looking forward to meeting the succulents, but her mood is contagious.

'Let's go outside.'

The balcony is just big enough for a two-person setting and a few potted plants. There's only a glass fence between me and a six-storey drop.

Mum smiles when I press my back to the wall and sidle along it. She laughs when I choose the chair furthest from the corner where two glass panels meet. 'Scared of falling?'

'Scared of landing.'

'How's your smoothie?'

I take another sip. The flavour hasn't improved. 'It's interesting.'

'It's good for you.' She points to something below. 'See what I mean?'

'I would if I could move, but I can't.'

'The childcare centre. It's just down there.'

Now she mentions it, I can hear children's voices, but

they're so far away it's only a pleasant hum—nothing like O's screaming at close quarters.

'Do you want to go for a swim?'

'I didn't bring a change of clothes.'

She holds up a finger. 'Wait.'

I wonder how much a place like this costs. It must be heaps. Then again, there's no one around, hardly any cars on the street. Maybe it's one of those apartment blocks built during a boom, before there was a bust. A ghost condominium. Maybe no one fell for the whole 'beach living' thing, or maybe the old blokes in waders scared them off.

I lean forward in my chair. The sky stretches for miles, broken only by other high-rise apartment blocks. The air smells like mud.

'Here.' Mum tosses me a pair of board shorts. 'They're probably too big, but they'll do. I'll pick some up in your size for next time.'

I hold up the shorts by the waistband. They must be the boyfriend's. They look new. They're way too big but there's a drawstring waist.

'Thanks.'

'Get changed in my bedroom if you like. There are spare towels in the bathroom.'

I go inside.

The bathroom is a two-way: doors leading off the lounge and the bedroom. The apartment must be about half the size of our flat, and the flat is tiny. I'm not sure how we're going to make this cohabitation thing work in such a small space, but I'm willing to give it a shot.

I open the double doors in the bathroom expecting to

find a linen cupboard, but it's a mini-laundry with a washing machine and dryer. In the cabinet above the basin, there's no razor, no Lynx—only perfumed girl stuff. Just a single purple toothbrush on the counter. I peel back the shower curtain. I'd smash my elbows if I tried to wash my hair in there. Again, only one set of Herbal Essences shampoo and conditioner, pink bottles. There's no evidence the sponsor boyfriend stays over regularly.

This is a good sign. If I got a job, Mum and I could trade up to a two-bedroom, two-bathroom apartment. This could work.

I fold my clothes and leave them on the toilet seat. The shorts are too long and bunched up around my waist, and my chest is white and concave. I put my T-shirt back on.

Dec was right: I look like a hairless whippet on two legs. Maybe I *should* start lifting weights. If I moved in with Mum I could work out every day.

There's a spare towel in the cupboard, like she said. I tie it around my waist and it comes to just above my knees.

Mum's waiting at the apartment door, wrapped in something that looks like a giant handkerchief with palm trees on it. 'Are you ready?'

We take the lift back down to the third floor. The pool and gym are behind ceiling-to-floor clear glass windows—anyone walking along the corridor can see in. The pool is long, narrow, deep-blue, too classy for bombs.

'It's nice, isn't it?'

'Amazing. It's like a hotel.' I take off my T-shirt and leave it with the towel on the side of the pool. I wade in using the steps. 'It's warm.'

'Solar heating,' she says. 'This place is green-energy rated. Whatever that means.'

I duck under and swim along the bottom. When I come up, Mum's checking her phone. I breaststroke two laps and tread water in the deep end until she looks up.

'Are you coming in?'

'Oh, I'm not swimming,' she says. 'My hair will frizz. I'll just sit over here and watch.' She kicks off her thongs and stretches out on a pool lounge.

Ten lazy laps and Mum's still on her phone. My body has acclimatised, and my teeth are chattering. The pool doesn't feel quite as warm. There's a hair tie tangled with a clump of long hair floating in the skimmer box, and a used bandaid stuck to the side of the pool. If it's true that one in five people pee in swimming pools and each swimmer contributes 0.14 grams of fecal matter, I worry the chlorine in this one has been neutralised. At this temperature it's the optimum environment for Crypto.

I get out of the pool and dry off.

'Good timing,' Mum says. 'I didn't realise it was so late.'

'What time is it?'

'Nearly twelve.'

'Lunch?' A grass-clipping smoothie is not food.

'I have to go out in half an hour. Can we do lunch next time?' She picks up her thongs and slips her phone into her bag.

'Oh. Okay.'

Fifteen minutes later, I've put on my dry clothes and Mum's getting changed again. While I wait, I take a bread knife from the cutlery drawer, flip the coffee table upside down and tighten the screws.

'What are you doing?' Mum asks as she emerges from the bedroom in a fresh set of gym gear.

'Fixing your table.'

'You didn't have to do that.'

'I don't mind.'

I turn the table over, put the knife back in the drawer and pick up both smoothie glasses. The green stuff has turned to sticky froth. There's a dishwasher, but I don't know how to use one, so I fill the glasses with water and leave them in the sink.

'You have to come and stay soon. Okay? We'll make this work.' Mum stands awkwardly by the door.

I don't know what she means by stay. Stay for a night? Stay for a week? Stay for as long as I need? I've been here less than two hours. She could have warned me this wasn't a day trip before I caught three buses and skipped a whole day of school.

Nice. Positive. Helpful.

'Thank you for having me,' I say.

Everything seems back to normal at Youth. The rec room's packed, Macy's in the kitchen burning macaroni and someone's playing the jukebox. Of all the billions of people on the planet, I wonder how many are triggered when they hear the song 'Runaround Sue'.

Tash materialises wearing a paint-spattered pair of denim overalls and a yellow knitted beanie. Not exactly low-key.

'Good. You're here. Did you sign the petition?' she asks.

'What petition?'

She lets out an exaggerated sigh and pulls me by the elbow

to a table near the entrance. 'You walked straight past it.' She watches as I sign my real name and the usual fake address, although she has no way of knowing it's fake. 'Macy says if every member signs we'll have a hundred and sixty-two signatures.'

'Is that—' I check her expression. She's frowning. 'not good?'

She sighs. 'I've started one online and I already have over a thousand.'

'Well, that *is* good. Right?'

Macy's watching us through a cloud of steam. I steer Tash away from the kitchen in case she offers us something to eat.

Tash shrugs me off. 'It means shit. Half the signatories aren't even from this continent.'

'So? Do they even check who signed?'

'Petitions are passive. People will sign anything as long as they don't have to get out of their seats. We have to make them uncomfortable—then they'll get involved.'

'And do what?' I ask carefully.

'Be aggressive. Make them think doing something is more worthwhile than doing nothing.'

Macy's heading in our direction.

Tash spins on her heel and walks away, which is a relief because she talks too fast and in circles. I really want to sit alone, do nothing and be passive for the next three hours until closing.

Macy is suspicious. 'What are you two up to?'

'Nothing,' I mumble. 'That was the original plan, anyway.'

She thrusts a bundle of worksheets at me. 'Well, make yourself useful and copy these for the weekend's workshop.'

She drops the office keys in my hand. When I don't move straightaway, she adds, '*Please* and *thank you.*'

I flick through the pages.

The Body Positivity workshop is my all-time not-favourite. We're supposed to sit around and say flattering things about each other. If you're shy, you can make anonymous comments or confessions via The Box—this is after you've documented Ten-Things-I-Hate-About-Me and shared them with the group, apparently an exercise designed to exorcise self-loathing, but it only works if each member of the group is willing to talk you out of every bad thing you ever thought about yourself. It's a bloodbath. After the first workshop, Macy said under no circumstances should delinquents like us be given anonymity, a permanent marker and total freedom of speech, but then she smiled and flicked someone with a tea towel and we knew she didn't mean it. Macy always thinks the best of people. I thought she wouldn't make the mistake of letting us read comments from The Box aloud ever again.

'Mace. We all know how that turned out.'

'None of your snark, mister. I'm not in the mood.'

'Let me run a ninja-star workshop. Come on. Just once, before we're all out on the street.' I bat my eyelashes. 'I'll be good.'

Macy snorts. 'It's against the rules, and it would be a massive breach of my duty of care. Thirty booklets, pronto, and knock on the toilet door—Povey has been in there for fifteen minutes.' She gives me a gentle shove. 'Hurry up. I need ten extra hands today.'

I've often thought Macy is the closest thing I've had to a

mother since mine took off, so I do as she says: bash the toilet door until Povey stumbles out blinking, unlock the office, load the sheets into the photocopier, program the machine to print thirty collated copies, slump into Macy's office chair and spin slowly until the booklets are ready to be stapled. I look around for other things I can do to help Macy, but the best I can come up with is to make ten copies of my right hand and leave them on her desk.

The door creaks open. Tash pops her head through the gap. 'I've been looking for you. It's almost ready.'

'What is?'

'This.' She steps inside and dumps a black portfolio case on the desk. 'Lock the door.'

I shake my head. 'We'll get in trouble.'

'Bloody *hell*.' She closes the door, turns the lock, unzips the case and slides out a sheet of heavy plastic-coated card with letters cut out of it. 'I've kept it small so we can be in and out in, like, twenty seconds. Uses less paint, too. Tricky as shit with all those letters, but it's clean—I've tested it and timed it. No serif, and the counters are hanging by a thread so we can't saturate or it might fall apart. I reckon it's good for fifty, maybe more, if we're careful.'

I have no idea what she just said.

She whips out something that looks like a scalpel. Clocks my expression. 'Relax, I'm not going to stick you.'

'What *is* that?'

She looks at the knife. 'X-Acto.'

I raise my eyebrows.

'Stencil-cutter, you newb.'

'What are you—a freaking *professional*?' I hold the stencil up to the light. It's my quote from the wall in block letters, enclosed within the shape of a house, two windows and a flame curling from the roof. 'This is awesome.'

'Yeah. I know. Let's go blow some tiny minds.'

'Apathy,' I say, nodding wisely. 'Indifference.'

Tash is unimpressed. 'Huh?'

'They're our biggest obstacles. That's what my teacher said.'

She rolls her eyes. 'The biggest obstacle is buying the paint. I'm on a ban list.' She tucks the stencil inside the portfolio and closes the zip.

I'm thinking of the locked utility cupboard in Tech, and the key stuck in a blob of Blu Tack on the inside of Mr Trask's desk drawer, and the unsupervised access I have to the Tech workshop because I am, essentially, a trustworthy kid.

I'm feeling restless and pissed off. I've been good all day.

'I can get the paint.'

She smiles. 'Red and black. Lots of black. But it's not completely finished. We don't have a tag.'

The words have never come more easily. 'Ungrateful Youth.'

Tash swears under her breath. 'Short words are not your strength. This is going to take a bit longer.'

TWENTY-ONE

I'm supposed to be copying detailed theory notes on Archea, single-celled organisms. Archea thrive in extreme environments previously considered unable to sustain life: the Dead Sea, hot springs, salt evaporation ponds and acid lakes—shitty places like that.

Our Science teacher never bothers to check our notes, so I'm faking. He always speeds through theory to get to prac so he can play 'Clash of Clans' on his iPad for the rest of the double period. I hate prac. I prefer to work alone. Especially since Abe Farrugia is my lab partner for the term and he's a methanogen: a single-celled organism that produces large amounts of methane gas as a by-product of his digestive and energy-making processes.

I zone out.

Tash texted this morning to say tonight's the night. She said it's a new moon. I'm not sure if that means it'll be safer in the dark, or she believes in astrology. I add Bairstal and Rowley Park High to my list of inhospitable environments, close my notebook and doodle a burning house on the cover of my textbook.

It's not until we're packing up to leave the lab that I notice another foul odour. When I wasn't paying attention, Kobe Slater switched seats to sit behind me. I suspect I'll find the rotten-egg bomb in my bag or my hood later. On the upside, it means I pass through the halls without bumping into anyone because they all give me a wide berth.

I make it to English a full two minutes before everyone else.

Mr Reid looks up, surprised. 'To what do I owe this newfound enthusiasm?'

I shrug and slide into my seat.

He strides to the whiteboard, picks up a pen and writes:

If you would rise above the throng
and seek the crown of fame,
you must do more than drift along
and merely play the game.
—*Edgar Albert Guest (Ambition - 1881)*

'Not games again,' I mutter.

'No, not games.' He bows. 'Role playing.'

Role playing? I bang my head on the desk. I dropped Drama so I wouldn't have to do this stuff.

'For someone who demands originality you sure use a lot of other people's words.'

I think I've pushed him too far this time, but he nods.

'I have to play the game too,' he says.

The rest of the class arrive. Mr Reid closes the door and I don't get to find out what he means.

I vague out again and sketch another house with finer detail. This one's even better. I'm thinking of the paint I have stashed in my locker, wondering if it will be enough.

'Claim your future,' Mr Reid is saying. 'Visualise your goal. Go towards it every chance you get.'

Kobe Slater stands.

'Where are you going, Slater?'

'I'm moving towards my future Big Mac.'

'Sit down, please. It's time to devise your plan, people. For your homework assignment you are to write several scenes featuring *you* as the hero.' He points to the board. 'Think about something that's happened—or could happen—where the outcome could have been changed by reacting differently. Identify your fatal flaw in each situation, overcome it, rewrite history and move towards your future.'

I must have missed the fatal flaw speech, but Reid has rammed enough Ibsen and Shakespeare down our throats over the past two years that I get the gist.

'What's your fatal flaw?' I ask Peros on our way out.

'Time mismanagement,' he says, without missing a beat. 'I'm a gamer.'

'Makes sense.'

'What's yours?'

'Can we only pick one?'

Mr Reid stops me. 'McKee.'

'*Uh-oh*,' Peros says. 'Good luck.'

When everyone has left, Mr Reid gestures for me to sit down. 'I need to—elaborate,' he says.

'Looking forward to it.'

'Ask me anything.'

'What do you mean?' He's so intense. It's making me nervous.

'Go ahead.' He crosses one leg over his knee and leans back in his chair. 'Anything.'

He's wearing retro Air Jordan 1 Off-White. Merrick would probably swap his entire deck for a pair of those.

'Okay, what do you call those plastic things on the end of your shoelaces?' I say.

'An aglet or a Flugelbinder. Originally made from shrunken sheep intestine.'

I'm sweating. I unzip my jacket and lay it across my legs. Another blast of rotten egg spreads through the classroom. It's definitely coming from the hood. 'Who invented the zipper?'

'Whitcomb Judson.'

'What's that awful smell?'

'Ammonium sulphide. Come *on*, McKee.'

I shrug. 'So you know more than me. You're supposed to.'

'Did you know the answers to the questions you asked?' he says.

'Yeah. Of course.'

'You played it safe.' He leans forward. 'So how do you expect to learn anything new?'

'What's your point? What happens if neither of us knows the answer?'

'Poetry.'

'Poetry?'

'Poetry, art, human endeavour,' he says. 'The quest for the unknown. True science is about worlds already explored, but great poetry speaks to something deep inside you. It's not just *words*. It lights a fire in your belly—it alters the way you see yourself and the way you see the world.'

'I'm missing lunch.'

Blink. Blink. 'Ask me something I don't know.'

'How would I know what you don't know?'

Doesn't he get it? He's picked the wrong student. He's like a caricature of every Robin Williams character ever, and he's making me play a game I'm not interested in playing.

'Can I go to lunch or what?'

He waves his hand. 'Yes. Go.'

I gather my things and kick the chair under the desk. He should try to convert someone who actually cares, like Zadie or Will, not stack his fragile teacher ego-eggs in a busted basket like me.

He's doing the wet sandcastle thing again.

'Sorry,' I say, and I mean it.

He opens his lunchbox, slowly unwraps a sandwich, and takes a bite. 'It's fine.'

'I like poetry,' I offer. 'But nothing you say will convince me to love it. I just don't give a shit.'

A torpedo of chewed crust exits his mouth. '*Pah!* You think I'm talking about *poetry*?'

'Aren't you?'

He shakes his head. 'Look, you can end up an under-educated smart kid or an overeducated robot—that's up to you. This institution wants to teach you to learn. But teachers aren't textbooks. We're here to teach you to think.' He taps his head. 'I have answers, thousands of them. But ask me something I don't know—ask *yourself* something you don't know—and we crack open the universe.'

I have questions I've never asked anybody. Worries I've never shared. Thoughts that circle and collide and die screaming because they never make it outside my head. What Mim said is true: stuff like that, if you let it go, it's a survival risk. You can't let it go unless you feel safe.

—

Tash is picky. She says we're aiming for the trifecta: low visibility for us at night, high exposure for the artwork during the day and peak curiosity about the message, which means a cluster of works in a concentrated area will be more effective than an opportunistic hit. And we need to complete this operation over a single night.

We've been scouting the area around Youth for over an hour. So far Tash hasn't opened her backpack once, and my heart rate has been over a hundred the whole time.

Finally, she stops at a stobie pole near the corner shops. 'Here.' She snaps a pair of rubber gloves from her pocket and hands them to me. 'Put these on.'

'Fingerprints?'

'It's messy. You hold and I'll spray.' She opens the backpack containing the paint cans—four black and one red. 'If we're busted, grab the backpack, run as fast and as far as you can and ditch it somewhere. Then keep running. Right?'

'Why me?'

'You have longer legs. You'll cover more ground.'

'What will you do?'

'The same, except I'll set fire to the stencil.'

I pull on the gloves. 'I guess this makes me an accessory.'

'Press hard and don't let the stencil slip. My reputation is at stake.' She shakes the spray can. 'Are you scared?'

The sound of ball bearings rattling inside the can is ridiculously loud.

'Yeah,' I confess. 'Is that pathetic?'

'No. It's smart.'

Tash lines up the stencil and starts spraying. For the tag, she tilts the smaller stencil on an angle, and adds a dash of red for the flame.

She pulls the stencil away and steps back. '*That* is fucking *beautiful.*'

I have to admit, it is.

'Having fun yet?' she asks, smiling.

It feels good to fight back, even if what we're doing is illegal. 'I'm not sure. I'll let you know when I do.'

We hit nine more stobies along the main road, the rear walls of Bunnings and Officeworks, the fence outside Jack Berry Dog Park, four bus-stop shelters and the concrete retaining wall near the Macca's drive-through. Nothing privately owned, but that was only because I managed to convince Tash that stencilling Agnes's Corona would be a step too far. The Macca's one was tricky—even at 2 am there's hardly a break between customers—but it's by far the most visible. Tash reckons it'll be cleaned up by the afternoon, but by then hundreds, if not thousands, will have seen it.

We walk for half an hour, through backstreets and alleys, Tash singing quietly. She has her phone on shuffle. One minute it's R&B, the next it's a soppy love song from the sixties, or it's techno or house, and she skips tracks partway or messes with the volume until my nerves twang.

'Can't you just let one track play all the way through?'

She starts a different song. 'If I'm not feeling it, I skip it.'

'So make a playlist of songs you *do* like.'

She stops. 'Why? How do you do it?'

I pull out my phone to show her. 'Top 100 of all time. This way I'm never disappointed.'

She passes my phone back in disgust. 'God, that's like when people ask what would you eat if you could only choose one meal for the rest of your life, and you say pizza—and you mean it.'

'What's bad about pizza?'

'Pizza isn't bad. Eating it voluntarily for the rest of your life is. It's a dumb question.'

'It's a *hypothetical* question. It's not about food—it's about having a standpoint.' I put up both hands. 'Are you pizza? Or are you ice cream?'

'Neither,' she says. 'I eat whatever I want whenever I want.'

It gets me thinking about Merrick and our similarly pointless discussions. He'd choose pizza, for sure. And it's all fine for Tash to say she'd eat whatever she wants, but what if the question isn't purely hypothetical at all? What if your choice is chips or…chips?

Now we're at the underpass. Tash decides it's too high and too dangerous—we'd definitely be spotted if we tried to spray upside down from the top of the bridge. We take a break underneath, on the slopes, and Tash opens her bag. She shakes the cans. All but a single black one are empty.

'What do we do with them now?'

Tash frowns. 'Dispose of them responsibly, of course,' she says.

I laugh. Apparently she's serious, which makes me laugh harder. There's a pain in the back of my thigh: I'm sitting on a sharp stone. I shift my weight, leaning towards her, and—she kisses me.

The mad beat in my chest isn't a nice feeling. It's panic. I thought I'd give anything to be kissed by a girl, but this is all wrong—wrong time, wrong place, and I have a strong suspicion it'll become another bad memory.

Tash notices I'm not kissing her back. She pulls away. 'Is it me?' she says in a small voice.

'No. I don't want to get with anybody, really.'

'Are you shy?'

'No.'

'Gay?'

'I don't think so.'

'What then?'

I shrug. 'Just—busy.'

'Busy?' Her mouth goes slack. 'Okay. Fine.'

'I mean I've got too much stuff on my mind.'

She folds her arms and pulls her knees to her chest. 'It was just a kiss.'

I stand up and dropkick an empty can. It ricochets off a pylon. 'Yeah, that's where it starts.'

'I don't know what you mean.'

'Then you want to come to my place and you hate where I live because it's tiny and it stinks, and we can't be alone because I share a room with my brothers. And you can't handle the way my old man looks at you and he makes disgusting comments about us, so the only way we can be together is at Youth, which will probably be shut down anyway. We end up doing it one night in the middle of the school oval and it isn't romantic at all, and the condom breaks and six weeks later you tell me you're pregnant. It's likely you'll have twins and when they're born one of them won't be right in the head, and we'll have to live in a Housing Trust unit—like we do already—and I'll spend all our money on drinking and gambling and you'll cry all the time and—'

She holds up a hand. 'Wow. You've got it all worked out, don't you?'

'Not me. Statistics.'

'You're right. We're doomed. We have to break up.'

'But we weren't even—'

'I'm *kidding*. It's okay, I reckon you'd be shit at it anyway.' She kicks my leg gently.

'At what?'

'Kissing.'

'Probably.'

She makes eye contact with a shrug and a sniff. 'My house stinks too. It's noisy. My stepbrother has his mates over all the time and I don't feel safe.'

'That sucks.'

'Hey, it could be worse.'

'Worse *how*?'

'We know things could be different. What if we didn't know any better? Like, imagine being okay with the way things are, you know? That would be so much worse.'

'No, it really wouldn't.' *Not* knowing sounds better.

Tash jumps up. 'We shouldn't hang around in one place for too long. Let's go.'

I want to go. I also want to stay. How is that possible? Sometimes I think I'm still so far from willingly approaching another human being, I might as well be my own postcode.

Tash has already moved on. 'Are you coming, or what?'

'Wait.' I point to the eye on the underpass. 'You have to yawp. It's tradition.'

Tash thinks for a long time before she lets out a sound like a barking seal. Walt would be pleased.

TWENTY-TWO

Claim your future. Visualise your goal. Go towards it every chance you get.

I'm lying on my bed, staring up at the ceiling and visualising the hell out of eating a meat-lovers' pizza since the new neighbours had a Dominos delivery an hour ago.

I've been waiting until everyone's asleep to start the hero assignment. I thought this one would be fun and easy (I'm a master at imagining alternative realities and I'm all too aware of my own flaws), but try rewriting history with the distraction of Jake muttering in his dreams and the sound of sirens, plus stains on the ceiling that seem terrifyingly symbolic, shaped like mushroom clouds and burning buildings.

I left my English workbook in my locker, so I pull out my current notebook. By the light of the torch on my phone, I flip to the last few blank pages.

Maybe I won't bother starting a new one. Thoughts and words only take you so far—like expecting to represent your country in the luge when you've only ever practised in the bathtub and you've never seen snow. (I have a sudden, painful urge to trade *Cool Runnings* quotes with Merrick.)

I check the rubric I copied from the board. It doesn't say

we need to consider obstacles or setbacks, nor does it specify anything about not being allowed to inherit a large sum of money from a mysterious benefactor.

At the top of the page I write: So You Want to Be a Hero.

SCENE 1:

By some miracle, I get to the laptop cart first.

'Hey, thanks, McKee,' Kobe says. 'Give it up, wanker.' He grabs one end of the case and pulls.

I yank it back. 'No.'

'Last chance.'

'No.'

He lets go and dead-arms me.

I hug the laptop to my chest and wait for Mr Reid to notice there's an uprising. There's enough noise that Reid could remain ignorant of the standoff until there's blood.

Kobe punches me again. 'Give it up now or you're fucked later, dude.'

'It's a laptop, dude.'

He lowers his voice. 'I'm coming for you.'

I raise mine. 'Look, I'm flattered, I really am. But I have to be truthful—I'm a less than experienced lover.'

'As if.' Kobe's eyes dart around the room. 'You're weird, you know that?'

'Yes. I know. I'm still not giving you the laptop.'

'You don't have a choice.'

'Actually, I do. I have possession and you don't. I can give it to you or I can wait for you to take it.' I tuck the laptop under my arm. 'I'll wait.'

He lunges left. I do a half-turn, forcing him to step past. He corrects

223

and comes back the other way. I spin again. To everyone watching it must look we're playing a game of invisible totem tennis.

Kobe is running out of options, and so he commits social hara-kiri by stepping forward and giving my chest a vicious pinch.

I turn to my now mostly silent classmates. 'What is this strange ritual? Should I reciprocate?'

'Cripple nipple?' Will offers. 'And probably not.'

I rub my middle finger in a circle around the sore spot. 'I'm sorry. I'm just not that into you.'

(If Mr Reid was paying attention that would be his cue to tell me to be more original, but he's not.)

Zadie delivers the killer blow by offering her laptop to Kobe.

Kobe is forced to turn it down, or look like a pre-schooler. He turns red and slinks off to his seat.

On my way back to mine—victorious!—I whisper to Zadie, 'I've seen our futures. None of this will mean anything in a few years. You and me are going places.'

This scenario has several variables. It'd pay to slip Mr Reid a strong sedative and wear my 'I killed it. Sir' T-shirt, and if he ever asks us to share our scenes with the class I'll be back to square one on the game board.

SCENE 2:

Rat and Pug are following Owen Kleinig after school again. This time I'm the last caboose, and I'm packing a flick-knife I snatched from the security guard's tray of confiscated items. (This is feasible—he doesn't pay much attention on the way out.) I leave a large enough gap to allow Rat and Pug plenty of time to catch up with Owen and, when I hear him shriek, I burst into the clearing brandishing the knife.

'Stop!'

Rat sneers. 'Says who? You?'

Pug presses Owen's face closer to the rusty tip of a broken couch spring.

'Here are your options,' I tell them. 'Public shaming, or private mutilation. You both roll up to school tomorrow and tell Miss DeVries all about your sustained bullying campaign, or I'll let Owen Kleinig here engrave his initials on your bums while I hold you down.'

'Okay,' Owen says.

I hold up my free hand. 'Patience, Owen Kleinig. Let them choose.'

'Oooooo,' he repeats. 'Kaaaaay.' He contorts his body and, so swiftly Pug doesn't realise what's happened, Owen has his arm twisted behind his back. 'O. K. They're my initials.'

That took an unexpected turn. Mr Reid was right: I've got nothing original. Anyway, I think Owen Kleinig might just save himself, so I put a line through his scene. It would be funnier if Owen's name was Fyodor Uglov.

Jake gets out of bed and wanders down the hallway to the toilet. I turn off my torchlight. When Jake comes back, he drags the shared quilt and pillow from Otis and crawls underneath the bunk with them. Otis whimpers and pats the space Jake left behind.

I hold my breath, ready for the screaming, but after a few minutes their breathing is synchronised again, even though they're apart.

SCENE 3:

I'm perched on the roof of one of the abandoned warehouses on Smith Street, peering through a broken window slat (reminiscent of the warehouse heist scene from 2 Fast 2 Furious*). Brock Tuwy and Shaun Fallon are presiding over their one-person sweatshop, Merrick,* who's stripping copper from a coil of cable taller than he is.

'Faster,' Tuwy says.

Merrick holds out his hands. 'I'm bleeding.'

Fallon kicks him and he falls onto his side.

He crawls to a dark corner on his shredded hands. 'No more,' he whimpers.

Fallon laughs like an evil overlord and drags him by the collar, back to his station.

I wait for my white-hot fury to subside. I must be patient; I have to out-think them. Everyone knows you can't run a successful crime racket with two enforcers and zero brains.

Silently, I remove four glass slats to allow myself entry, dropping them (also silently) over the edge of the roof. I crawl through and balance on a narrow steel beam like a cat.

Merrick has spotted me. Tuwy and Fallon are too deep in conversation to notice. Merrick stares up at me with his tear-streaked, hopeful face; he points to the roof, and the gloomy interior of the warehouse lights up with an otherworldly glow. (It's Merrick, using his superior mathematical ability to calculate the sine, cosine and tangent of the triangle that is a me, a vicious hook on a long chain, and Tuwy's head.)

This is going to take faith, athleticism and brute force—not Merrick's equations. Sometimes you just have to close your eyes and jump.

I leap. I grasp the chain with both hands, slide down and grip the hook between my feet. The chain (conveniently attached to a metal conveyor thing) carries me with increasing momentum towards Tuwy and Fallon. The racket makes them look up, but it's too late—at the last second, I strike out with both feet and the hook embeds itself in the fatty flesh of Tuwy's chin.

He's dead before he hits the ground, but not before the stunning *realisation hits him: Nathaniel McKee is one sick assassin.*

I roll to my feet and prepare to take on Fallon, but Merrick has him in a chokehold with a length of cable tightened around his throat. Fallon's eyes glaze, then he twitches and stops kicking.

'What took you so long?' Merrick says.

'It doesn't matter. I'm here now.'

It's obvious my fatal flaws are fear and apathy, but I write them down and underline them, just in case. It's not bad. Probably a decent pass. But why not shoot for the moon?

BONUS SCENE:

I become a leading neuroscientist after a mysterious benefactor offers to pay my full tuition and, on my first day of theatre, I perform a marathon first-of-its-kind operation to rewire O's brain. Dec is proud of me and we're all equal favourite sons. Nance is happy.

Full tuition? A mysterious benefactor? A roll of fake turf from The Man is one thing—the gift of a several-hundred-thousand-dollar tertiary education is something else, and that's assuming I can get my shit together enough to ace Year Twelve. And I'm struggling to see how I can change my present or future without completely rewriting the past.

I'd have to change *me.*

BONUS BONUS SCENE:

The biggest goat takes a step forward and paws the dirt.

'Man up,' Dec hisses, tugging my shorts.

Brett comes around to the side of the ute. 'Might be better to let him take a rabbit his first time.'

'I've got this,' I say. 'Go get me a beer.'

Dec hands me the gun. I take the weight of it, cup my left hand under the barrel, hook my right forefinger around the trigger. *Neither hand shakes.*

'I can do it myself. Only way to learn, right?'

Dec slaps me on the back. 'That's yours—the dumb one in the middle. Right between the eyes. Don't nick him.'

I line up the sight.

'Shoot,' Dec says.

Shoot the goat.

Shoot the goat.

Shoot the goat.

Bang.

TWENTY-THREE

We're sitting on the kerb outside the flats. It's after ten. Merrick is fidgeting like crazy: plucking weeds from the verge, scraping dirt from the tread of his Yeezys with a stick, checking his phone every ten seconds. He lights a cigarette, puts it out after three puffs, tucks it behind his ear and lights it again ten seconds later. When he's finished he uses the butt to set fire to the pile of weeds.

'You'd better go. They'll be here any minute and Tuwy hates you,' he says.

One of his front teeth has a fresh chip. It makes him look tougher, except now he has a lisp.

'Mutual.'

'You know why he hates you, right?' He blows the embers until they burst into flame.

'The question is, why does he like you?'

'FYI, he hates you because you always pull that face.'

'What face?'

'Like everything he says is stupid.' He points at me. 'That face! You're doing it now!' He stands and gestures for me to put out the fire. He doesn't want to burn his tread. 'Anyway, I wouldn't call it like. It's a business relationship.'

'It's not business. It's illegal.'

'Says the guy with a forest of weed in his bedroom. You're such a hypocrite.'

'It's not my weed.'

'See, this is the problem. You're always an accessory.' His phone pings. 'Shit. I've gotta walk. Catch you later.'

'Where are you going?' I jump to my feet and stamp out the flame. 'I'll come with you.'

'Why?'

'Nothing better to do. I could help.' Not the truth, but the only way I can think to get Merrick out of this is for me to get into it.

'They won't cut you in.'

'I don't care,' I say.

'Yeah, you do. I just don't know why you care *now*.'

I fall into step beside him. 'I always cared, you dick. You might be the freakin' love of my life.'

Merrick laughs. 'You're shitting your pants.'

'It's that obvious?'

'Yeah.'

'If I come with you, will you tell them you're out? Will you quit?'

He seems relieved to accept it as a new short-term goal. 'Yeah, I might.'

As we cross the main road we pass a stobie pole sporting one of Tash's burning houses. It's visible from the road and, when oncoming headlights hit the flame, it seems to flicker.

Merrick doesn't notice.

'Where are we going?'

He throws me a warning look. 'Don't start anything.'

'Who's the hypocrite now?' I slip into dialogue. 'Where the hell are they?'

Merrick catches on. 'About ten degrees off your starboard bow. You take...'

'Don't give me that shit! Point!'

Jaws one is arguably better than *Jaws* two,' Merrick says, sighing.

'Are you joking? Man versus beast is one thing, but all those kids looking out for each other—heartwarming as all shit.'

He stops. 'Is that what you're doing? Looking out for me?'

The worried expression is back. He looks like he's in pain. His face doesn't know what to do with itself when it isn't smiling.

'We're prey animals. Safety in numbers.'

'Whatever.' He jerks his head. 'Come on. This way.'

He squeezes through a gap in the temporary fencing and cuts between a couple of the warehouses on Smith. I follow. The ground is scattered with shredded boxes, rubbish and syringes. At the rear of the building, fifty metres away, Tuwy and Fallon are squatting next to a large plastic container.

'What's that?' I whisper to Merrick.

'Water meter. A big one.'

'And?'

'It's about twenty kilos of brass—a hundred bucks for scrap.'

'Seems like a lot of work for not much.'

'There are four of them.'

'Oh. Okay.' Four hundred bucks split three ways—except Merrick said he only gets twenty per cent. 'I don't get why they don't just split it fifty-fifty and leave you out of it.'

He flips his tool belt to the front. 'Skillz,' he says, which I take to mean that his superior mathematical brain has transitioned seamlessly to plumbing.

It's cold out but my palms are sweating. Voluntary sacrifice isn't exactly what I had in mind when I decided to pick up our friendship where it left off. I hang back until Merrick has made his presence known.

'What's up?' he says. 'Is it disconnected?'

Tuwy and Fallon look up. They're both wearing canvas overalls.

'They look like Mario Bros,' I whisper, and Merrick gives me a nudge.

Fallon's holding a long black torch shaped like a base-ball bat.

I say, 'Hey.'

'What's he doing here?' Tuwy says.

Fallon doesn't speak.

'Couldn't shake him,' Merrick says. 'He can go lookout.'

Tuwy shrugs. 'No cut and you're still ugly.'

This time I try really hard not to make the face.

Tuwy kicks the plastic cover until it cracks through the middle. He yanks the two pieces apart and inspects the meter. 'Can't be connected. This shit's about a hundred years old.'

Merrick squats. He lays a small hacksaw on the ground and pulls a huge adjustable spinner from his tool belt. The thing must weigh more than the meter.

'Where's the trolley?' he says.

Tuwy points to the alley between the warehouses. 'You passed it.' He looks at me. 'The security guard from the car

232

yards buzzes every half-hour or so. If he comes, give us a signal and we'll kill the torch. Go on.'

Fallon still hasn't said a word. It's freaking me out.

I do as Tuwy says and wait in the alley. I have a clear view of the street. I'm not sure how I'll be able to tell who's coming or what kind of signal I'm supposed to give, but I am reassured by the fact I have three possible exits: back the way we came, over the rear fence and into the adjacent paddock, or up a piece of scaffolding and onto the warehouse roof. And I have no idea how covertly carting eighty kilos of stolen brass in a Woolworths shopping trolley is going to work out, but I'll leave that small detail to the professionals.

I check my phone: it's just after eleven. A couple of cars drive by without slowing. It's so quiet and nothing happens for so long that my heart rate almost returns to normal, but then I hear Merrick swear, followed by a ringing clank and a sound like a thousand thongs slapping pavement.

I leave my post and peer around the corner.

Merrick, Tuwy and Fallon are drenched. Fallon has the torch trained on a geyser of water, about the thickness of an elephant's trunk, shooting ten metres into the air like an illuminated fountain.

In seconds, the dirt has turned to mud and a flash flood is finding its natural course past my feet, through the alley and out onto the street. I hoist myself onto a window ledge to avoid getting soaked. Boxes float past like boats.

'What happened?' I shout, but the noise drowns me out.

The water gushes, carving a channel through the alley to pool and swirl in the middle of the road. Another car passes. Arcs of water spray up on both sides.

Holy shit. That's an insane amount of H_2O, down the drain, wasted.

Worry, worry, worry.

'What do we do now? Can't you turn it off?'

Merrick shakes his head. He's trying to retrieve his tools without getting swept away. He manages to find the hacksaw, but the spanner is a lost cause—the water is already up to his ankles.

Fallon has picked his way carefully through the mud and out of range. He shakes himself like a wet dog. 'Let's go!'

The torch flickers out.

I feel a stab in my ankle and try to scramble higher on the window ledge. I lift my leg. In the dim light I can see a syringe, dangling, its needle caught in my sock.

'Oh, Jesus fuck!'

I snatch it out and flick it away just as Merrick and Fallon run past, skidding and laughing. I hop down and wade through the river. My jeans are soaked, and without Fallon's torchlight I can hardly see where I'm going. The sound of the water is deafening, but luckily there doesn't seem to be anyone around.

Merrick and Fallon are long gone.

Wait. Where's Tuwy?

I wade upstream, back to the source. I can just make out the figure of Brock Tuwy on his hands and knees, thrashing around in the mud. Is he hurt? Stuck?

'Hey!'

Tuwy looks up.

'We have to go! What are you doing?'

'Looking for the spanner,' he yells.

'What for? Leave it!'

Tuwy raises a muddy middle finger.

The water pressure has eased off, but the area behind the warehouses is turning into a lake. Lights are starting to come on in the estate.

I move closer, picking my way carefully through the water across uneven ground. 'Come on! The others have gone.'

'So go.'

'We'll get caught.'

'I have to try to shut it off!'

It's all I can do to drag a hundred kilos of soaked Brock Tuwy away from the broken pipe, through the river, between the warehouses and out into the street. We leave a trail of footprints along the path until we reach the spot where we go our separate ways.

Tuwy shakes his head. He says, 'It's such a fucken waste.'

In another life, when I'm looking back on this and not cursing Merrick's rapidly disappearing shadow, obsessing about millions of litres of wasted water and wondering if I'll die young after contracting a blood-borne disease from a dirty syringe, I might be able to laugh about it.

'Yeah,' I say. 'I'm gonna have nightmares about this for years.'

Back at the flats, Merrick is hanging around under the visitors' carport, swinging his wet Yeezys in one hand.

I give him a filthy look and sit down on the kerb. 'Skillz.'

His ears turn red. 'The pipe broke.'

'No more whining about loyalty.' I kick off my own squelchy shoes. 'We're even.'

'Jack Berry offered me a part-time job at Tunza. My six weeks is up.'

'Why didn't you tell me?'

He shrugs. 'Never a good time.'

'You get busted for scamming and he offers you a job? How does that even work?'

Typical. A hundred applications and I get nothing; Merrick lands the best part-time job on earth without trying.

He chuckles. 'It's probably like when they hire hackers to catch hackers.'

'So you're one of the good guys now? Do we get a discount?'

'Yeah, but we can't scam the hoops anymore. I have to think of my reputation.'

It was just unlucky Merrick got caught. We both did it: double-team on the hoops game and you can go to triple or quadruple overtime which can pay out hundreds of tickets, and 'Whack-a-Shark' is lucrative if you dump the hammer and use four fists. We could make five bucks stretch to over a thousand tickets—as a result, Merrick has six lava lamps and three plasma balls in his bedroom.

'How's your mum?' I ask.

'Dunno. I haven't been over there.'

'Why not?'

His mouth twists. 'She's busy with the baby and stuff.'

'Mine's back,' I say. 'She has an apartment near the beach. I'm thinking I'll go and live there for a while.'

'Sweet.' He pokes a thumb at our flat. 'What about your old man?'

As usual, the flat is in darkness. It doesn't look like anyone's home, but I know they're in there.

'He probably won't notice. He has Nance and the boys.'

Merrick nods. He inspects his bare feet and turns over his

hands, cataloguing his cuts and scrapes. 'What took you so long anyway? You were fifteen minutes behind us.'

'Tuwy was trying to fix the pipe. I went back for him.'

Merrick gives an incredulous snort. 'Your sense of loyalty is fucked up. Whose side are you on?' He holds up a finger. 'Wait. Tuwy was doing what?'

'Trying. To. Fix. The. Pipe.'

Merrick knows about the wasting-water thing. He cracks up. When he catches his breath, he wipes his eyes and says, 'Life is weird sometimes. People are weird.'

Things haven't exactly gone to plan. Instead of murder-ing Brock Tuwy with a hook, I seem to have upgraded him from a plain old dickhead to a dickhead with a conscience.

TWENTY-FOUR

I get home from school to find the flat in a mess and Nance in a panic. Jake is tearing around outside with the hose, squirting people's windows and tracking mud everywhere; Otis is running a temp of thirty-nine point five and lying starkers on the couch while Nance sponges him with a wet towel.

'His breathing's not right,' she says.

'Did you call the doctor?'

There's only one clinic within walking distance of our place. Guaranteed, if you weren't sick with something when you walked in you would be by the time you walked out again. Nance hates taking the boys there. The doctors are on such high rotation she has to go through O's history every time.

She wets the towel in a bucket of water and squeezes it. 'They're fully booked. They said prepare to wait for hours or take him to Emergency if it's urgent.'

'Is it?'

'I think I've given him too much Panadol already.'

'Is that why he's like this?' He's pale and clammy and his eyes are glassy. His expression reminds me of the stray dog that sometimes hangs around the Rage Cage: humans aren't to be trusted.

'No, no. I don't think that's it.'

'Should we call an ambulance?' It would mean breaking Dec's rules: no police, no ambulance. Not ever. No one outside of family or Dec's friends is ever to come through the front door. 'Has he got a rash?'

I ask this every time O's sick. I've seen those kids who look like they're plain old sick, but they develop a rash that spreads faster than you can connect the dots, and the next thing you know they have to amputate their arms and legs. There's a vaccine you can get for it. Nance has asked Dec for the money before, but he says Jake is tough, I'm too old to catch childhood diseases, and vaccines make kids like O worse.

'No rash,' she says.

'We should call a locum.'

'We can't. Is Jake still outside?'

'He's okay.'

She wipes O's red cheeks and checks his temperature again. 'I need someone to tell me what to do.'

Helpless is about the worst thing you can be.

'I don't know.'

'It's like he's looking straight through me,' she says.

Until now I've felt relatively calm. Otis is sick, like, every two weeks; something is always coming out of one end or the other. We adapt. We clean him up. We sleep through it most of the time and the next day, or the one after, he wakes up and he's fine. But now Nance is staring at me and I know whatever I say, that's what she'll do, because she's not thinking straight. And what if I'm wrong and O dies, or they have to cut off his arms?

'We have to call Dec.'

'I did already. *God!*'

'I'll find him.'

Nance breathes out. She nods once. She knows it's never the easy option to find Dec when he doesn't want to be found.

I jog to the pub. The sign out front says 'The Queen's Head' but mostly everyone calls it The Job Centre. Not having a car means Dec will be within walking distance, unless he's gone somewhere with Jarrod, but Jarrod lost his licence for DUI so it's not likely.

I check the front bar first. There are a couple of faces I recognise, but Dec's not here.

Jimmy Black is. I ask him, 'Have you seen Dec?' and he jabs his thumb in the direction of the pokies room.

I'm under eighteen. I'm not supposed to go in there, but now that they have twenty more machines they've expanded the saloon bar and added another entrance. The last time Nance asked me to find Dec he was there all right, but I lied and said I couldn't find him. The time before that went badly—I got him home, but the fighting went on past midnight and Nance had to sleep in our room until Dec sobered up.

But this is an emergency.

I go outside and come back in through the new entrance. Bad move: the gaming-room manager is standing just inside, leaning on a machine.

Eilish has been working here for about a year. She has a thing for Dec—he says she's always hanging around when he's on the machines, making eyes at him. Dec calls her Champ because she reserves his favourite machine. I call her Eyelashes for obvious reasons. Sometimes she sends Dec a text if someone else looks like they're playing his machine too hard, or she switches it off and fakes maintenance if she has a hunch it might pay out. Dec says The Jewel of Arabia owes him a fucking fortune and Eilish has dibs on fifteen per cent if he ever hits the jackpot.

Eilish has her back to me. From behind, she looks a bit like Nance.

I slide past the ATM so I can see The Jewel: it's reserved and the stool is on its front legs, leaning against the machine. The jackpot is over fourteen thousand.

My phone jangles in my pocket.

It's a text from Nance. *Have you found him?*

Not yet.

'You can't be in here.'

Up close, Eyelashes is much older than Nance, but there's still a resemblance.

'I'm looking for Dec. Have you seen him?'

'You're his little brother, right?' She smiles.

I'm confused. 'He's not my brother. He's my dad.'

Now *she* seems confused.

'The baby's sick. We need to take him to the hospital.'

Her expression changes. 'How old are you?'

'Sixteen.'

'Dec is your dad?'

'Yeah.'

She digs her nails into my shoulder and steers me towards the door. 'You can't be in here,' she says again. 'I could lose my job.'

'But was he here today? I need to find him.'

'He *was* here, but clearly he isn't now.'

She seems angry about something. A bit green in the cheeks. After she shoves me through the automatic doors she strides back to The Jewel. I follow her, watching as she tips the stool onto four legs and stabs the Reserved button with her finger.

'How much earlier?' I say. 'Like, hours or minutes?'

'Out.'

'Please.'

She plants one hand on her hip and spins around to face me. 'About an hour, I guess. What's wrong with the baby?'

'We don't know yet.' I turn to leave. 'Thanks.'

I can feel her staring after me as I wave my hands to open the doors. I suppose she's surprised that I'm Dec's son, not his brother—that lie could easily knock ten years off his age—but I'm not surprised at all. It's not the first time he's said that.

Nance's second text comes through just as I'm entering the front bar at the Rowley Park Tavern. I ignore it. Dec's here—I've spotted him through the window—and there's no point replying until I know whether he'll come or he won't.

He's leaning on the bar, watching a horse race on the big screen with the form guide spread in front of him. He slaps a ten-dollar note down. The guy behind the bar pulls a fresh pint and slides it across.

I take a step closer. 'Otis is sick.'

I want to say *I want you to come home* or *you need to come home* but it's always better to let him make up his own mind. I add a few degrees to help him decide.

'His temp's over forty. Nance is freaking out.'

The bar guy reaches for the glass and says, 'If you have to

go I'll tip it, mate. No charge.'

Dec's hand shoots out. He grabs the pint. His eyes slide to me and I can tell he's pretty far gone. He must have lost big today.

He taps the form guide. 'Pick a nag in the next one, Nate. Change my luck.'

'But O's really sick.'

'O's always sick.'

The bar guy pulls his arm back. He's no match for Dec, and he knows it. All the rules about having the right to refuse service don't mean jack unless you're tough enough to enforce them, and Dec knows it too.

'Race Nineteen,' he says, and taps the paper again. 'Anything but the roughie.'

'What's the roughie?'

'Long odds.' He points to the screen. 'Win big. Lose big. The last roll of the dice. Nobody bets on the roughie unless they're playing get-out stakes.'

I check my phone. I've been gone nearly half an hour. If I beg and he refuses, I am less and he is more. 'If I pick one will you come?' It's a fair trade.

He hands me a twenty and swallows half his beer. 'He'll be right.'

Who'll be right?

'Capernicus Rex,' I say.

Dec shakes his head. 'Gelding. Got no knackers.'

'Mystique.'

'Filly. Too green. Likes the wet.'

In desperation, I pick the horse with the dumbest name. 'Boogie.'

Dec places the bet. He hands over the twenty like it's nothing. Doesn't matter how hammered he is, he always knows how much money is in his pocket or hidden around the flat. He tests me. He tests my honesty, my loyalty, my bravery, my commitment, my toughness, and he's always waiting to catch me out, for me to let him down.

'How long until the race?'

He doesn't answer. He's leaning on the bar with his head on his arms, eyes half-closed.

The bar guy pours a schooner of Coke and puts it in front of me. 'Freebie.'

'Thanks.'

So now me and bar guy are watching the screen as the race starts. Dec's snoozing. The caller says Boogie is fractious in the gate and I don't know what that means but it doesn't sound good. The gates fly open. Mystique gets a clean start. Boogie misses the jump.

'He's missed it,' the bar guy says, but quietly.

'We could cancel the bet.'

'You can't. It's too late.'

I scull the Coke. Boogie is still about fifteen metres behind the second-last horse and the jockey is swinging the crop in ever-faster circles, but there's no closing that gap. Mystique wins and the horse with no knackers comes third. The caller says Boogie is knocked up.

The bar guy says, 'Sorry, mate.'

I can tell by his slow breathing: Dec has passed out. His wallet is still on the bar next to him. I pick it up and check the note section: it's empty. I reach out to touch Dec's shoulder, but bar guy is watching me with a look in his eyes that matches the feeling in my stomach. He shakes his head.

A piece of me agrees with Dec—Otis gets sick all the time and Nance has a tendency to overreact. Another piece is so epically tired of everything, and I'd probably feel better if I walked out and kept walking in the opposite direction until the hard part was over. Still another piece—and it's a tiny one—wonders what would happen if I toughened up and poked the sleeping bear. But if I wake Dec and try to drag him home it will end badly for everyone, including the bar guy, who I want to punch right now because *he's* the adult and the law has his back—he can refuse service and kick Dec out, or call the police if he needs to.

But maybe we're not so different. He's just scared, like me.

Bar guy opens his wallet and takes out a twenty-dollar note. He winks at me and slides it under Dec's empty pint glass.

'When he wakes up I'll tell him he broke even.'

He waits for me to thank him.

When I get back to the flat, Jake has left the hose running outside. I turn it off.

He's sitting on the floor in the kitchen, covered in mud, eating a biscuit. The water's running in the bathroom, too. Someone is crying, but I don't want to go in there in case I embarrass Nance if she hasn't got any clothes on.

'O's sick,' Jake says, spitting crumbs.

'Yeah. I know, mate. Is he having a bath?'

'O won't wake up. Can I go outside?'

My skin prickles. It's Nance crying, not Otis.

I've got the same feeling I had after Mim was attacked and

the day I met Mum in the cafe—as if something irreversible is happening and life will never be the same. If I open that door, everything changes.

So I hold off for as long as I can.

I pour Jake a drink and hand it to him. More water. Thousands of litres, pouring down the drain and the gutters, wasted. The next bill will finish us. *Worry, worry, worry.*

I sit next to Jake on the floor. I hang on to normal.

It takes no more than a few minutes, but it feels like a lifetime—I realise I always think everything is about to change and I'm always wrong. It doesn't. It goes back. Stuff happens and things goes back to the way they were. Somehow that's worse.

'Go outside,' I tell Jake. 'Play with the hose.'

I wait until he's gone and knock on the bathroom door. My heart is in my throat. There's no answer, so I hit it with the palm of my hand. 'Nance?'

'Dec!'

'It's me. It's Nate.'

The door's unlocked. I open it.

Nance is standing under the shower, fully clothed, O draped over her shoulder. His face is bright red and he looks stiff, like he's frozen solid. His mouth and lips are blue.

Nance's teeth are chattering. 'He was too hot. I had to cool him down.'

I step forward and put my hand under the water. Freezing. I try to take O from her but she tightens her grip.

'Nance.' I tug her arm. 'He's not hot anymore.'

She shakes her head.

'Nance. Let me take him. You need to call an ambulance

now.' My voice is steady, but I'm terrified. I'm terrified she'll hand his tiny, slippery body to me and I won't know what to do next.

'Did you find Dec?'

'Dec isn't coming,' I say.

'He'll come.'

'He won't.'

'He'll come.'

'Nance, let go.'

TWENTY-FIVE

We're at the Women's and Children's. I don't know why people say they hate hospitals—what's to hate about state of the art machines and beeps that tell you your brother is alive and being cared for by no-bullshit people who know what to do? Do this, do that. Keep calm. Make rational decisions. Cool hands on his forehead, steady fingers on his wrist. Cleverness. Kindness. A nurse bought Jake hot chocolate from the machine down the hall.

Jake has curled up with a board book on a giant cushion on the floor.

Otis is sleeping. How he can do that with bright lights overhead and tubes up his nose, I don't know. His oxygen levels are pretty much back to normal but the doctor said his body is tired. He had a febrile convulsion, which is a kind of seizure. They're fairly common and usually harmless, except Nance cooled him too rapidly—the seizure intensified and lasted longer than it should have.

I'm thinking about the emergency operator's voice on the phone. She told me to check that Otis was breathing. He was. She told me to dry him gently and keep him warm, which sounded all wrong but it was the right thing to do. She said

I was doing a great job and that O would be fine and he is. I wish I knew her name.

I'm picturing the paramedics in their green suits and boots, the way they gave all their attention to O, paid none to the smell of the flat and the mess on the floor or the stain on the ceiling.

I fucking love these people.

My body feels light. The worry has left. I wonder if Nance feels the same way, but she just looks stunned. Like me, she keeps thanking everyone who comes in the room, as if she doesn't know any other words.

A nurse checks O again.

'Thank you,' I say when she leaves.

I could stay here forever, eating food from a vending machine and watching the minute hand on the clock ticking around and not caring about what comes next.

Nance starts talking, slow and slurring, like she's in a dream state. 'The doctors are going to refer O to a specialist. They said they might be able to help him with his growth and motor skills.'

'That's good,' I say. 'Isn't it?'

'It'll be expensive.'

'Nothing good is free.'

'Free,' she repeats, like a robot. 'You told me about something you read once. Do you remember? They took two kids—one was brought up in a loving home, and the other one wasn't—and they measured the growth of their brains over a couple of years. The one who didn't grow up feeling loved, his brain was almost third smaller than the other kid's.'

I remember. It wasn't that the boy with the smaller brain

was stupid, though. He was smart, but there were all these rooms in his mind that were locked to him. Like, he could only travel one way along a dark corridor, because he was following a pattern of restricted behaviour. He hadn't been shown that those doors were meant to open.

It bothers me that Nance is bringing up some dumb article I talked about ages ago, and now she's trying to make it about our family. You can make just about any theory fit if you're that desperate for answers.

I offer to get her a coffee but she doesn't answer.

'I should have done more.'

'What do you mean?' How could Nance have done *more*? 'You have to stop worrying. There's nothing you could have done to change what happened to O.'

'What if O is less because I loved him less. I don't mean now—I mean when he was born. He needed me too much. And then he stopped needing me and I loved him more, but what if it was too late?'

She means Dec—Dec loves O less—but she won't say it aloud.

I repeat what the doctors said when O was born. 'Nobody is to blame.'

But I can't help thinking of all the times we say Jake took a piece of Otis. It's family folklore by now. How has that affected Jake? And I worry it could be true—if the world thinks you are less, and treats you like you're less, it's a tiny brain and locked doors for you regardless of what you *could* have been. Potential is nothing without options.

Fuck potential. I'll settle for not being afraid anymore.

—

Dec and Nance are fighting again. I don't mean they're yelling—it's more of a low buzz, like the sound powerlines make when there's a storm coming. I've tried to fall asleep, but it's impossible.

Jake is crashed out on the bottom bunk, nestled around an empty space because Otis isn't there. When I came to bed, Nance had a bag ready by the door. It was a small bag, so I assumed she was going back to the hospital, but then Dec came home and the fight started.

Nance is pleading now, and her voice is getting louder.

I press my ear to the wall. Maybe tonight Nance will win.

She's saying Dec needs to stay home, stop gambling, drink less, get rid of the plants, give me back my bedroom, be around for the kids, get a real job, treat her with respect, be more, more, more.

It's too much.

Dec punches the wall separating our bedroom from the lounge; pieces of paint flake from the ceiling and land on my face. The deadbolts on the front door slide back. By the sound of it, he's going out again.

Nance sticks to the rules and locks the door. *Chick-chick.* Quiet. A low *thunk* as she throws herself into the couch and curls up in a ball, sobbing as quietly as she can so she doesn't wake us.

I don't need to see what's happening to know what's happening. It's all in the playbook.

I was supposed to be grateful that Dec stayed when Mum left. Dec never goes far and he always comes back. But the fact that he leaves us every day is somehow worse.

I pick up my notebook. It's all there—how things could be.

Man up. Man the *fuck* up.
Dream—Goal—Plan—<u>Action</u>—Reality.

Before school, I go to administration. Just walking up the ramp and pushing through the doors turns on all my defence mechanisms and makes my guts queasy. I can't recall a single positive experience I've had in this building. Like so many instinctive responses, it's hardwired, but I'm trying to be optimistic.

Mrs Gough takes her time looking up. Maybe her experiences haven't been so great either.

'Nate? What can I do for you?'

I realise every time I've been here, it was to ask for something. I hand her the envelope.

'What's this?'

'It's nothing. I wondered if you could pass it on to everyone who helped pay that school account. You know, for the stationery.'

She shakes the envelope. 'There's money in here?'

'Not much. Just enough to cover the notebooks you gave me a few weeks ago.'

'Do you need more?'

I shake my head.

'Can I open it?' She's already sliding her fingernail underneath the opening.

'Later, okay?' I blush.

It's a cheap, ugly thankyou card. It's embarrassing, really. It's not enough.

'Oh.' She seems to be having trouble catching her breath. She presses her palm to her chest.

'I just wanted to say thank you. Could you pass it on?'

'I will,' she says. 'Thank *you*.'

'And could you give this one to Miss DeVries?' I try to hand her the second envelope but she ignores it.

'She's still here. I'll check.' She heads down the hall, clearing her throat a number of times along the way. 'She says come on in.'

'Look, could you just give this to—'

'Gratitude is best delivered in person, Nate,' she says, smiling.

'Oh, it's not—' I sigh. 'Okay.'

When I enter, Miss DeVries is eating a tub of salad.

'Please excuse me.' She holds her hand over her mouth until she's finished chewing. 'Take a seat. Any news about Connor?'

I sit. 'I think he'll come back.'

'When?'

'I don't know. Soon. When he's ready.'

'Well.' She snaps a lid on the tub. 'I only hope that's not too late.'

'Too late for what?'

Her eyes narrow. 'What can I do for you?'

I place the envelope on her desk. 'I wanted to give you this.'

'What is it?'

It might not make much sense—or it might. I don't know. But if it makes a difference then I'll be glad I gave it to her. And if it doesn't, that'll come as no surprise to me or Owen Kleinig.

'It's about Owen Kleinig.'

There it is: a twist to her lips. Distaste.

'What about Owen?'

'Just read it. It's everything I know and a few things I've seen. And something I wrote a while ago about how this place works, just in case it's not in the procedure manual. Nobody else will tell you so I am. Telling you. So you can—I don't know—do something.'

Fuck. I suck at monologues. This is why I should stick to writing things down.

'Okay,' she says slowly. 'I'll read it. Will you come back if I have questions? We might need to put something on record.'

I stand and put the chair back in place ready for the next student.

'I'm not coming back. You can put that on record.'

I'm ready. My chair is balancing on two legs. I no longer desire to like or to be liked by my oppressors. What's the worst that could happen?

I've always been at a disadvantage (my second-row desk near the classroom door couldn't be further from the laptop cart, and why try too hard when the odds are against you?) but now I have the element of surprise. And, over the past few weeks, I've been paying attention.

Mr Reid is a creature of habit: he slips off his shoes under the desk, picks up whichever epic fantasy novel he's currently reading, puts his feet on the desk and smooths out the crease of the page he's marked, and then—

'Laptops. Be quick about it.'

I'm already halfway across the room before anyone else has their chairs away from their desks. I must look like a crazed shopper who's been camping out for three days, waiting for a sale, willing to crush small children underfoot, but it's a price

I'm willing to pay to upset the natural order of things.

Andrew Brink gets in my way. I shove him aside easily—he's short and he's wearing a moon boot.

Kobe Slater is right next to the cart, as usual. He only has to stand up to be first in line.

There are still plenty of laptops on the cart. I snatch one and handpass it to Zadie, who, as usual, hasn't bothered to get out of her seat. She gives me a nervous smile, but she takes it. I dash back and there are still two left, but I leave them for Will and Chris. Instead, I wait until Kobe turns around with three in his arms and I lay the move on him—one I've perfected over hours of practice in the Rage Cage with Cooper and Deng—a smooth twist and rip he doesn't see coming.

Kobe's too stunned to react. But the challenge isn't getting them. It's keeping them.

I deal two like playing cards, one to Gurmeet and another to Leila. Kobe taps me on the shoulder, and now I know what Merrick meant by feeling hot breath on his neck. Kobe is blowing like a mad bull.

Mr Reid is still reading.

I'm not sure if I'm more terrified or exhilarated. It's all very undignified, but I've rehearsed enough times and the variables can be overcome if we stick to the script.

Hey, thanks, McKee, Kobe says. Give it up, wanker. He grabs one end of the case and pulls.

'Oi. Wanker.' Kobe holds out his hand.

I pull back. 'No.'

I shake my head.

'Last chance.'

'Give it up.'

Ever predictable. Still on track.

No.

'No.'

Now the class is quiet and people are catching on. Mr Reid glances up, frowning. If he steps in, it's a Kobe slam dunk. Here's the part where Kobe's supposed to make a vague threat that I can turn into sexual innuendo, but he's not playing—to make things worse, the case isn't zipped properly and I can feel the laptop sliding down my thigh.

'You have a tablet,' I squeak.

The laptop shoots down my leg, somersaults off my shoe and lands upside down on the floor.

Kobe smells blood. He rocks back on his heels and holds out his hand again, waiting. 'Pick it up.'

I've got the works—nausea, shakes, dizziness. We're way off script and I can't improvise. On the outside I'm a statue, like Deng said, except the reason I'm not moving is that on the inside I'm curled in a tight ball.

Fuck. I *am* an armadillo.

Benjamin Peros picks up the laptop, lifts my stiff left arm and tucks the laptop underneath. 'You dropped something, buddy,' he says, and ruffles my hair.

Kobe takes a step forward but Will Farnsworth cuts him off. 'You can have mine.' Kobe brushes him away, but he insists. 'It's okay. It's nothing to be ashamed of,' he says, entirely without context, but it's more effective than anything I could have written in a script.

Gurmeet stands. 'Here. Take mine.'

Leila catches on. 'Here, Kobe. You obviously need it more than I do.'

And Zadie deploys her most perfectly timed long-suffering expression ever. 'Use your words, Kobe. You only had to ask.'

He mutters, 'Forget it,' and starts to sweat. 'Anyway, you don't even go here,' he says to Peros.

Peros laughs. 'I don't even *exist*. Say no to the drugs.'

Just like that, Kobe Slater's currency is spent and six of us are better off.

'All right, all right, everybody sit down,' Mr Reid says. 'Slater, do you need to borrow a pen?'

Kobe slides into his seat without answering.

On my way back to my seat—victorious!—I pick up my dropped lines and whisper to Zadie, 'I've seen our futures. None of this will mean anything in a few years. We're going places.'

'Together?' she says, her eyebrows raised. 'I don't think so.'

But she's intrigued. I can tell.

I wait to speak to Mr Reid after class.

'It's almost the end of term. You still owe me an essay, McKee.'

'You originally said any form I like.'

'What form are you proposing?'

'Does my dramatic performance count?'

He sighs and begins marking papers. 'How *was* the laptop experience?'

'Disappointing. I couldn't log in.' He's waiting for something, but I don't know what. 'I'm up to the part where I fight my enemies. You know—*action*.'

'I noticed,' he says.

'I should have punched Slater.'

'No, you shouldn't have. You lot make it easier for the powers that be if you're all killing each other. It matters *how* you win, McKee.'

I stare at my feet. 'I wouldn't call it a win, exactly.'

'Often the aim of resistance is not victory, but progress.'

'I couldn't even *speak*.'

'Mute protest is as good a means as any.'

'Peros had to step in. And Will and the rest.'

'Nobody will take your hand if you don't reach out.'

'I'm probably going to die later.'

'We're all going to die, McKee. The question is, do you want a walk-on part in the war? Or a lead role in a cage?'

He's messing with me.

'You're a walking quote generator, Mr Reid.' I'm trying to make him laugh. It's not working. I walk back to my desk and D&G pedals past right at that moment. I pick up my bag and shove my things inside. 'Last year you said something about us surrendering the only weapon we had.'

He gives the tiniest nod.

'You meant our education, right?' I'm rewarded with a smile. 'You should pay attention. This has been a teaching moment.'

He shakes his head. 'It was never about me.'

'I've been wondering, why did you let me off easy with the board game thing?'

He puts down his pen and rubs his hands over his face. 'Because I was wrong. I made assumptions and you were right to call me out. I don't know anything about what it's like to be you.'

'And why did you leave Saint Monica's?'

'So I could make a difference,' he says flatly.

It's my cue to tell him he did make a difference, but the words get stuck. It's like hugging Jake—I know it's what he needs and what he deserves, but it's just so hard.

He supposedly has all the answers, so I give him the next best thing.

'Mr Reid?'

'Yes.'

'What if, in an alternate reality, my fatal flaw is actually a superpower? Do I ditch the flaw, or find a new reality?'

He closes his eyes. 'Thank you, McKee.'

The truth is, I kind of, possibly, maybe, might be starting to give a shit.

TWENTY-SIX

Peros waits for me by my homeroom door after school. In the time it takes to walk to the bus stop, we dissect the Siegfried Sassoon poem we're supposed to be studying, discuss what we're doing on the weekend, diss Kobe Slater and swap phone numbers.

Peros is even more clueless than I was about poetry. I say science is the answer and art is the question, and I tell him about the fire in my belly and that it's not all shapes in clouds and paint by numbers—and at the end of my monologue he looks even more confused, so I offer to send him a copy of my own analysis to give him some ideas. And when he tells me how hard he's trying to get decent marks, I have no urge to make fun of him.

'Has Slater come back at you?' he says.

'Only if you count death stares.'

'He's not as tough as he acts.'

'Well, he had me fooled.'

Peros produces a crumpled band flyer. 'Hey, do you want to come on Saturday? They're mostly thrash and screaming, but the guitarist's good.'

'All ages?'

'Karl will get us in. You'll just need a clean shirt with a collar.'

It takes me a full ten seconds to realise he's teasing. 'Ha-fucking-ha.'

'You'll come?'

'Yeah. I'll come.'

'Later.'

'Seeya.'

Another street over, my phone rings. My phone never rings unless it's Nance. I get a sick feeling before I even look at the screen, but it could be about O so I pick up.

'It's me.' Tash.

'Hey. Tell me you're not calling to say we got busted.'

'Not exactly. Did you hear?'

'About what?'

'About Youth?'

'Did we win?'

She goes quiet for a moment. 'Macy has been given a date. June thirtieth. The Freemasons are moving in.'

I slump down onto someone's brick letterbox. 'Who are they? Some family?'

Tash sniggers.

'Great. I finally do something and it's all for nothing.'

Tash yells down the phone. 'It doesn't mean we *stop*.'

'What now? Burn some real houses?'

Tash makes a gasping sound.

'Are you laughing? How can you laugh about this?'

'The Freemasons aren't a *family*. It's a kind of club.'

'Never heard of them. Anyway, it's not that funny.'

'Yeah, I know. Hey, where are you?'

'Heading home from school.'

'So, are you up for something?'

I hesitate. 'Depends what it is.'

'Macy says she'll let us run a stencilling workshop.'

'She knows, doesn't she?' Silence. 'Are you nodding?'

'Sorry, I forgot we were on the phone. Yeah, she worked it out.'

'What did she say?'

'She said we might as well get started because we're running out of time.'

'Started on what?'

'Training an army, of course.'

I wave at the grumpy old guy who has the only green lawn on the street. He's standing on his verandah, surveying the grass. I should slip one of Bob the Lawnmower Guy's cards in the letterbox—get him closer to breaking even.

The old man smiles and waves back.

'Are you still there?' Tash says.

'Yeah.'

'You know what? I love Macy. I mean I *love* love her.'

'Yeah. Me, too.'

'So, are we still friends?'

Something catches in my throat. 'I don't really have *friends*, as such.'

'Perfect. Me neither.' She hangs up.

I wish I'd known sooner that everyday conversations on an ordinary day can have an extraordinary effect. Maybe this is what can happen when you yawp at the world instead of yelling down the well.

—

When I get home, Nance is bashing plates around in the kitchen. Something smells amazing. O is lying on the couch watching *The Lion King* on DVD, and Jake's trying to catch a fart in a plastic cup. Dec's here, too. Nance is whistling.

Everything seems normal, but somehow different.

'Hey,' I say to everyone and no one.

'Naaaate!'

O is back.

I go into the kitchen. 'Youth's closing.'

'I'm sorry, bub.'

'Want me to dry up?'

'You are ace, Nate McKee.'

'What are you making?' The flat has never smelled this good.

'It's lasagne—I think. I've never made it before.' She points to the ceiling. 'I'm making it for Margie upstairs. Kelly died last night.'

'Oh.'

'It's sad. She just went to sleep and never woke up.'

I wonder if anything I could have done would have made a difference. I guess it doesn't matter. I didn't do it.

I pull a tea towel from the hook inside the cupboard under the sink and pick up a wet plate. Nance isn't really paying attention to what she's doing: the plate still has tomato sauce on the bottom. I scrub it away with the tea towel, wondering if Nance has any clue what else is under the sink.

An odd sound makes us turn around. It takes forever to make sense of what's happening: Jake is holding the plastic cup over O's nose and mouth, pressing so hard O's cheeks are puffed up around the rim and he's trying to scream and thrash, but it only suctions the cup more tightly to his face. And Dec is laughing, which makes Jake press harder.

Nance moves first. 'Jake, let go! He can't breathe!'

'Lighten the fuck up,' Dec says. 'It's just a cup of cheese.'

Nance grabs Jake by the arm and wrenches him away. She doesn't stop there—she yanks his shorts to his knees and delivers a stinging slap to his bare backside.

Jake wails and hits her across the face.

Nance reels back and rubs her cheek, shocked, but Otis has taken a deep breath and when he lets it out it's like a siren going off.

Jake goes to run away. I catch him by the arm and haul him back. 'Don't hit your mother!' I smack him again, and now he and Nance have matching cheeks.

Until now, Dec hasn't stopped laughing.

For a big guy he moves fast. He shoots Otis a look of such intense hatred, it hurts like he's kicked me in the guts. He peels my fingers away from Jake's wrist and bends my hand so far back I have no choice but to kneel on a pile of dry cornflakes Jake spilt at breakfast. The instant agony makes my eyes water. With his free hand, Dec grabs my throat and digs his fingers into my Adam's apple. He forces my head back until my neck burns and I think I'll pass out, but Nance grabs his forearm and clubs the side of his face.

Dec lets go and everything stops.

'Oh, God,' I say, and Nance whispers, 'Dear God,' at the exact same time, when neither of us knows the first thing about praying.

Everyone has been hit, except Otis, who still has an O-shape around his mouth. My legs are jelly. My fight or flight response is on hold—it feels like whatever I do next could spark another chain reaction.

Jake pulls up his pants and retreats to the bedroom to sulk.

Dec runs his tongue over his bottom lip as if it's bleeding, but it isn't. It's not even fat.

Nance quietly gets Dec's wallet from the kitchen table. She passes it to him. Her face is pale except for Jake's tiny hand-print on her left cheek. 'Go,' she says. 'I give up.' She runs to her bedroom and closes the door.

It's just me and O and Dec, staring at each other. I've finally worked out what's different: he's completely straight, and Dec sober is more terrifying than Dec off-his-face any day.

This is the fallout from Nance's ultimatum.

Dec pulls on a T-shirt, picks up his keys and walks past me, swinging his shoes like nothing happened. He stops to bump my clenched fist with his, opens his wallet and slips me a twenty-dollar note and a wink on the way past.

I accept both because I don't know what else to do. It feels as if I've passed the test.

I hold it together until he's gone, until my throat is too choked to breathe and my nose is burning like I've snorted paint thinner.

None of us ever cries together. We all go to different rooms, so no one can see. I slide into the space behind the kitchen door, bite down on my knuckles, press between the bones of my wrist. Someone once told me there's a pressure point to relieve stress in there, but all it does is make my hand ache.

I splash my face over the kitchen sink and drink a glass of water.

Jake is confused. He doesn't know whether he's been bad or good. He watches from the doorway, scratches his arm until it bleeds, says nothing until I unlock the front door.

'Where you going?'

'Out.'

'Where?'

'Just out. Away from here.'

I'm confused as well.

Good things happened today: Slater's humiliation, Peros's invitation, Tash's workshop. Bad things, too. It's like if you swing the pendulum one way, it's going to swing just as hard on the way back. Perpetual fucking motion. And I don't know why, after everything that doesn't pass for normal in my family, it's Kelly dying because Margie loved her too much, and O refusing to say Dec's name because he doesn't trust him, it's Jake's fart in a cup and Dec laughing like it's all a big joke, that makes me realise this has to stop somewhere.

Someone has to make it stop.

D&G lights the community barbecue using a match. He unwraps five sausages, cuts them and places the sausages on the butcher's paper an equal distance apart. He opens a sweating bag of ninety-nine cent bread and eats a slice the same way I do—peels the outer crust, feeds it into his mouth like a noodle, squishes the rest into a dumpling and stuffs it in his cheek. When the barbecue starts to smoke, he transfers the sausages to the hotplate in exactly the same order.

I'm sitting on the edge of the track, dangling my legs. I was hoping Merrick might show up, but it's only D&G and two kids on scooters riding the shallow track. When they switch tracks, I swing my legs over and move to the bench under the shelter.

Up close I can smell D&G's body odour, his unwashed clothes and greasy hair. There's an unzipped bag strapped to the back of his bike and it's full of things people usually leave at home: clothes, shoes, books.

D&G might be the loneliest man in the world and I don't have the time or the energy to be his friend. That makes me another shit human being in an entire world full of shit human beings. Connections complicate things—I almost wish Jake and Otis had never been born, otherwise I'd pack a bag right now and take my chances somewhere else.

He pays me no attention, although I'm only a few metres away. I'm just a secondary character in his life, too.

I wipe my nose on my hand and sniff.

'Are you all right?' D&G says.

His voice is deeper than I expect, and he has several missing teeth.

'I'm fi—' I start to say. But I'm not fine. Things are not fine. 'Actually, I'm just trying to hold it all together.'

He looks as if he's about to say something but decides not to. He turns his sausages one-eighty degrees and pulls a bottle of BBQ sauce from his bag.

'Hungry?' D&G asks. 'Bread.' He points. 'Sauce?'

I stand and take a piece of bread.

He chooses a sausage, cuts it lengthwise, and flips both pieces over to blacken the inside. After about a minute, he squirts parallel lines of sauce between the halves, reconstructs the sausage and places it squarely in the middle of the bread.

It's not how I do it, but it looks edible. 'Thanks.'

He nods once, and indicates I should eat.

While I wait for the sausage to cool, I watch his movements. His clothes are filthy, but his hands and nails are clean. He slices another sausage, squirts the sauce. Repeat. He eats his meal slowly and thoughtfully, and when the hotplate has cooled enough he cleans it, using a scraper and a few pages from a newspaper. Everything has to be just so; it's like a choreographed ritual performed to a beat playing inside his head.

'Thanks for the sausage.'

He turns sharply as if he'd forgotten I was there, nods again and goes back to cleaning the hotplate.

I think we're finished, but then he says, 'Moments. Just moments, one after the other. You only have to hold it together for one moment at a time.'

I dig in my pocket for Dec's twenty, thinking I'll pay D&G more than the sausage is worth and I won't take change. But he's so dignified. He probably won't accept it for the same reasons I wouldn't. The guy rides around on a kid's bike—he probably sleeps on benches and squats to shit, but the crappy life he's having is so ordered, so completely within his control, and this upsets me more than it should because I'm so fucking undignified, even though I have *more* than him.

When he's not looking, I slip the twenty in his bag. This way I don't owe my old man anything, D&G keeps his dignity and everyone is better off.

'Man is no island,' I say to D&G, and leave him there.

'No *man* is an island.'

I tell myself he was just repeating what I said, but deep

down I know I misquoted. He was correcting me.

Just make it through this moment. And then the next. And the one after that. I repeat this all the way home, until I get to the flats and I see Margie sitting on the top step, alone.

I think moments are the problem—I've never been able to see past the next one. How can you choose a future like that? Margie took things a moment at a time, but even-tually those moments piled on top of one another and her dog exploded.

Like Owen Kleinig, the twins and I are at the losing end of a whole string of bad transactions. And when we grow up to be nothing, people will say it's because we have character defects, not because we grew up in Bairstal and we never found our way out.

Mr Reid was right—they stole our futures. And I'm finally fucking angry about it.

TWENTY-SEVEN

Otis is lying on his stomach on the floor, chewing his fist. I wonder how long he's been there. The bedroom door is still closed and I can't see Jake anywhere.

Something's burning.

O reaches for me, but I brush past him and head to the kitchen. Inside the oven, Nance's lasagne is a smoking corpse. I use the pot-holder to pull it out, slam it on the sink, open the window and fan the smoke.

'Nance?'

No answer.

'Jake?'

I scrape the lasagne into the bin and fill the pan with hot soapy water. Otis is starting to whine so I hand him his sippy cup.

While Nance still hides in the bedroom, I shove almost everything I own in my school backpack: a few clothes, my phone, my toothbrush and notebooks—nothing I don't need in the next few days, or that can be replaced. I can't find any more cash lying around but I steal Dec's phone charger from the kitchen, wondering how many people could travel this light. I've been kidding myself that my life is huge and complicated, but here it all is, stuffed in a bag. There has to be a cosmic reason why I have so few possessions; there has to be a pay-off.

And it's this: I can leave. I'll go to Mum's apartment by the beach. If that's not an option, I'll create another option. I'm a *master* plan-maker. I've been planning my whole life.

Leave through the front door and tell the people you love that you love them.

'Nance?' I knock on the bedroom door. 'I need to talk to you.'

Nothing.

A familiar odour is overpowering the smell of smoke. Otis has oozed shit all over the carpet.

I worry about leaving him like this, so I pick him up, carry him to our bedroom, and lay him on a towel on the bottom bunk. In the five seconds it takes me to grab a nappy from the top drawer of the dresser, he rolls off the bed and crawls towards the hallway. I haul him back by his nappy, and he's paddling like when you hold a dog above water, and now there's shit on my hands and the carpet needs scrubbing. I use about fifty wet-wipes to clean him up, change him and stuff the dirty nappy and wipes into a plastic shopping bag. I spray the marks on the carpet with toilet bleach (that's all I can find in the laundry cupboard) and stomp on paper towel to soak it all up.

Otis has commando-crawled back to the lounge room. I prop him between two pillows on the couch and press play on *The Lion King*. It should keep him quiet for a while. He doesn't remember he's already watched it about a hundred times. I wash my hands, dry them and look for a piece of paper. I'll write Nance a note. There's a sheet of discount vouchers for Dominos on the fridge; I tear it through the middle and flip to the blank side, but I'm having no luck with the mighty pen—luckily, I find a half-eaten black crayon on the floor, but I don't get beyond *Dear Nance* before I realise I can't write small enough to say everything I need to say, and anyway, it looks like a ransom note.

I worry the boys will be hungry and Nance might be too upset to remember dinner, so I slap together two cheese-slice sandwiches, cover them with cling wrap and finish the note with: *here's dinner for the boys.*

I worry about the trail of dirty washing leading from the front door to the hallway. I scoop up as much as I can and stuff it all in the washing machine, which is still in the middle of the laundry after the last time it shuddered so hard, it walked. I turn the machine on but, partway through filling, the pipes rattle and the water stops. I make sure the taps are turned on. I check the kitchen taps, too—water runs for a few seconds, then the same thing happens. *Clang-clang.* Nothing in the bathroom, either. I can't imagine why the water would be turned off unless the bill wasn't paid, and I can't imagine the water bill hasn't been paid, or the electricity bill, because Dec's plants would die without both, and *priorities.*

Fuck.

I pull the washing out again so it doesn't stink.

'*Run away, Simba…run. Run away and* never *return.*'

'I'm *trying*,' I mutter. By now, I could probably quote *The Lion King* in its entirety. In Swahili.

'Simba! Run!'

It takes me ages to realise it's Otis, not Jake, speaking.

And when I turn around, Otis has rolled off the couch. He's standing, no holding on, like he's been practising in secret the whole time.

Now we get our miracle.

'Ruuuuuun!' O raises his fist and stares at the TV, his eyes filled with tears.

'Nance!' I bash on the bedroom door. 'Come look! Look at O!'

Jake opens the door a crack.

'What's going on?'

He scowls. 'Nance won't get up.'

I push the door open and peek through the gap. Nance is lying on her stomach, the quilt wrapped around her body, the pillow over her head. Her fists are bunched around her ears.

'Nance, you have to see.'

She doesn't answer. Now Nance isn't functioning. This completely screws up my plans.

I cross the room and tug at the pillow. 'Are you trying to suffocate yourself?'

'Yeth,' is the muffled reply.

'Won't work. It's like holding your breath until you black out—you can't die, because as soon as you pass out, your brain tells you to breathe again. Survival instinct. Come on.' I grab one of her hands. 'Please.'

She flings the pillow aside. 'He cheated.'

'What? Who?' But I already know.

'It was that Irish girl from the pub. She might be pregnant.' Her eyes are swollen like she's been crying for a long time. 'Give me one of your alternative realities. I do *not* like the one I'm in.'

I know nothing I've ever imagined will make Nance as happy as what is real in the next room. 'O's walking.'

'What?'

'Well, he's standing.'

Nance leaps out of bed. As she throws back the quilt, a biscuit tin clatters to the floor. She pushes me aside and bolts for the door.

I grab the tin and carry it to the lounge room. Jake follows close behind.

Nance has picked up O. She's laughing and crying at the same time, spinning in circles.

Jake is still as confused as all hell, but he punches the air and yells, 'Yeah, little buddy! Go, little man! All right!' with an American accent, like a kid from a seventies sitcom.

Nance holds Otis so tightly his face turns purple. As she spins him like they're dancing, his head whips around so he can see the screen—he doesn't want to miss a thing.

Nor do I. I can't leave. My little life is huge and complicated. 'What's this?'

Nance glances at the tin. 'Money.'

She puts Otis down gently. He wobbles and falls on his arse, and she lifts him under his arms. The second time he stays up.

'Oh.' Her hand flutters to her cheek. 'What do we do now?'

It scares me to say what I'm about to say aloud, and I don't know what she's really thinking—but if she's think-ing what I'm thinking, she's wondering how long this moment will hold us before we crash.

Dec will never leave his family.

Dec will never let his family leave.

'Just…go. Leave. Take the boys.'

Her eyes brighten. As quickly as it appears, the spark goes out. She shakes her head.

'Your folks would come, wouldn't they?'

'In a heartbeat.'

'Then why? Why stay?'

But I know why. Dec has worn us down, like water over stones—he just keeps running over us, wearing us down, until we offer no resistance.

Nance takes the tin and gestures for me to follow her to the kitchen. 'This is all I've got.' She opens the lid and tips the contents onto the table.

I stare at the cash. It looks like a lot. 'How long have you been saving all this?'

'About a year. I had to do something. I needed a plan.' She rubs her eyes with her fists. 'Nate, it's not enough.'

'What do you mean? It's like—'

'It's exactly four hundred and forty-six dollars and fifteen cents. I counted.'

'Yeah, a lot.'

'Not enough.'

I take a deep breath. 'I know where there's more.'

Nothing has changed in so long. Now it's all changing too fast.

Nance has only packed the basics, but the rooms already echo. I wander through the flat, tidying up after her, keeping one eye on the boys.

Nance races from the bedroom to the kitchen clutching an armful of clothes. She shoves them into a duffel bag. Her eyes are wide and panicked. 'How much time do you think we have?'

'Pub shuts at twelve.' I shrug. 'Five or six hours?'

She grabs my elbow. 'You shouldn't be here when he gets back.'

'Will you leave a note?'

'I'll call him. When things settle down.' She wipes her nose with the back of her hand. She seems on the verge of tears. 'We're going to get picked up at the shops so no one sees. We have to go before—'

'—Dec comes,' I finish.

'Before I change my mind.'

'You won't.'

'You have to tell him you were out. You don't know anything.'

'Okay.' All around me is chaos, but I'm eerily calm.

'That's everything.' She surveys the lounge room with her hands on her hips. 'I think.' The pram is near the door, the basket underneath loaded with nappies and shoes.

I pick up O and press my face into his neck. He wriggles and kicks his legs against my thighs. He doesn't want to be held and I don't want him to start screaming, so I put him back down.

Jake is sitting on the edge of the couch with a Sponge-Bob backpack between his knees. 'Bye,' he says cheerfully. 'We're going to a farm. I'm going on a tractor.'

Nance's face crumples and she pulls me into a brief, hard hug. Her bones are jangling, her heart beating crazily against my chest. She straps Otis into the pram, slings the duffel bag over her shoulders and takes Jake by the hand.

Then they're gone.

TWENTY-EIGHT

I've been sitting on the verandah with the front door wide open, wondering if Nance and the boys are safe and far enough away. I don't remember ever having the place to myself this late.

Out on the street, a single working streetlight flickers on. It's getting dark and I'm getting hungry.

I head inside. On the way past Dec's surfboard I give it a flat-handed shove. It moves the tiniest bit. I wiggle it using both hands, but it must be buried deep. I step away, kick out sideways and it gives a little more. Five more hard kicks and my ankle is throbbing and the board's leaning backwards at twenty degrees, but that's as far as it will go. Something is stopping it. Another kick. The board makes a sound like a branch breaking; it falls over, leaving its tail fin in the dirt.

Something inside me breaks, too.

I rip Nance's hydrangea out by the roots, fling it out onto the driveway, go inside and open the door to my old bedroom.

The day the cops came to the door, Dec asked what would happen to all of us if he was locked up. In a few days or weeks, the plants will be gone—right now there are twenty-two of them, plus an unregistered gun in the roof space, and there's still some cash taped to the bottom of the kitchen sink. There's a good chance he won't even come home tonight, but Nance needs more time.

If Dec is right, that's two years right there.

I take some leftover change from Nance's forgotten jar in the kitchen and walk to the phone box near the service station.

I'll become the monster to defeat the monster. One phone call, anonymous, the flat will be raided, Dec will probably be held for at least forty-eight hours, and Nance will have a better chance at full custody of the boys. For most people, this wouldn't even be a choice—it's simply right or wrong. For me it's like deciding between doing nothing and waiting for the asteroid to hit, or doing something to change its course. These are my options. Either way, probable mass destruction.

I step inside the phone box, sweep cubes of broken glass from the counter, lift the handset, feed the coins into the slot and jab the buttons—my hands shaking, heart speeding, pits sweating—and I can't dial the final number. I physically *can't* do it.

I'm part of the problem. I have been for a long time.

I go to Youth.

I lean against the wall, wishing I smoked so I'd have something to do with my hands other than pretend to scroll through non-existent messages on my phone.

I text Nance—*Are you okay?*

The court light's working again. Cooper and Deng are taking a smoke break in the far corner. Povey is half-asleep, leaning against rear of the wall with a melted Zooper Dooper in his hand.

Someone goes in; somebody else comes out. Business as usual. A blast of warm air from inside brings the smell of burnt toast.

Cooper calls out. 'Shoot?'

I give him a thumbs-down.

The doors open again.

'Hey, Nate.'

'Hi, Mim.'

'What are you doing out here by yourself?'

I shrug.

'I'm just checking on Mr Povey.' She takes the Zooper Dooper from between Povey's pinched fingers and touches his neck. 'Didn't spill a drop. Are you coming inside?'

I shake my head. 'I've got things to do.' I point at Povey. 'Is he dead?'

'He's fine. But what about you?'

'Good.'

She smiles. 'That could mean you're fine, or you want everyone to think you're fine, or you're absolutely not fine.'

'You stole my line.'

She grabs my hand. 'I'm asking, Nate.'

I feel like crying again, so I change the subject. 'Mim? After what happened—are you, like, different?'

She frowns. 'Different? Do you mean am I afraid?'

'Yeah.'

'I was,' she says. 'I am. I'm angry, too.'

'At the guy?'

'No?' More firmly, 'No. It wasn't personal. I'm angry because I felt helpless.'

'Maybe he just needed drugs.'

'He probably needed not to be alone,' she says. 'The other stuff came after.'

I can hear the clack of cue balls and the jukebox playing. My heart's beating so fast—I wonder if Mim can tell. 'Do you remember what you said about not closing the door behind me?'

'Yeah.'

'What did you mean?'

'I meant something like it's fine to escape, but you shouldn't leave the people you love behind. One day you might want to come back.' She waves her hand. 'Look at me.'

'What if I don't?'

'Well, that's up to you. Advice shouldn't come one-size-fits-all.' She flips the lid on the rubbish bin near the entrance and drops the wrapper inside. 'So, how's it going?'

'How's what going?'

'The get-out plan.'

I think of Dec and how helpless I feel. It *is* personal.

'I have to go.' I take a few steps towards the road and stop. 'Tell Macy…'

'Tell her yourself.'

Macy is standing by the door, fists on hips, scanning the car park for trouble. She's wearing green army pants, a Slasher hoodie, red Converse, and she looks like nobody's mother. I want to slick down her cowlick.

Mim catches my eye and jerks her head in Macy's direction. She says nothing, but sighs and gives me a gentle shove. She goes inside.

'Tell me what? Did you burn your own bloody house down?' Macy tries for a grumpy expression, fails, and ends up looking scared.

'Mace, I just want to say—' I don't know what to say.

She blushes. 'I know.' She rummages in her pocket for a cigarette and lights it. She pulls a fifty-dollar note from a different pocket and holds it out. 'Here.'

'What's this for?'

She twirls me around by the shoulder and tucks it in my back pocket. 'I've always said the only time I ever want to lose a kid is when they don't need me anymore. Then I'll pack their bags and pay for their ticket myself.'

'But—'

'It's for your fucking ticket. Now take it or I'll be offended.'

I don't like to hug or be hugged. Seems to me it's something you have to practise, like learning to cross a busy road: you have to judge the gap or somebody will get hurt. Macy isn't a hugger either, so we kind of lean in, brush cheeks and pat each other on the back.

'Thank you,' I say in her ear.

'What's your hurry?' She pulls away. 'Come inside—I've made your favourite.'

'I can't. I have to go.'

'Right now?'

'Yeah.'

'Well, we'll be here if you need us.' She doesn't look convinced. 'You just call me, okay?'

'Okay.'

She sniffs hard, wipes her nose on the back of her hand, hitches her pants. 'Be good.'

'I will.'

'Don't be a dickhead.'

'I'm trying.'

'Go on, then.'

She storms inside and immediately breaks three of her own rules: cigarette in hand, yelling profanities and invading people's space.

Nance asked me what we do at Youth once. I told her we played pool and hung out, but the truth is Youth gives us a place to do normal things: eat regular meals, do homework, access wi-fi, even take a hot shower. There are plenty of kids who don't go home for dinner, then don't go home for lights out, and one day they just don't go home. Youth gives us a place, because if you have nowhere to go you have nothing to lose, and that's dangerous.

TWENTY-NINE

I forgot to lock the front door.

It's wide open. Splinters of wood and shards of glass are scattered across the verandah. The bottom half of Dec's surfboard is jammed in the space where the glass panel used to be.

I have a burning sensation between my shoulderblades and a feeling of impending doom. Dizziness, fatigue, nausea—basically all the symptoms of a heart attack. I worry I'll flop about like a dying fish and stop breathing right here on the verandah, but the panic fades when I realise it can't be Dec. He wouldn't leave the door open, not even if he came home to find Nance and the boys were gone.

I step inside and flick the nearest light switch. There's no power. I turn on my phone torch.

The TV is gone. The Xbox is missing, but I can't remember if Nance took it with her. The kitchen cupboards have been raided—it's not like there was much to eat but everything has been pulled out and ripped open. A line of ants march from the kitchen to the lounge, carrying cornflakes. A crazy trail of clay balls leads from my old bedroom and the door hangs from its hinges. Only the pots are left. The flat smells of damp gyprock and rotten floorboards. The back door is open too.

The flat has been looted, but there's no movement—whoever's been here has left. It's as if a natural disaster hit and everyone evacuated in a hurry, taking only what they could carry. Which is kind of true, but it wasn't like this when I left.

I slam the front door. The frame is bowed and the dead-lock won't catch, so I push the TV cabinet across to use as a barricade. I can see lights from the adjacent windows through the splintered wood. I check the yard and close the back door.

Dec and Nance's bedroom is trashed: clothes and cornflakes all over the floor, smashed pictures, wet, stinking carpet. The worst part is, when I go into our bedroom, Jake's drawings have been ripped off the wall. Nance didn't have time to pack Jake's Lego or O's toys and they're mostly gone too. I find one jar of Lego two-blocks under the bed. When I twist off the lid they smell like pickled onions.

Any sign of weakness and the pack will turn on you—well, to be accurate, wolves don't do this. Humans do. And ants. Ants are the only species besides humans that pillage and make war and enslave their own kind. Who steals *toys*? Who steals from *children*?

I pick up a soggy pack of cigarettes from the floor. Six left. The find would be a bonanza for any other person on any other day, but this day is the opposite of ordinary. I find a Bic in the kitchen, light a cigarette and let it burn.

I don't inhale but I might as well—loneliness is ranked as high as smoking as a risk factor for mortality. Natural selection favours people who need other people. W.H. Auden said we must love one another, or die. One is science and the other is poetry and neither is fucking helpful in this situation.

Should I wait for Dec to come home? Will he finally hit me?

Do I stay?

Do I have a *choice*?

The cigarette goes out.

Our bedroom still stinks like O's piss. The sheets are still on the bed, but my quilt is gone and there's a fresh crack in the window. I climb the ladder and curl up with my phone on the pillow.

I press the home button and the screen lights up the dark room. Maybe an hour of battery left if I avoid using it.

If you don't reach out, nobody will take your hand.

I text Mum.

Does the couch offer still stand? I need somewhere to crash.

When there's no reply, I type *Please*.

An hour has passed. I must have dozed off, and that scares me. Anything could have happened.

My phone has two new text messages. The first is from Mum.

I'm still getting on my feet. Maybe next year ok?

And a later message, *Let's do lunch*.

There is no world but this: walls, ceiling, floor, bed and things left behind.

Fuck you, I type. *And the horse you rode off on. Fuckyoufuckyoufuckyou.*

Delete.

Twenty minutes later I type and send: *No worries. Never mind*.

Mr Reid was right: first you fight your allies, then your

enemies. But he didn't warn me about the intersections: allies can be enemies and enemies can be allies, and fighting apathy is like swinging at an enemy who isn't even in the same room.

When I wake again it's still quiet. Cold.

I check my phone for the time but it's dead. I regret shooting the sensor light and telling Clancy next door to shut up so many times. I miss music and light.

'Oi.'

Merrick is outside the window, his breath misting the glass.

'Jesus, Merrick.' My body tingles with adrenaline.

'I'm Winston Wolf. I solve problems.' *Pulp Fiction* again.

'Good. We got one.'

'So I heard. May I come in?'

'Uh, yeah. Please do.'

I climb down from the bunk and twist the catch. As I lift, the crack makes a crunching sound. A triangle of glass pops out.

Merrick's teeth glow in the dark; his Yeezys, however, do not.

'Are you all right?' He sticks his head through the opening and looks around. 'This is all kinds of messed up.'

'Yeah. Did you see? Do you know who did it?'

He climbs inside. 'It could have been anyone. Everyone hates your old man.'

He's not telling. I don't blame him. He has to live here too.

'What are you going to do?' he says.

'Wait here until he turns up, I guess.'

'I'll wait with you.'

'I don't know what will happen when he gets back. Nance

has taken the boys. It could be bad.' I try to close the window but it jams. 'Everything is broken.'

He cocks his head. 'What's that from?'

'I don't know. Original, I think.'

Merrick goes into the lounge room and lets out a low whistle. 'This is what our flat looks like all the time.' He glances at the open door to the third bedroom. He doesn't seem surprised.

'I stole Dec's cash stash and I gave it to Nance.'

I've broken a law—not the kind you'll find written in any rule book, but just as binding.

Merrick jams his hands in his pockets and kicks at the clay balls on the carpet. 'You're dead.'

Two cats are wailing at each other outside. Someone yells and throws a bottle to scare them off. The sound of breaking glass makes us jump.

'This is bad. This is the worst thing to ever happen to us.'

'It's not happening to *you*.'

Merrick backs up against a wall and slides down to a squat. 'Not sure I can offer any protection,' he says.

'I'm not asking—'

'But you'll need a witness.' He pulls his slingshot out of his pocket and picks up a clay ball. He loads it. He aims the slingshot at the wall opposite and fires. The ball punches a neat bullet-sized hole. 'Did you see that?'

I laugh. 'Straight through.'

'I reckon you've got one shot.'

'I'll aim between the eyes.'

'Drug kingpin murdered with clay ball. Huh. Ironic.'

'Now he gets it,' I say.

'I always got it. I was just messing with you.' He grins. 'Anyway, it won't go through. It'll probably just bounce off his pecs.'

'I know that. But it would be *symbolic*.'

'I'm not convinced a symbolic death will save you,' he says.

I look around. The flat is borderline uninhabitable. This is Page Three, poisonous comments stuff. We'll be another example of a family of ungrateful, feral slackers who shat in their own nest, except that's not our whole story.

'Give me that thing.' I hold out my hand.

'I was joking,' he says.

'You're the one who said you'd rather swing and miss than duck and run.'

He laughs shakily and stands. He hands me the slingshot.

I pick up a handful of balls. I aim, fire and the ball punctures another clean hole next to the one Merrick made. I shoot again. This one ricochets off the ceiling and lands on the carpet.

'Incoming. I can see lights.' Merrick peeks through the broken blinds. 'I don't recognise the car.'

'One of Dec's mates?' My mouth has no spit. 'Is it Jarrod?'

'I don't know. Wait. Oh, it's nothing.'

I breathe out, pull back the sling and aim at a greasy head-height stain on the wall.

'You can crash at mine,' Merrick offers.

'I'd rather face my old man than see yours on the couch with his hand down his pants any day.'

'Fair call.'

The next two shots are wild.

Merrick picks up the cigarette packet and shakes it.

'Can I have these?'

'Knock yourself out.'

'Why don't you call your old man? Give him the heads-up?'

'We have no power. My phone's dead.'

'Here.' He offers his.

I shake my head. 'I'll wait.'

'And then what? Turn up to a gunfight with a slingshot?'

I have an idea. I don't know why I didn't think of it before. Once an idea has taken hold of the brain it's almost impossible to eradicate.

'You'd better go.' I hand him the slingshot. 'Take this.'

Merrick snatches it away and tucks it in his waistband. 'You had me for a minute.'

He stares at me as if there's something different, but he can't put his finger on it. I've changed, but change on the inside is just a bunch of neurons firing in a different pattern. You can't see that.

He looks back once before leaving the way he came. 'You know where I am.'

Yeah. I do.

I close the window behind him and check the catch is tight. To make sure, I drag the dresser over—it's not high enough, but it'll make entry more difficult—and I go back to the lounge room. This is ground zero. Things can't get any worse. But the more time goes by without Dec showing up, the less scared I feel. I'm not worried—I'm numb. You can't worry about shit that's already happened.

I dreamed a dream.

I had a goal.

I made a plan.

I put my plan into action—and this is my reality. There is no alternative. You can only take control of the reality you're in, and maybe it's okay to close the door behind you. Like, forever.

THIRTY

Waiting for Dec is like waiting for a snake to come out from beneath the woodpile.

I've moved the TV cabinet back to its original position, and I'm sitting on the floor with my back against the wall, a direct line of sight to the front door. That's where he'll come in. That's the way he always comes in.

The gun isn't as heavy as I remember it. I hauled it down from the roof space, unwrapped it, checked its parts. I cleaned it as best I could, but I'm worried about the quality and quantity of ammo: only two bullets left in the box, both of them corroded and pitted with rust.

They could jam. Or they'll fire but they won't fly true.

Both ends can hurt, loaded or not.

A police car siren blares nearby. I will it to come closer, to keep coming until the flash of red and blue is right outside the flat, but it eventually fades.

I listen for the sound of footsteps on broken glass. My hands are steady enough, but my index finger is twitchy on the trigger; every tiny noise sets off a fresh adrenaline shot. Fighting it leaves my muscles with a dead ache. I keep bawling, on and off; it sneaks up on me, like a wave I don't see coming.

I shift my weight to stretch out a cramp in my calf.

The lights in the block are turned off except for one: Merrick's bedroom, across the way. I'd like to think he's keeping watch but sometimes he still sleeps with the light on. It's been about forty-five minutes since he went home. The rest is guesswork—maybe eight hours since Dec went to the pub and around five since Nance left with the boys. They could be halfway across the state by now.

My eyes droop. My chin bounces off my chest. I clear my throat to wake myself up and pinch the skin on my wrists. I taste blood where my bottom lip has cracked; I'm itchy with dried sweat. I wonder if there's any water left in the pipes, enough to rinse my mouth at least, but I'm wary of leaving my post in case I don't have time to reset.

I lift the gun to feel its weight, line up the sight, recalibrate. Let it fall. Too much time has passed; the certainty I felt when I loaded the gun is starting to waver. I could put it back in the roof space. Dec would never know.

Pussy.

Another wave approaches—my heart swells in my chest and it feels like if I don't let it out it'll split clear through the middle—and when it passes, I'm left with rage and a clear head.

Toughen up. I can't put the gun back. I'll be defenceless.

Salt and sweat make my eyes burn. I blink it away. My muscles burn from strain and my back is stuck in a hunch, as if the vertebrae have fused together.

Tough it out.

I flex my fingers, stand, stretch. I take a cushion from the couch, jam it behind my back and resume the position.

More long minutes pass. I doze again, only struggling to

pull myself back when a dog barks, and the room is illuminated by a moving beam of light. I listen without breathing.

It's a car, pulled up out on the street. The engine idles, and
I strain to hear the *thunk* of a door. Then it comes: a footfall on
broken glass. The beat of silence when someone freezes, then
takes another step.

Crunch.

I tense and lean forward.

Crunch.

I stand and steady myself with my left heel wedged against
the wall. Raise the gun. I'm a statue—no move, no fear. The
only way to change the world is to destroy it.

Never aim if you don't mean to shoot.

I aim.

Back straight, chin up, steady, aim, breathe out—

A tentative knock. A flat-handed shove, then a dull thud as
a shoulder hits the door, once, twice. On the third, the front
door flies open.

Shoot the goat.

Shoot the goat!

SHOOT THE GOAT!

A million moments, all leading to this.

Squeeze.

The bullet whistles. It punctures something solid. An
explosion of light turns everything white.

The second bullet never makes it. I can't tell what the first
bullet hit—I only know that I missed.

I'm not sure how I end up on the floor; I don't remember
falling. Instinct tells me to protect my head and my ribs, so
that's what I do: fold down, curl up around the gun, make

myself small. This must be what it's like to drown in the wave; it drags me down so deep, I don't know which way is up. I cover my ears but all it does is amplify the *whoosh* and trap the repeat sound of the gunshot inside my head.

I wait for the punch or the kick.

Nothing happens.

One by one, things come back: the scratch and tickle of carpet on my cheek, the smell of rotting wood and hot metal. Enough light to hurt my eyes and a cool hand on my back. There's a voice on the other side, telling me to get up.

'Give it to me.'

Not Dec.

'Bub, give it to me.'

I let go of the gun. Nance stumbles backwards, gripping it with two hands. She places it on the floor, carefully, as if it might bite. Then she's pulling me up, squeezing my neck, forcing my head between my knees.

'Breathe.'

'I can't.'

'You've been doing it your whole life. Breathe.'

Nance waits for my breathing to steady and takes her hand away. She spins slowly, playing the torchlight of her phone over the wrecked room.

'Did he do this?'

'No.'

She looks at me sharply. 'You?'

'No!'

Her gaze skitters to the back door.

'He's not here.' I glance at the gun. 'You should have stayed away.'

Nance's face is ghost-white. 'I didn't come back for him. I came for you.'

You shouldn't leave the people you love behind.

She won't look me in the eye. The light from her phone hits the neat hole above the door frame and her mouth sets. She's all business: she picks up the gun, empties the chamber, and puts the bullet in her pocket. A brisk rub with a wet wipe and our prints are gone. She stands on the chair in the hallway and places the gun back into the roof space.

She darts into the boys' bedroom and comes back with my backpack.

'Is this all you need?'

She's being careful not to give anything away, but I know she's thinking about the second bullet.

I nod.

'We have to go. You can come home if you—just tell me and I'll bring you back to him. Okay?' She grabs my hand and squeezes it to still the shaking. 'We have to go *now*.'

Suddenly it's important to me that she understands.

'I missed.'

'I know,' she says. 'I should have called out. I scared you—it's my fault.'

Mr Reid asked if I ever did anything with intent. I did. I do.

'Nance, I *missed*.'

'*Please*—'

She doesn't get it.

She pulls me along the path and out onto the street, where a white twin-cab ute is idling, headlights still on. She pushes me into the seat and fastens my seatbelt, like I'm a child, and jumps into the driver's side. The door slams and she checks the rear-view mirror.

'Another day, bub. What do you think?'

I think it wouldn't have mattered if it was Dec who came through that door at point-blank range and I had all the time in the world—I still would have aimed to miss. I'm not like him. Everything he ever did made me lean in the other direction. Maybe *that's* my golden ticket.

'What about the flat?'

Nance glances over her shoulder. 'We can't live here anymore. You'll see—my parents have a big house.' She tries to smile. 'You'll have your own room.'

'What about school?' I'm not ready to get off that train. Not when it feels as if it's finally going somewhere.

'You can go to school there too.'

'What about my friends?' Merrick, Tash, Peros—

'It's not goodbye. You can come back when things have settled. You know, when Dec has had time to calm down.'

'Come back,' I say.

'Yes.'

'Later.'

'Yes, later.'

'When I'm grown, with a full set of teeth.'

Nance stares as if I'm speaking a different language, but it all makes perfect sense to me. I couldn't shoot the goat. I *am* the goat.

Nance checks the mirror again. 'If we're going, we have to go now. I don't know what's the right thing, so you have to tell me.' Her hands flutter on the wheel. 'Tell me—what do *you* want?'

There's a wheat stalk caught in the wiper. I want to touch it to see if it's real.

'I'm coming with you.'

I want to sleep for a thousand years.

'Are you sure?' she says.

I want enough headspace to write something happy for Nance. I want to hug the boys.

'I'm sure.'

I want to find my way out of the jungle and save the world. For the first time ever, it seems possible.

ACKNOWLEDGMENTS

Each book I write tends to colour real life in some way, and this one was harder than the others. I'm grateful to all the people who give me support, time, advice, love and patience:

the team at Text Publishing, brilliant cover designer Imogen Stubbs, and my extraordinary editor Penny Hueston (who always knows exactly what's missing—and brings it);

my agent, Sheila;

my family and friends, who put up with my disappearances (love you guys!);

the readers, writers, poets, artists, teachers, dreamers and revolutionaries;

and to 'Nate': kids like you change the world. It's up to you how you do that.

Thank you. You are ace.

Loved *This Is How We Change the Ending*?
Now read Vikki Wakefield's extraordinary debut novel.

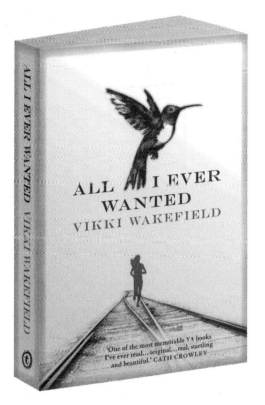

WINNER, Adelaide Festival Awards for Literature, Young-Adult Fiction, 2012
SHORTLISTED, Victorian Premier's Literary Awards, Young-Adult Fiction, 2012
SHORTLISTED, Queensland Literary Awards, Griffith University
Young-Adult Book Award, 2012
NOTABLE BOOK, Children's Book Council of Australia Awards, Older Readers, 2012
SHORTLISTED, NSW Premier's Literary Awards, the Ethel Turner Prize
for Young People's Literature, 2012
SHORTLISTED, REAL Awards, 2012
SHORTLISTED, Gold Inky Award, Centre for Youth Literature, 2011

**'This is one of the most memorable YA books I've ever read.
The voice is original, the characters are real, the language is
startling and beautiful. And the plot keeps you trapped till
the dangerous but hopeful end.' Cath Crowley**

'A stunning contribution to young adult fiction. 5 stars.'
Books+Publishing

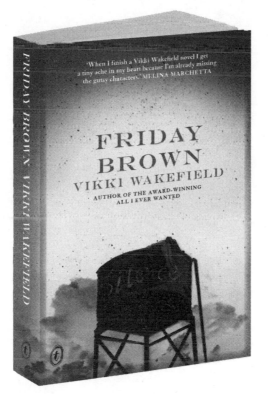

WINNER, Adelaide Festival Awards for Literature, Young-Adult Fiction, 2014
SHORTLISTED, Victorian Premier's Literary Awards, Young-Adult Fiction, 2013
HONOUR BOOK, Children's Book Council Awards, Book of the Year, Older Readers, 2013
SHORTLISTED, Prime Minister's Literary Awards, Young-Adult Fiction, 2013
SHORTLISTED, Queensland Literary Awards, Young-Adult Fiction, 2013
SHORTLISTED, Western Australian Premier's Book Awards, Writing for Young Adults, 2013
SHORTLISTED, Gold Inky Award, Centre for Youth Literature, 2013

'A pull-no-punches story about learning the truth and growing up,
full of the preciousness of friendship and love.' *Herald Sun*

'A gritty, heartfelt read for teens and adult readers alike.'
Readings

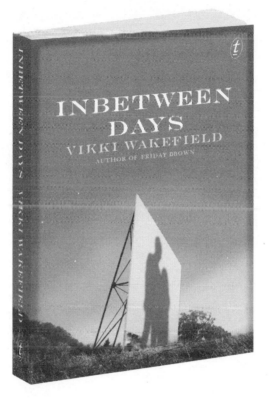

HONOUR BOOK, Children's Book Council of Australia Awards,
Book of the Year, Older Readers, 2016
COMMENDED, Barbara Jefferis Award, Australian Society of Authors, 2016
SHORTLISTED, Prime Minister's Literary Awards, Young-Adult Fiction, 2016
LONGLISTED, Gold Inky Award, Centre for Youth Literature, 2016

'Memorable, intriguing, perceptive and often very funny,
this is an unforgettable YA novel and a most unusual love story.'
Magpies

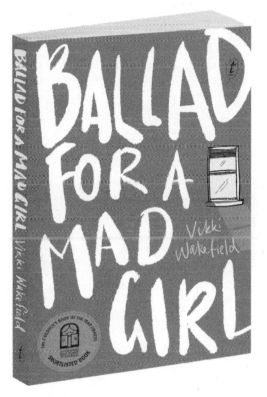